Adventures Aboard
S/V
Casablanca

A Novel
Inspired by True Events

Terry J. Kotas

with Artwork by Travis Johnston

Black Rose Writing | Texas

ISBN: 978-1-935605-68-3
PUBLISHED BY BLACK ROSE WRITING
www.blackrosewriting.com

Printed in the United States of America
Suggested Retail Price (SRP) $18.95

Adventures Aboard S/V Casablanca is printed in Chaparral Pro

*As a planet-friendly publisher, Black Rose Writing does its best to eliminate unnecessary waste to reduce paper usage and energy costs, while never compromising the reading experience. As a result, the final word count vs. page count may not meet common expectations.

Enjoy!

Terry J Kuntz

7-14-21

To Heidi, you're the best.

Adventures Aboard

S/V
Casablanca

RICK AND JACK SAIL AGAIN!

PROLOG

I'm not sure what time it is, but now, right now, this very instant I am in heaven. Well, not literally in God's House, but as close as I can be here on earth.

I am floating in an aqua blue sea, the temperature of the water is just slightly below the 88 degrees of the warm, softly blowing wind that is gently pushing the air mattress, that I'm laying on, to the full length of its tether. The other end is fastened to *Casablanca*, my 35 foot sailboat that is in turn anchored in a nearly unpronounceable cove in the Sea of Cortez in Mexico.

My consciousness is hovering just on the edge of unconsciousness and my brain is telling me that it really wants to take a time out and grab a nap. Instead, scenes from my past start to unroll in my head and it's like watching a movie of my life. Depending on my mood, different scenes are picked out for viewing, but generally it starts when I was young and progresses through my teens then early adult life. Sometimes I make a big deal out of an event and sometimes I leave something out that was an important part of the journey. But the one thing that is always the same is the ending, or rather the here and now. Today it's on an air mattress, yesterday it was a hike to the top of a volcano and tomorrow.....who knows? It's all about the journey.

Today the story began with me as a mischievous kid growing up in the small fishing village of Gig Harbor, Washington. I was surrounded by boats though I only held a passing interest in them at the time, but it set the seed for my lure of the sea.

My early teens were spent doing my best to stay out of trouble, and then one day I discovered the world of hang gliding. Well, much to my mom's chagrin, I was building and flying hang gliders with barely a thought as to the potential problem of falling out of the sky. Then one day I got a wake up call. Some air turbulence coupled with poor decision making had me crash landing in a lake with near fatal consequences.

Before the month was out, I had traded in my wings for another form of wind assisted transportation: a small sailboat. It was a one person craft and I could just squeeze my lanky 6 foot frame into its confines.

It was love at first sail. I was able to use what I had learned flying and applied it to skimming across the lakes near my home town. So, when a salesman at a large boat show encouraged me to move up in boat size, I couldn't say no.

The problem of not being able to afford a new boat was remedied by purchasing one that was "semi-complete" - one that I could finish as I had the money. All the major components would be installed and I just needed to do a little trim work to have a finished yacht. Unfortunately, the economy works in strange ways and the boat company that was building my "semi-completed yacht" went bankrupt, leaving me with next to nothing: a fiberglass deck and hull that weren't even attached to each other.

The next several years were spent learning to be a boat builder. Nothing like on the job training. Eventually those two pieces of fiberglass became the semi-completed yacht that I'd originally intended to purchase. Then, after a few more years and a considerable amount of work, I finally had a sailboat.

All the while I was building the boat that I'd dubbed *Rick's Place*, mentally I was planning a voyage that would take me to places in the world that were exotic, warm and had swaying palm trees. Those places were a long way from Gig Harbor, where the boat sat, next to my mom's house.

It was one of the proudest days of my life when *Rick's Place* was finally launched. But it took another couple years to get the boat, and myself, ready for my long held dream of a blue water cruise.

Originally, I was to sail *Rick's Place* by myself to Hawaii, but at the last minute, for reasons I still don't understand, I picked up an unlikely crew member, with the even more unlikely name of Sparky. The voices in my head were against this guy as crew, but I didn't heed their warning. After Sparky spent a long week of mal-de-mar at sea, we made an unscheduled stop in San Francisco, so he could become an ex-crewmember.

During my layover in San Francisco, I met two individuals that would change my life forever: Sheryl and Jack.

After nearly a month in the bay area, I once again set off for Hawaii. I tried to talk Sheryl into sailing with me, but as the owner of a flower shop, she couldn't just leave on the spur of the moment. With promises to meet somewhere down the line, I resumed my cruise to the islands, this time with Jack as my traveling companion. As it turned out, he was very good company.

Jack and I had a fantastic time in Hawaii. That is if you don't count the time we nearly crashed the boat making land fall on the Big Island, or hurricane Iniki that destroyed several boats in the area where we were anchored. But, as the saying goes, God watches out for idiots and drunks, and I definitely fell into one, or both, of those categories.

After spending several months in those beautiful islands, it was time for us to push on. We aimed the bow south and headed toward the equator and a small atoll with the name of Fanning Island. That would be my first foreign port of call. While there, I was able to help the remote islanders with a small electrical problem that had plagued the islands only TV, and that charitable act brought me huge rewards. I never had to crack open my own coconuts again.

The month on Fanning went by in a blur. Saying goodbye and pulling anchor was much harder than the journey to get there had been. I found, once again, that leaving a place and new acquaintances was one of the toughest parts of cruising.

Bora Bora, with its history and charm, was *Rick's Place* first stop in the southern hemisphere. Beautiful coral and expensive hamburgers made for a real love-hate relationship to this part of Polynesia.

Pressing on to the Cook Islands, the hamburgers got cheaper and the snorkeling was magnificent. Paradise just kept getting better and better.

All the while, during the months since leaving Sheryl in San Francisco, we attempted to meet up in the various tropical ports in which I stopped. I felt a bond with this tall blue-eyed blonde and I wanted to nurture our relationship. But, fate had its own agenda and plans always fell through, so Jack and I kept moving west.

Our next stop was the Kingdom of Tonga. Now that sounds exotic and it was. With many islands, big and small, completely surrounded by a barrier reef, traveling and snorkeling there was very pleasant indeed. I wanted to spend more time in Tonga, but the need to explore, rather than stay put, drove me on. It was a decision that I have replayed over and over again in my mind.

Fiji, the land of the cannibals, was the next destination. A short sail from Tonga and again the snorkeling was beyond words. The days were glorious with blue skies dotted with cotton ball clouds and azure water.

Ruku Ruku was a village on a small protected bay on the island of Ovalau, in which *Rick's Place* was anchored during my stay in Fiji. I was invited to join in a Kava Kava ceremony with the local chief and I brought my own Kava to share. This endeavor made it possible for Jack and me to stay in the bay and be welcomed as part of the village. Here I helped hook up the village's first generator for lights, learned to weave palm fronds and sharpened my skills at reef fishing.

This was truly the paradise I had been searching for. Many times in life, the expectation exceeds the reality, but in the case of Ruku Ruku, the opposite was true. It was more wonderful than I could ever have imagined.

But, Mother Nature follows her own rules: rules that don't always conform to a set calendar. So when an out of season cyclone struck that small bay, my life was changed forever.

"Rick are you listening to me?" came a slightly irritated voice forcing me out of my long day dream. With the mental dexterity of an idiot savant, OK, maybe just an idiot, I snapped back to the present.

"I've been talking to you for the last ten minutes, have you heard anything I've said?" she asked with a knowing smile.

"Of course, Sheryl, you said something about something else and concluded with what a great guy I am."

With that, she yanks the small line that's holding my air mattress to *Casablanca* sending me into the warm clear water. And so it goes.

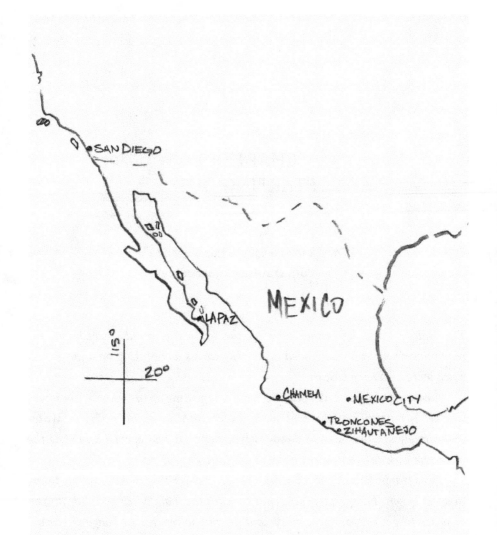

PART 1
MEXICO

CHAPTER 1
STARTING OUT

"Who knows what the tide will bring"
—Tom Hanks in *Castaway*

The thunder and lightening were occurring nearly simultaneously as the remaining daylight quickly faded away. The waves were taking on a larger and much more menacing posture.

According to my instruments, the wind was gusting up to 60 knots, but it was still eerily quiet. Then the boat hit the reef with a sickening THUD. Water immediately started to pour through the crack that had opened up below the waterline – a crack that wore an evil jack-o-lantern grin.

I was trapped inside the cabin and the water was rising rapidly, quickly filling to waist height. I desperately stretched to reach the main hatch and slide it open in order to get out of the watery confine, but it refused to budge. I started pounding on the stubborn hatch with all my might as the water swirled up to my chest. Complete panic was setting in. Rick's Place began to lean at a 45 degree angle as it was beaten by the relentless waves.

The salt water was burning my nostrils as I thrashed around searching for another way out. Something outside the porthole caught my eye and as I strained to see what was there, a bolt of lightening illuminated the sky and I realized it was Jack, my traveling companion of more than a year, staring in at me and he was calling my name, "Rick, Rick!"

"Rick! Wake up! You're having a nightmare," Sheryl said, gently nudging me back to reality.

As the fogginess of the dream lifted, I realized I was actually safe inside the dry cabin of my 35 foot sailboat, *Casablanca,* and I could see Jack was sleeping comfortably on the V-berth. Sitting up and finger combing my curly brown hair out of my eyes, I noticed I was covered with sweat, an occurrence that seemed to be happening with increased frequency.

"It's that weird dream again," I told her, getting out of bed and stumbling to the table to sit down. "I am back at Ruku, on *Rick's Place,* during the storm. Water keeps pouring in but I am trapped below and the hatch won't open."

"This month will be the three year anniversary of ....you know....losing your boat on the reef," Sheryl said soothingly. She reached her delicate hand across the table, and softly placed it on mine. "You're just subconsciously beating yourself up over that terrible loss."

"In my dream, Jack gets out OK and I'm the one trapped. What's with that?" I ask rhetorically.

"It shows you were really worried about his well being. You love him as much as I do."

"Listen," I said looking up, "that miserable cat got me into more trouble....."

"Oh, pleeeeze! You wouldn't have known what to do without him to keep you company on *Rick's Place,*" she said smiling as she scratched the sleeping cat behind the ears.

With that, Jack, Sheryl's docile, and somewhat overweight, tabby cat, stretched and yawned, then continued on with what he does best: napping. Jack and I had gotten to know each other pretty well in the past several years. He had inadvertently stowed away on my previous boat as I set sail across the Pacific Ocean. Luckily, Sheryl had toilet trained him at a young age, so he wasn't as much of a bother as he might have been. In fact, she was probably right when she said I wouldn't have known what to do without him on that voyage.

"It's nearly sunrise. I'll make some tea and cocoa then meet you out in the cockpit," Sheryl spoke trying to coax me out of my dream induced funk. Sheryl's compassion was just one of the many qualities that makes her very special. I was grateful she was able to take time away from her successful flower shop and share this adventure with me.

"See ya out there," I said, my mood brightening. I climbed up the stairs and flopped onto a cockpit cushion and began reflecting on the differences between *Casablanca* and *Rick's Place*. *Casablanca* was only five feet longer in length, but coupled with its three foot wider beam, it felt like twice the boat. But the biggest difference between the two boats is that *Casablanca* has a center cockpit, which sets higher above the water and helps keep errant waves at bay. *Casablanca's* design also allows for easy movement as the teak decks are nearly two feet wide the entire length of the boat between the cabin top and the life lines.

As I looked around, I was happy to see the seas were smooth and we were still bobbing gently at anchor. I relaxed into the silence of the predawn. The temperature was a very comfortable 73 degrees and I knew that the water temperature would be about the same. I was hoping to enjoy a little swim before breakfast, as soon as it was full light.

Sheryl, Jack and I are anchored in the Sea of Cortez, off of a resort called *Perry's Landing* just 15 miles north of La Paz, Mexico. The resort is only a few years old and it is built on the rocky, cactus covered hills that are about 200 feet from the crystal clear water of this inland sea. Once called the aquarium of the world by Jacques Cousteau, these waters are a treasure trove of aquatic life.

The resort consists of a stucco building that is two stories high and divided into 12 rooms. Each room is decorated with furniture, wall hangings and artifacts that depict different themes of the rich Mexican culture. From the Aztec Room to the Gold Coast Room the owner spared no expense in bringing authenticity to each unique unit.

Outside, there is a wonderful infinity pool with waterfalls, hidden caves and a swim up bar: definitely an ideal place to go for low key relaxation.

There are also eight small bungalows designed for the sport-fishing crowd. Each of the two bedroom thatched huts is stocked with fishing gear and also has a small runabout boat assigned to it. Of course, a larger charter boat is available for extended fishing trips.

Once caught, the fish are tagged, cleaned and deposited to the resort's freezer until its owner is ready to leave. The catch can also be flash-frozen and shipped anywhere in the world or prepared that night by the chef for a delicious dinner.

The resort has a landing strip that can accommodate medium sized corporate jets complete with aero fuel service. The opulent accommodations, coupled with the rather obscure location, have made

Perry's Landing a favorite for those who like to, and can afford to, get away from the crowds. Celebrities, sports figures and the rest of the stinking rich seem to gravitate to this little remote piece of heaven which sits on one mile of white sand beach.

Unlike the guests that come here to "get away from it all", I had the good fortune of enjoying this luxury because I just so happen to know the man that owns the resort.

The story of our first meeting and subsequent friendship began back when I was only twelve years old....

I grew up in a small town on Puget Sound in Washington State. Life in Gig Harbor was slow of pace even though it was only removed from the chaos of Seattle's high rises and traffic jams by about 30 miles. The town consisted of about 5,000 people at that time and the mainstreet, Harborview Drive, meanders around the shoreline of the almost triangular shaped bay that is Gig Harbor. Net sheds, some a hundred years old, were built out over the water. Fishing trawlers, purse seiners and long liners filled the docks attached to the sheds. The toll bridge on the main highway to Gig Harbor acted as a deterrent and helped it to maintain it's quaint fishing village charm for many years.

Our neighborhood, which was several blocks inland from the waterfront area, consisted of wood frame houses built in the 40's and 50's complete with picket fences, neatly trimmed lawns and tidy gardens. It was your typical middle class neighborhood.

My three best friends growing up were Steve, Donnie and Randy. Steve, a thin blond kid, was the oldest in a family of three boys and the most mature of our bunch. He, too, didn't have a father and had kind of taken on that role to his younger brothers. Randy, however, came from a very large family, eleven kids in all, and didn't feel the heavy responsibility that Steve did. He was the risk taker. Donnie was slightly cross-eyed and just a little "off". He'd moved into the neighborhood later than the rest of us and we always teased him about how his mother doted over him by calling him a momma's boy. He was the most cautious of the four of us; nonetheless, we could always depend on him to go along with whatever we cooked up.

We called our little group the "Adventurer's Club". The unspoken motto of our small membership was simply to find as many things to do after school or during the long summer days to keep from getting bored, or even worse, getting roped into doing work around the house. We would construct forts and tree houses, dam up streams and build rafts to float across ponds. We constantly walked that thin line that separated good behavior (boring) from bad behavior (exciting). When our parents would say, "Stay out of trouble" we knew they weren't kidding, but those were words we heard a lot.

I came from a single parent household. Mom, who was built like a fireplug, short and wide, came from the wilds of Northern Canada where she learned to be tough. Her red hair matched her fiery temper and the justice that she dispensed to her only child was swift, but fair. She had to raise me by herself from day one, as my father, the love of her life, was tragically killed in a motorcycle accident before I was born. She never remarried, and I suspect it was because between me and the two jobs she worked to support us, she didn't have time for much of a social life. Like many women of her age group, she had an infatuation with Humphrey Bogart, so she named me Rick in honor of his character in her favorite movie, *Casablanca*.

Our little group thought that we were pretty darn clever and we balanced on the tight rope between good and evil with a master's skill. But, one winter week, our smugness caught up with us.

It was mid-January and the first snow of the season had been falling sporadically for several days. The roads were being kept passable thanks to the city's one and only snowplow. We were having loads of fun, taking great pride in our many snow creations which included snow forts and giant snow balls which we'd occasionally roll out into the street to attempt to block the traffic. Of course, we never tired of writing our names in the snow.

Unfortunately, the teenage drivers of Gig Harbor had no respect for our creative snow sculptures. Almost before we would finish a work of art, an old dented car or truck would swerve off the street and purposely crash into whatever we had just fashioned. After a couple days of repeated destruction of our labors, we came up with a sure fire plan to put a stop to, and get even with, the rampaging snow bullies.

We chose my yard for "Operation Get Even" because we had a corner lot and it would attract the hoodlums from two different streets: location, location, location. After selecting a large rock from our terraced garden, the four of us struggled with the weight of the 2 by 3 foot stone, finally getting it on to a snow sled. Dragging it to a spot visible from both streets we strategically placed the boulder about 6 feet from the road. Then, with fresh snow beginning to fall, we proceeded to build a snowman. Instead of rolling a big ball for the base, we simply packed snow around the huge rock we'd just relocated. That done, we rolled two balls of snow to complete Frosty in the more traditional way. We went all out to decorate the bait, giving him a hat, scarf, charcoal eyes, a carrot nose and we even had him holding a broomstick. All that was missing was a corncob pipe. It was a masterpiece and the whole scene cried out "Run me over!".

So we waited. With the fresh falling snow, the cars weren't driving around and it wasn't until the next day that we got a strike. Around seven that evening I heard the tell tale sounds of a car engine revving up and I bolted to the window hoping to see our snowman extract revenge for all his fallen brethren. The streetlight on the corner illuminated the scene perfectly and my heart raced as I saw the truck turn off the road aiming for Frosty the Destroyer. I held my breath and watched as the vehicle sped in for the kill. There was a dull THUD and I was dismayed to see the snowman's head fly through the air while the truck that had attacked him didn't even slow down. He had driven right over the top of the rock that we'd hoped would put an end to the delinquent's reign of terror.

The next day we examined what was left of our failed trap. Picking up the crushed hat and broken broom, we were disappointed. Not because of the snowman's demise, but because we believed we were smarter than the knuckleheads that had run over our work. Walking down the sidewalk towards Donnie's house, we all stopped dead in our snowy tracks. The answer was sitting right in front of us! With peals of excited laughter we set about gathering the hat, carrot and all the other pieces we'd need to put Frosty together again. With bubbling energy the four of us proceeded to build the next great snow warrior. The job took us several hours, as we had to import some snow from adjoining yards. Just as the winter sun was beginning to dip below the horizon, our new manifestation was complete. We stepped back and admired our work, patting each other on the back, before Randy, Steve, Donnie and I split up to head home for the evening.

We hadn't gotten far when we heard the familiar un-muffled noise of the pickup which announced the return of the enemy that had been terrorizing the neighborhood. Quickly, the four of us regrouped and hid together in the shadows of a nearby laurel hedge. The truck passed right in front of us as it clearly took aim at its target. We heard the young driver and his passenger whooping it up as they began the charge, but suddenly, with just a couple car lengths to go, he must have realized his mistake and he tried to stop the truck. The icy road had other ideas and the pickup only managed to swerve slightly, unable to avoid the trap entirely.

There was a shriek of tearing metal, a grinding sound and then silence. When the snow had settled the vehicle sported a six foot long gash down the passenger's side which included the front fender and door. The silence was broken by a string of curse words as the driver got out of the battered cab. We could see the passenger trying to shoulder his door open, but unfortunately it was now inoperative having taken the brunt of the damage.

"Those little bastards built the snowman over the fire hydrant!" the driver was screaming to his still stuck accomplice and the rest of the world.

We stood rooted in our hiding spot, collectively holding our breath as we watched the angry teen get back behind the steering wheel and attempt to get the truck unstuck by revving the motor and rocking the pickup truck back and forth—first putting it in forward and then in reverse. After a few minutes there was a final metal ripping sound as the four-wheel battering ram was freed of the fire hydrants clutches.

As the pickup disappeared around the corner, we broke into muted cheers and back slapping.

Our reverie was halted when Randy's mom's voice boomed out from a few houses down announcing it was time to come in. The celebrating would need to resume in the morning.

That night I drifted off to sleep content in the knowledge that a bully had gotten what he deserved.

When Mom's not so sweet sandpaper voice tore me out of dreamland early the next morning, I hopped out of bed still giddy with the excitement of the night before. As I headed to the bathroom, something outside the bedroom window caught my eye. On the street, I saw the flashing amber lights atop a city utility truck and my curiosity soon turned to dread as I watched one of the two men in coveralls examining a tattered hat that looked way too much like Sir Frosty's chapeau. Craning my neck I could just barely get a look at the last known position of the snowman. There was a large area of standing water precisely where the hydrant came out of the ground. Instinctively I ducked below the window to avoid detection by the city workers and muttered one of the swear words I'd picked up from our

Turret's inflicted friend, Donnie. I dared to poke my head up slowly for another peek and observed one of the men using a long wrench to turn what must have been a valve to stop the flow of water.

"Ricky!" My mom's voice boomed nearly causing me to pee my PJ's. "Get a move on or you'll be late for school!"

As I washed up to get ready to go, the knot in my stomach told me I didn't want to come face to face with the city crew. So after a couple minutes of practicing my best "sick look" in the mirror, it was time to try it on Mom.

But, as luck would have it, just as I reached the kitchen table I heard the diesel roar of the city's repair truck leave our neighborhood.

"Slowpoke, are you feeling OK?" Mom asked as she placed her hand on my forehead.

"I'm fine," I said, even though I was still recovering from the sick-to-my-stomach feeling brought on at the sight of workers at the scene of the crime. But now that the danger seemed to have passed, there was no way I was going to be kept from going to school and talking to the boys about the snowman covered, truck damaged fire hydrant!

After hurriedly completing my morning tasks, I bid Mom a goodbye with the promise of being a good citizen and a learned scholar, or in her words, "Pay attention to your teachers and stay out of trouble."

The four of us made a habit of meeting together in the morning before Donnie's short bus came and picked him up to take him to a different school than the rest of us attended. We never talked about where he went or why, but I was pretty sure it had something to do with the language that he used.

"Shit Damn!" Donnie yelled when he saw the enormous amount of water around the hydrant.

"Donnie, relax," we all said nearly at once. We didn't need him going off right now and drawing attention to us.

Steve whispered, "Are we in trouble or what?"

"No way," I offered up, "we didn't drive that truck!"

"That guy sure messed up his truck, huh," Randy put in.

So we decided we would stay away from the area for a while. We could hang out in Randy's back yard until the whole thing blew over in a few days. As Donnie boarded his bus, I picked up the crumpled hat the repairman had been handling. Randy and Steve grabbed the scarf, broom and what was left of the carrot nose. We chucked it all into a trash can on our way to school so there would be no evidence of our involvement.

The next couple weeks were spent mostly indoors playing board games or taking stuff apart, like old clocks (who knew they were antiques?), and just plain laying low. Gradually our anxiety level returned to normal, as did the weather.

With spring fast approaching we were again ready to get back outdoors. The days were getting noticeably longer, much to our delight. Winters in the Northwest take a toll on kids and parents alike, as the short period of daylight hours limit "outdoor time" and every one gets cabin fever.

Walking home from school one mid-March day, we turned the corner at the end of our block and were greeted by heavy construction equipment working around the fire hydrant that had been deactivated since the time the truck had plowed into it. Luckily there had been no fires in the neighborhood in the intervening time.

There was a backhoe parked very close to the damaged hydrant. I'd seen those used when they dug trenches for pipes along the road, with their long arms and big scoops on the end. Next to it was a bright yellow tractor with a large flat blade for pushing dirt. Smoke was bellowing from its noisy engine as it slowly moved back and forth. There were no wheels; instead, it had belted tracks like on the combat tanks in old war movies. On the side of all the equipment in large letters were the words "Perry Construction" followed by a phone number.

So for the remainder of the week *The Adventurer's Club* would happily hang around the construction site watching the crew of three muscular young men dig holes, push dirt and yell obscenities. We found watching to be great fun, but what we really looked forward to was when the crew went home for the day and we were able to sneak a closer look at the tractor and backhoe. We'd ride our bikes within touching distance of the equipment or "inadvertently" kick a soccer ball underneath the tractor, anything to get up close and personal with the awe-inspiring machines.

Saturday rolled around and the four of us gathered together at the construction site. When it was clear that there would be no digging activities taking place on the weekend, we boldly climbed up on the tractor and took turns sitting in the seat. Perched so high off the ground on the massive piece of machinery, it gave one a real feeling of power. Our imaginations had us pushing up dirt piles or knocking down trees with the wide blade.

"Hey! You boys get off that thing!" yelled Mr. Fritch, an older white-haired man from the next block over. He was obviously coming back from the local Food King grocery store (the one I would later work at during high school, rising to the high position of Produce Manager) because he was pushing a shopping cart that should have been left in the parking lot.

"I'll call the cops on you little hoodlums," he threatened in a raspy voice. Donnie and Steve obediently jumped off the large yellow beast. Randy, who was sitting on the arm rest next to me, jumped up and in doing so he kicked an unseen switch with his tennis shoe. Suddenly, black smoke and a grumble of the diesel engine coming to life made the situation a whole lot worse.

"Shut the thing off!!" I yelled at Randy.

He fumbled around for what seemed like forever, but could not find the switch to stop the engine. He was getting kind of pale looking and said, "Look, we gotta get outta here."

"No, we have to shut it off," I said resisting the urge to just run and hide under my bed.

Meanwhile, Steve and Donnie were yelling at us from the ground, "Come on! The cops are on the way! Just push a button or something. We gotta scram!"

Randy jumped off the machine and yelled, "come on Rick. We gotta beat it!"

As I got up I hit a lever with my knee and the tractor lurched forward, flinging me back in the seat.

"Rick, get the hell off that thing! Stop it and let's go," yelled the guys, now in full panic mode.

The pace of the machine was just a little faster than a person walking, but to me it was way too fast. I knew I couldn't let this mechanical monster just travel on its own because it would surely knock down a house or two. At least if I stayed on it maybe I could steer it away from some disaster.

My friends stuck with me instead of running to save their own necks, and they walked right alongside the yellow behemoth calling out instructions:

"Pull that lever", "Push that button", "Flip that switch", even though nobody knew in the least what to do.

But soon I would need to make a decision because not more than one hundred feet in front of me sat the parked car and the distance was diminishing all too rapidly. No amount of twisting knobs, pulling levers or praying seemed to impede the progress of this dooms-day machine. And the thing that scared me most was that if I didn't stop it I would have to answer to Mom.

Fifty feet and closing and I still didn't know how to turn the machine, let alone shut it off, so I was trying to decide whether to bail off just before impact or ride it on in. I was hoping if I sustained some minor injuries maybe Mom would be a bit more lenient and not dispense the full blown punishment that I knew she was capable of. As my mind was racing through the different consequences that would probably follow me into adulthood and put an ugly splotch on my permanent record, I noticed that my friends were suddenly no where to be seen and then I saw why they took off: A bright yellow "Perry Construction" truck had just skidded to a halt right next to the Buick that I was about ready to plow into. A squat, thin-haired, deeply tanned man about my mom's age, was getting out of the truck and heading towards me. I recognized him as the guy that doesn't work at the site full time, but comes by nearly every afternoon to check on what's going on. He moved briskly to catch up to the smoke belching demon that I was riding, then he deftly jumped on the rotating track and walked on it like it was a moving sidewalk. Without a word he reached under the dash and pulled a plug that was painted red. Suddenly there was silence as the tractor lurched to a stop. I heard a bird chirping in a nearby tree and then he spoke, "You kids could-a caused a lot of trouble or run somebody over," he said sternly. "Your buddies all beat feet. Where do you live?" And before I could answer he added, "I'll take ya home and let your dad deal with ya."

"I don't have a dad....my mom's a widow," I stammered.

"Where do ya live?" he repeated.

"That brick house on the next block. The one on the corner," I said with dread as I pointed to my house.

"Let's go," he demanded and we started walking to what I knew would be a very messy situation.

"What's your name," he asked as we walked in the direction of my demise.

"It's Rick, sir,"

12

"I'm Joe...have you lived here all your life?"

"Yes."

"Just you and your mom?"

"Yes."

"Where does she work?"

"She works at the hospital at night and for the schools part time during the day," I answered wondering where all this was leading. I was fearing I had even gotten Mom in deepwater with this screw up, but then Joe stopped and looked at me with eyes that were much softer now then they had been minutes ago.

"Your mom going to tear you up over this?"

"Yes sir!"

When we arrived at the front door of our house he stopped and put his hand on my shoulder and said, "Rick, you let me do the talking."

"Yes sir," I choked out, feeling the blood drain from my face. God was I scared!

As I opened the door I was surprised to see Mom already walking toward us.

"Mom, this is Joe," I said awkwardly.

"Hello Joe, my name is Muriel. How can I help you?" Then she added, "Is Ricky in some sort of trouble?" glancing at me like she was trying to read my face.

Here it comes, my life will never be the same....I'll never see the light of day again. I was about to throw myself on the floor and beg for forgiveness when Joe spoke.

"No, no... He's not in any trouble. Actually he helped me by pointing out that one of my men left a master switch on in the tractor out there. I own the construction company repairing the water hydrant down the street."

My jaw dropped to the floor and I just stared in amazement as Joe continued on with his story.

"I just wanted to ask your permission for Rick to come down to my shop and do some sweeping and cleaning up....you know, after school....pay is $5 per hour."

"That's a very generous offer, Joe," Mom said, stealing another suspicious look my way.

"Well then, it's settled. I'll see you on Monday Rick".

"One of the guys working on the hydrant will bring you over from here. We're only a couple miles away. Muriel, it's been a pleasure...talk to you soon." And with that Joe turned and opened up the front door and started down the stairs

"That seemed odd Ricky. Are you sure there's nothing going on?" she started to grill me.

"I'll be right back Mom, I gotta tell Joe something," I said as I rushed out the door to avoid the question.

I caught up with Joe just as he was getting into his yellow pick up.

"Thank you very much," I said softly.

"No problem kid. Just stay out of trouble and off my equipment," he said as he slammed the door. The truck coughed to life and started to pull away, then suddenly it stopped and he backed up and rolled down the window. Leaning out he said, "By the way, I heard the reason the hydrant got broken was that some kids built a snowman around it and some jerk hit it with a truck trying to mow it down. You wouldn't know anything about that, would you now?" Before I could say anything he added smiling, "I didn't guess so..."

So I ended up working for Joe Perry for a couple of months after school, cleaning up the shop and learning some basic mechanical skills. It was my job to clean the dirt off the machinery when it was brought in to the yard. I also learned to grease and maintain the equipment and even got to drive the tractors around the property on occasion. Looking back, that job, and Joe, probably kept me out of a lot of trouble.

When school was letting out for the summer, Joe "cut me loose" as he said so I could pursue other interests, but we remained friends throughout my teenage years. And Mom, well, I think she knew something didn't smell quite right that March day, but ignorance being bliss won out. She also thought it was a good idea to keep me working, both for the extra cash and to occupy my time, hopefully keeping me out of trouble. It wasn't long before she insisted I get a summer job: a newspaper route.

L.O.A.	34'-6"
L.W.L.	27'-6"
BEAM	11'-0"
DRAFT	4'-8"
DISP.	21,000 lbs.
BALLAST	7,200 lbs.
SAIL AREA	630 Sq. Ft.
POWER	DIESEL
FUEL	120 GALLONS
WATER	215 GALLONS

CHAPTER 2
MOVIN' ON

"If you don't know where you are going, you're going to end up somewhere else."
—Laurence J. Peters

The tea kettle whistling atop the two burner propane stove in *Casablanca's* galley, brought me back to the present. Sitting in the cockpit, I soon heard the tinkling of a spoon hitting the sides of my favorite mug, as Sheryl prepared our morning drinks: hot cocoa for me, English breakfast tea for her. She then joined me in the cockpit just as the sun's first rays graced the desolate, cactus strewn hillside of Mexico's Baja Peninsula.

"This never gets old, does it?" She said smiling at the promise of another beautiful day.

"Yeah, kinda tough to take, alright," I replied sarcastically, and then added, "you know I only have a couple more sailing classes to teach then I'll be done here."

"I'm just about finished with the landscaping at Perry's compound as well. It looks like we'll be moving on soon," she said with a tinge of bittersweet in her voice. This would be Sheryl's first experience of what I have always considered one of the hardest parts of cruising: leaving a place and new found friends when it's time to set off on a new adventure.

It was quite a stroke of luck that Sheryl and I were able to get jobs in the Sea of Cortez. We were living in this beautiful spot and both doing things we loved, plus fattening up our cruising kitty (and I don't mean Jack). Life doesn't get much better than that.

Several months earlier, while we were in San Diego, getting ready to head south of the border into Mexico, I received a call from Mom. She had been talking to Joe Perry (who had remained a family friend since that incident with the tractor many years ago). She wanted me to know that since he'd retired and sold his construction business he'd bought a resort near La Paz, Mexico and was now looking for someone to teach sailing lessons for a couple months. He was hoping I could lend him a hand. Sounded like a win-win situation to me. The pay wouldn't be that much, but we'd have the run of the place. It sounded like a great spot with nice little bungalows, a good restaurant and bar with live music during the busy season.

With jobs waiting for us, we then had a plan and set sail from San Diego. Our first stop, a mere 60 miles away, was Ensenada, Mexico. We chose to clear into the country there, because they've streamlined the process in that city, putting all the agencies that you must visit in one building. In other ports of entry the Customs, Immigration, Port Captain and bank are scattered all over town making it an all day scavenger hunt in a strange and foreign city.

After a short stay in the busy city of Ensenada we set off for Turtle Bay, a dusty little village about 300 miles south that offers the most protected anchorage on the Pacific Baja coast. There we were able to top off our fuel tanks and wait for a good weather window to continue on.

Cabo San Lucas was the next stop. Just a four day sail from Turtle Bay, but a world apart. Cruise ships, condos and high rise resorts greeted *Casablanca* and her crew as we rounded Lands End, the most southern point on the Baja Peninsula. Once we left the hustle and bustle of Cabo, we headed north, into the Sea of Cortez toward the city of La Paz, another 150 miles away.

A month after that call from Mom, we were anchored off the resort, near the city of La Paz, having dinner with Joe. Much to my embarrassment he loved telling everyone about our calamitous first meeting and it seemed to get worse with each telling. When he found out about Sheryl's green thumb and landscaping background, he hired her to be the official gardener to get the grounds around the compound up to his high standards.

So we lived this idyllic life for two months, but our work there was nearly complete and Sheryl asked, "Where to next?"

"Troncones!" was my reply. That had been my goal when I first decided to head to Mexico, because I'd found out that Sparky, an old crewmate of mine, was living down there and had just gotten married to a girl named Tami. I went on to explain, "Troncones is a ways down the coast: just a bit north of Zihautanejo and there's some nice stops along the way."

"Sounds great to me," she replied as she finished the last of her tea. She set her cup down, stood up and kissed me on the forehead. Already in her bathing suit, she gracefully dove off the side of the boat into the clear, warm, Mexican water. She surfaced nearby and called up to me, "Make sure you feed Jack Cat—I'll see you on shore!" And with that she was off to work. We had use of one of the bungalows at the resort where we could shower and both kept a change of clothes which meant we could swim to shore and not worry about clothing.

The sounds of commotion drew Jack up into the cockpit to check things out and I turned to him and said, "Nice commute, don't ya think?" giving his head a little scratch. As always, he bit my hand in reply.

Jack the cat and I have a history. I first met this large tabby in Emeryville, California, where I made an unscheduled stop on my way to Hawaii in my first cruising boat, *Rick's Place*. There I spent several weeks at the dock readying the boat to continue on to the islands and Jack became a frequent visitor. He'd happily accept handouts, but he usually just liked a nice place to sleep. He was the most laid-back cat I'd ever encountered and I realized Jack was special from the first day. First: because he was trained to use the toilet. No litter box required for this cat. And second, his owner was a statuesque woman with long blonde hair and captivating silvery blue eyes set above her lightly freckled nose. A small scar creased her left eyebrow, the result of a run in with a shovel when she was just six years old, the tiny imperfection only added interest to her face. I quickly fell in love with the lovely, quick-witted free spirit in her bohemian style clothing. I was happy to have both Sheryl and Jack sharing *Casablanca* with me as we meandered through Mexico, enjoying the cruising life. Jack actually sailed with me before Sheryl had, when he inadvertently stowed away as I left San Francisco Bay to continue my solo crossing to Hawaii. We ended up sailing more than 3,000 miles together. His undocumented presence made entering Hawaii and every port after a bit of a challenge.

Jack was a good companion and he was with me three years ago when I lost *Rick's Place* as it crashed to shore during an out of season cyclone. We then lived in a hut on a beach in Fiji until Sheryl was able to fly down and take him back home. I followed a short time later, after I sold the bar I had built from the remains of my coral battered boat.

I bought *Casablanca,* a Fantasia 35, so I could continue the cruising lifestyle I'd come to love. She's a roomy, solid ocean going boat, built in the late 70's in Taiwan. Her teak interior gives a warm, cozy ambiance much like a log cabin in the woods. With it's spacious layout, it was easy to convince Sheryl to come along and explore the world with me. Arranging to leave her flower shop in the capable hands of her sister, Joni, she was finally free to go. Of course, Jack was part of the deal, so Rick and Jack were together again.

"Rick, hey Rick! Ya comin' in?" came a voice from shore once again breaking into my thoughts. Young Hector, my 15 year old helper from the resort's sailing class, was calling out to me. It was about time for lessons to begin and I could see that Hector had six of the small, one person Laser's lined up on shore with their colorful sails up. There were a couple of teenage students milling around the beach awaiting their instructions, and I called back, "I'll be right there!"

I quickly put some dry cat food into a dish and told my feline friend, "Stay on the boat, see ya later Jack!"

I grabbed my backpack and tossed it into our 10 foot inflatable dinghy which was tied to the stern of *Casablanca.* Sheryl had christened our small commuter boat with the very appropriate name of *Exit Visa.* After all, you always needed an exit visa to leave *Casablanca.* I climbed in to the tender and untied the line which held it to the mother ship. When I pulled the starter cord on the old 10 hp outboard nothing happened. I adjusted the choke, pulled again.....silence.

"Dammit," I said under my breath and I tried three more times. Each time tugging harder than the last. I was hoping my building frustration would somehow be channeled through the pull cord into the motor. By then the wind had picked up and it was blowing me away from *Casablanca.* I should know not to untie the dinghy until the outboard starts.

The kids on shore were all shouting instructions to me.

"Did you choke it?"

"Are you out of gas?"

"Is it flooded?"

"Is class cancelled?"

I stopped pulling to have a heart to heart with the reluctant propulsion system.

"Look, start you stupid SOB and I promise to give you a tune-up. Please start!" I begged. And with the next attempt, the engine coughed a cloud of blue smoke, missed a beat and then smoothed into a low idle.

I had drifted about a quarter of a mile from *Casablanca* while trying to get *Exit Visa* moving in the right direction, so I put it in gear and roared toward my awaiting sail class. There was a small round of applause to greet me as I stepped from the boat into the shallow water.

With six pubescent faces staring at me, I made a mental note as to which of my charges would have trouble with the rising wind and choppy water. I was lucky because the class was small and for the most part the kids were happy to be sailing in the sleek, fast boats. Their parents were all staying at the resort, having come down on a retreat paid for by the company where they worked: something to do with housing loans. Their unofficial slogan for the 10 day retreat was "Let's put the "treat" back in retreat". So, whole families showed up and they had booked nearly the entire resort for themselves.

Two girls and four boys made up the class. Right from the start the girls seemed to be natural sailors, partly because they paid attention while the basics were being taught and more importantly they weren't nearly as caught up showing off to the opposite sex as the boys had been.

The oldest "sailor to be" was Candace, who lives near Santa Cruz, California. Average height with long auburn hair and a splattering of freckles she was a real cute California surfer girl and very comfortable around the water. Courtney, who was from San Francisco, immediately connected with Candace and they became fast friends. Courtney was always smiling, not the least bit self-conscious of her mouth full of braces. Things have certainly changed since I was a kid. Back then NOBODY wanted braces and if they had to succumb to the torturous bands they would smile behind their hand to hide their embarrassment. Now they are a status symbol.

Then there were the twin boys, Travis and Evan. They had sandy blond hair, tan skin and were constantly punching each other. Always in competition, showing off, with nonstop yammering, they were two tall, wiry bundles of high energy.

A real character in the group was Vinnie, who was 14 but thought he was 18. He always wore earphones presumably listening to music, which combined with his dark wrap-around sunglasses kept him distant from the rest of the world. Sporting jet-black greasy hair and wearing low hanging pants that revealed his shorts underneath, he always made me think of that 'hoody' caddie in *Caddyshack*. He'd grown up near Oakland and was a bit antisocial. It was very apparent he wanted to be there the least of anyone. I'm sure his parents were hoping a structured class would help his stand-offish attitude, or at least force him to dress better. Plus, it would be impossible for him to light his cigarettes out on the water.

The youngest sailor was Jared. A stocky, blond haired kid that was eager to please and always had the right answers, but was a bit shy. I thought he was having a little trouble fitting in, since the girls had 'buddied' up, the twins had each other, and Vinnie was... well... Vinnie.

Hector was already setting up buoys in the water that the class would use as "marks". He placed them in a rough triangle, each being 50 yards from the other. They were laid out this way so the kids could practice sailing up wind, down wind and a beam reach, which is where the wind is hitting the sails at nearly right angles.

After the mandatory safety chat the group paired up to check each others life jackets to be sure all the straps were buckled.

"OK, it's going to be 3 laps around the course, stay to the outside of the buoys. This means you, too, Vinnie." He was one of those kids that always cut the corners trying to get an advantage.

"As always, we'll use that palm tree as the start/finish line," I said pointing to the tallest coconut palm on the beach. "There will be a 'one minute to go' horn, then the start horn. Today there is a prize for the winner in addition to the bragging rights: a DVD of *Captain Ron* that was donated by the resort. So let's go out there and have some fun!"

With that my charges walked the short distance to the beached sailboats and began the final preparations. One by one, they began pushing the small sleek boats into the azure water.

The bantering between Travis and Evan started immediately.

"I am going to kick your butt."

"Eat my wake!" came the response and so it went, on and on.

Candace displayed her usual quiet confidence as she walked to her boat with Courtney in tow. Courtney, being nervous, was rambling on about some off the wall subject.

Jared was already about fifteen feet from shore and he had some lines wrapped around the rudder of his craft, so he was just drifting as he tried to untangle the mess.

Last to leave the beach was Vinnie, with his heavy "I don't give a rip" attitude.

When Jared finally got the rudder free he quickly caught back up with the rest of the small fleet. I then blew the horn indicating there would be one minute to form up at the starting line. The trick was not to be too early across the line because that meant the offending boat would have to circle back and restart. But if you were too late crossing the line you'd end up playing catch up. This group was good, and I watched with a sense of pride as they all circled just behind the start line, dodging each other with only an occasional bump into a competitor.

I blew the horn to begin the race and all the boats shot to the first mark propelled by the wind that was now blowing 12 to 15 knots. The water hadn't gotten choppy yet, so they were off to a good start.

Surprisingly, Jared had the lead coming out of the first buoy, with Courtney close behind, followed by both twins, then Candace and finally Vinnie. I was pleasantly surprised that Jared was putting everything he had learned to the test.

The order remained the same after completing the first lap and the smile on Jared's face was from ear to ear. Candace was finally passing the twins who were busy trying to spoil each others wind and for the most part seemed to have lost concentration on what the objective was. A short time later even Vinnie moved past the boys who were now more interested in trying to ram each other. Apparently they thought they were in bumper cars and not a sailboat race. Oh well.

By the beginning of the 3rd lap the wind had climbed to over 15 knots, which is a bit much for these small boats. I could tell Jared was sailing slightly out of control, but he was still in the lead. The rest of the pack followed with Candace, Vinnie and Courtney within a boat length of each other and rapidly closing on the leader.

Suddenly a strong gust of wind hit the fleet. Before Jared could react and release his main sail, the boat was capsized by the unseen force. Unfortunately, Jared was a better sailor than swimmer and even with the life jacket on he appeared to be struggling to keep his head above water.

I pushed my inflatable dinghy out from the shoreline, jumped in and pulled on the motor's starting cord: nothing. Dammit! Luckily it took on the second pull and I didn't have a repeat of the morning's problems. Swinging around I gave the outboard full throttle until I was within 20 feet of the boy. I coasted the rest of the way in neutral so I wouldn't injure him with the propeller. I reached down and grabbed Jared by the life jacket, just as he inhaled what seemed like another gallon of salt water. I dragged his heavy body into the dinghy and he started to vomit uncontrollably. I nudged him and got his head over the side of the boat and let nature take its course.

During the slow motor to shore, with the Laser in tow, the poor kid gave back to the sea everything he had swallowed plus breakfast. And so it goes....

With Hector's help we cleaned up my dinghy and dried out the Laser. The rest of the class had gone their separate ways once the race was over. The small boats stayed on the beach, so that other resort customers could use them for the remainder of the day.

It was about noon when I finally tracked down Sheryl to see if she was ready to have lunch. We sat down to enjoy our usual: the fresh fruit plate. It's the best I've ever had with plenty of melon, bananas, cantaloupe and papaya with fresh lime drizzled over the top

"Heard you made a big rescue today," she said with a bit of pride in her voice.

"Yeah, a regular Johnny on the Spot," was my smart ass reply. "I've got to tune up that outboard on *Exit Visa*. It would have been more than embarrassing to have that boy float away because the engine wouldn't start."

"What is it? Spark plugs or something?" she probed.

"Yeah, something," I said rather distracted by what I was seeing, and pointing to Candace, I said to Sheryl, "there's the winner of today's race. She's about the best kid in the group and I just don't understand why she is with Vinnie, the wannabe hoodlum."

The two of them were sharing a Coke in a corner table of the restaurant.

"They're cute together," was Sheryl's observation: "Kind of a bad boy, good girl thing, huh?"

Since Candace was occupied with Vinnie, it left Courtney on her own for once and I was happy to note that Jared was taking advantage of the opportunity to spend some time with her.

"So," I said changing the subject, "Dave's playing tonight at the resort, let's drop in and surprise him."

Dave being Dave Calhoun, a friend of mine from my days of living in Gig Harbor. He's an accomplished guitar player and singer who played throughout the Northwest. *The Tides Tavern,* my old hangout, was where I first saw him. He'd play Sunday afternoons on the deck by the water entertaining us with his 'TropRock' music which is kind of a Caribbean/Jimmy Buffett mix of tunes. He was just finishing his second CD when I last saw him back home, but I'd heard he'd grown in popularity and had produced several more CD's and was playing all over the US. And here he was in Mexico!

I found out that one of the guests involved in the retreat was a big fan and had arranged for him to come down and perform for a couple nights. It would be a nice short getaway for him, considering the Northwest weather. Three years ago he would have done it practically for free, but now he gets paid well. Good for Dave.

I thought it would be fun to show up unannounced and surprise him because even though Dave knew I was somewhere in Mexico, he wouldn't know that I happened to be working at the resort where he would be playing.

We finished our lunch and Sheryl still had a couple hours of work to do, so I headed back to *Casablanca.* Jack greeted me in the cockpit with a long stretch and as I reached down to pet him, he bit my hand for good measure.

That night at the *Panga,* the resort's bar, Dave Calhoun and his guitar were on stage bringing smiles to all the attendees with his warm personality. The setting was a large thatch roof palapa open on three sides with its one wall set behind a highly lacquered ship's hatch cover which served as the bar. The wall held shelves crowded with glasses and colorful bottles of liquor. It was very attractive and well stocked. Opposite the bar was a low rising stage offering a panoramic view with the sea of Cortez as its backdrop. There were about 15 tables scattered over the sand covered floor and it was nearly filled to capacity. Dave's performance was informal with him sitting on a stool and a single spotlight shining down. He played a short set of songs, most having to do with palm trees, warm water, sailing or rum. Sheryl and I had managed to sneak in without him seeing us and we grabbed a table on the outskirts of the room.

In his easy going style he would ask the audience for requests, so after he completed playing *Margaritaville* for about the millionth time in his career, I called out from the shadows, "Play *Eve of Destruction!*"

His reaction was priceless. His jaw dropped, he hesitated for about 5 seconds and then said, "I can think of only one person who would request that song!" as he peered through the darkness trying to find a face to go with the voice. As soon as his eyes locked on to me, a big smile spread across his face and he began to sing the old Sixties protest ballad.

After he finished my request he did several more songs before he was done for the night. As soon as the show was over, Dave came to our table and sat down. I introduced him to Sheryl and then the old stories just flowed along with the drinks. Sheryl just took it all in with her usual indulgent smile.

We continued to talk and drink, while the bar staff closed up and cleaned the room, raking the sand all around us. Finally it was time to call it a night: before it was actually morning.

"What's next for you two?" was Dave's question as the three of us walked out into the warm Mexican air.

"Well, in a couple of days we're headed south to meet up with an old friend," I replied. "How 'bout you?" I asked with a slight slur.

"Marcia and I found the perfect boat and we'll be heading to the Caribbean next year!" He said with great enthusiasm as this had been a long-time dream of his. I was happy he and his charming wife Marcia were finally going to be able to cut the dock lines and experience the cruising life.

We promised to talk again the next day and Dave headed for his room at the resort. I rowed Sheryl back to *Casablanca*. I didn't want to deal with the ill-tempered outboard, plus I always hate to disturb such stillness with the grating sounds of an engine. Under the clear, warm, starry night we talked as *Exit Visa* slid across the water.

"So, let's leave the day after tomorrow," I offered. There was a long silence that had me kind of worried, until it was followed by the sound of light snoring. "I'll take that as a yes," I replied with a smile.

CHAPTER 3
WHEN NATURE CALLS

"If you haven't found something strange during the day,
it hasn't been much of a day."
—Frank A. Clark

Hauling up the anchor off of Perry's Resort, we sailed the short distance to La Paz, one of Baja's larger cities, to re-provision for our trip further south. Not having to rely on cruise ships for revenue, La Paz is a quiet, laid back city of 190,000. The town boasts several marinas and has a good anchorage off town at El Magote making it very cruiser friendly.

The Malecon, which is the three mile long tiled walkway along the waterfront, is always filled with joggers, bike riders and Mexican families strolling along enjoying their wonderful city. With it's colorful past there is a mix of older, historic buildings as well as new high rise condominiums and beautiful private homes.

La Paz has an international airport and Mexico's Highway 1 runs through town making it a major hub of the Baja Peninsula. Because of this, you can find almost anything you need in this friendly, slow paced town. We were able to restock *Casablanca* without want.

The next leg of our journey would be the 300 mile Southern Crossing of the Sea of Cortez to reach the Pacific Coast of Mainland Mexico, often called the Mexican Riviera.

After our crossing from La Paz to Puerto Vallarta, we found out rather quickly that the winds along the mainland coast of Mexico can be very unreliable. It was quite a contrast to my previous sailing experience in the steady trade winds of the open Pacific. The hills and valleys along the coastline have a profound effect on the wind patterns, causing them to accelerate without warning or die just as quickly, making it difficult to actually sail as much as we'd hoped. Luckily fuel was available along the way and diesel was relatively cheap.

From Puerto Vallarta we "harbor hopped" down the coast to break up the 400 mile trek to Troncones and our planned rendezvous with Sparky, my old crewmate. We'd enjoyed brief stops in Yelapa and Punta Ipala, but it was as we approached Bahia de Chamela that things began to get really interesting.

The morning was warm and a gentle swell was coming out of the north, but otherwise the sea was like glass. With the autopilot doing the steering, I was free to engage in one of my favorite activities: just looking around. I am constantly scanning the horizon, the water, the sky, searching for that one unique display of nature that tends to go unnoticed by most.

Six pelicans were flying in formation only inches above the water and just off of *Casablanca's* bow. They have learned that a boat moving through the water will disturb and panic schools of fish which makes for easy dining with just a short dive.

Sheryl was down below in the galley and I could hear her humming as she refilled her tea cup with hot water. Jack the Cat was lying on a cushion in the cockpit across from me with the rays of sunlight warming his fur coat and he looked quite content. All was well in our little world.

When we were a few miles north of Chamela the drone of the engine began having its usual hypnotic effect on me. First come the yawns, then the heavy eyes and before I know it my head jerks back as I wake up not realizing I had dozed off.

I looked around and there were no boats or other hazards in sight, the pelicans were still flying in close formation, Sheryl was down below and Jack was still sleeping across from me. My eyes were just starting to shut once again when.....BANG! The boat shuddered and Jack and I both sprang to our feet. He tore down the stairs passing Sheryl as she was coming up.

"Rick, what happened? What did we hit?" She asked with panic rising in her voice.

I was trying to clear my head and figure out what had happened. I couldn't let on I had been power napping and I had no idea what we might have hit in the short time my eyes had closed. Before I had a chance to answer her, our attention was drawn to the rear of *Casablanca* where a Pelican was struggling to untangle himself from the life lines. We hadn't hit anything in the water after all. Something had hit us from the sky.

"I think the poor guy was diving and missed the water and hit our deck!" I exclaimed, staring in amazement at our unexpected guest.

Upon hearing my voice, the prehistoric looking creature began to struggle and flop around the aft deck getting even more tangled up in the lines and rigging.

"Rick, do something or he'll hurt himself," Sheryl pleaded.

As I made my way back to where the bird was stranded, I was absolutely amazed at its wingspan, which was about 5 feet from tip to tip. I was also astounded by the amount of poop he was leaving on the deck. The more he thrashed the more he pooped.

I was soon within arms reach, but I really didn't know what to do next. The bird kept jutting out his beak as a warning to stay away. I figured I needed to get behind him and get his wings immobile so he wouldn't suffer serious injury.

"Grab a beach towel and hand it up through the hatch," I called back to Sheryl who was staring helplessly at the poor creature. She quickly disappeared below and in a few seconds the back hatch, near where I was standing, cracked open about an inch and a corner of a towel appeared. I slowly pulled it out, so I wouldn't disturb the bird any further, and quietly moved behind the big Pelican. I took a matador's stance with the towel as my cape then launched it forward trying to cover the massive head and body.

Missed it by that much. So now the bird had the towel in his beak and was more pissed than before. After a minor tug of war, I managed to get the beach towel back and I made one more attempt to subdue the feathered fighter. This time I was successful in getting the towel over his head and he immediately seemed to calm down.

I moved in closer and quickly untangled his wing from the lifeline. By that time there were a few feathers mixed in with the bird poop on the deck: what a mess. He was too large to fly off *Casablanca*, so I needed to try to lift him over the side and get him into the water.

"Slow us down," I instructed Sheryl, who was back in the cockpit watching the crazy goings on at the stern of the boat. She eased the throttle and slowly *Casablanca* lost its forward momentum.

I then wrapped my arms around the big bird that was still covered in the towel, and asked Sheryl to come back and take the towel off his head as I released him. I think that would have worked great, but the feathered creature had other plans. Sheryl did lift the head covering just as I was coaxing him over the side, and in one highly coordinated move, the gigantic bird turned his head, jabbed me in the forehead with his battering ram of a beak, pooped in my hand and then dove the short distance into the water.

We watched that guy for about 15 minutes to make sure he was OK, even though I don't know what we could have done had he shown any sign of distress. Then, just as if nothing had happened, he rose from the water and flew away.

"That was the weirdest thing," Sheryl remarked with awe. We were both still a bit stunned by the whole event. After all, it started out sounding like we'd hit something that could sink the boat, then when we discovered what had really happened it was all very surreal. Mother Nature always keeps us entertained. Better than TV.

I looked at the mess the Pelican had left on the deck and remarked, "I guess I'd better start cleaning up the poop deck." Sheryl just shook her head at my corny quip as she stepped back into the cockpit.

With that, I grabbed a bucket, tied a 10 foot length of rope to the handle and tossed it over the side. I scooped up bucket after bucket of the warm salt water and swabbed the deck.

Soon the wind picked up and we were able to turn the engine off, sailing the rest of the way into Bahia Chamela. We dropped the anchor just as the sun was dipping below the western horizon. It was a beautiful setting and a nice anchorage. Roughly a half mile across, the bay was rimmed with a white sand beach. After a light dinner I dropped off to a sound sleep exhausted from all the excitement of the day.

Early the next morning, I opened my eyes when I heard a strange sound: a low raspy vibration that seemed to be coming from the boat itself. When my grogginess lifted, I realized the sound must be emanating from something out in the bay, but I couldn't imagine what was making such an unearthly noise. I glanced out the port hole next to the bed in the aft cabin and didn't see anything out of the norm. I'd just convinced myself that it was part of a dream when I heard the rasp again.

Quietly, as to not awaken Sheryl, I padded up the stairs, opened the hatch and stepped outside. The first rays of light were creeping over the hills turning the inky black sky into another beautiful, bright Mexican day. Scanning our surroundings I didn't see anything that could have been making that eerie noise. There wasn't another boat of any kind in the bay.

Turning to go back downstairs, the strange raspy bellow came again from the bow of the boat. Suddenly there was the pungent stench of old fish enveloping *Casablanca*. Bile was creeping up my throat as I walked forward on the deck. Straining to see in the shadowy dawn, I did spot a large rock or log that was about 100 feet away. Then it happened. The "log" let out a breath of air that was a mix of misty salt water and something very rotten smelling. A WHALE! And he was huge: at least as long as our 35' sailboat. There he lay, sleeping and snoring.

I stood transfixed, afraid to move fearing any noise would awaken the sleeping giant. But I wanted to get Sheryl on deck as soon as possible. The sky was fully light by then and the details of the Herculean giant became more pronounced. Its eye, which appeared the size of a softball, seemed to be staring right at me. Then another big fishy spew erupted and I ran on my tip toes as fast as I could back to the main hatch. Trying to contain my excitement, I cracked the door open, leaned in and whispered forcefully, "Sheryl, Sheryl, wake up. Wake up honey, come here." I thought I heard her stir.

"Hon! Hey Sheryl!"

"Rick, what's wrong?" She asked sounding sleepy and confused.

"Come quick and don't make a sound, but hurry!" I told her, my excitement building just like a kid at Christmas when it's about time to open presents.

Shortly she was at the bottom of the stairs, dressed in an oversized t-shirt emblazoned with Jimmy Buffett's name, her hair was tousled and she had a worried look. Her eyes were searching my face for answers.

"Hurry," I said putting my index finger to my pursed lips and making a shushing sound. I reached down and grabbed her small hand to help her up the companionway stairs, and then practically dragged her down the deck to the bow of the boat. "Look!" I said with a flourish, as if I were a magician revealing what's under a magic scarf.

The look on Sheryl's face was priceless. Her sleepy eyes widened and her jaw dropped. She raised her arm and pointed at the sleeping giant as if she were in a trance, then the whale let out another burst of the fish scented mist.

"Come on, come on," I said, pulling her toward the back of *Casablanca,* nearly running.

"No, I want to look more," she whimpered trying to hold her ground.

"We will, I promise," I said, coaxing her to the cockpit. There I opened a deck box and pulled out our snorkels and masks. I handed one to Sheryl and her look turned to one of astonishment.

"Are you crazy? We can't go in the water with that thing! He could squash us and not even know it," she protested.

"No, no. We'll be fine, let's just go take a little close up look," I prodded.

"If we get killed you are in sooo much trouble, Rick!" She threatened.

I set the boarding ladder over the side of the boat, choosing to climb down into the water instead of diving in which would create a disturbing splash. We slipped in to the bay in near silence, Sheryl holding tight to my hand. Once we were floating in the warm water, we put on our masks and slowly swam toward our sleepy neighbor.

With our heads beneath the surface we could hear the whale breathing. His huge fins would occasionally move just slightly, reminding me of a person treading water. We swam within 6 feet of its head and could see the baleen, the curtain in its mouth that strains the sea water for food. His eye was still open, but it didn't seem to be following our movement, so I was reassured he was still sleeping.

We slowly moved along his body, keeping our distance. The urge was strong to go up close and touch the beast, but knowing any movement on the giant's part could launch us to who knows where, kept me well away. It was fascinating to see small fish poking at the whale's skin, eating microscopic parasites. Between these fish and the barnacles that covered much of his body, the cetacean was a regular ecosystem unto its own.

Sheryl and I had been in the water about 15 minutes when it seemed as if an alarm clock had gone off in the monster's head. He slowly started to move and our bodies followed along with him, due to the gentle current caused by the huge displacement of mass moving through the still water. It appeared our new found friend was on his way out to the open ocean to continue on his migration. We'd already been swept about a hundred feet from our starting point, so it was time for us to head back to the boat.

Once aboard, we were like a couple of teenage girls at a slumber party, talking at each other non-stop. We were excitedly recalling our impressions and observations from our close encounter of the aquatic kind.

After having a late breakfast we readied the boat and began motor sailing to our next destination, Tenacatita, a large bay about 40 miles south. We had clear bright blue skies for the entire, thankfully uneventful, 9 hour trip.

We'd put up the bimini cover, or sunshade, that Sheryl had made during our stay in the Sea of Cortez. We'd found out rather quickly, while anchored there, that the cockpit can become unbearably hot in the intense sun. To remedy this, she built a canvas cover that hooked on to the back of the dodger and stretched over the cockpit. Happy to be out of the sun's searing rays, we motored along, Sheryl enjoying a novel while I searched the sea, hoping to spot Big Gray from this morning's adventure.

Tenacatita is an indentation in the Mexican coast line that measures roughly 3 by 4 miles across. What struck me most when entering the protected waters was the lush jungle that rimmed the clear blue water. Unlike the stark scenery of the Sea of Cortez, here there were many shades of green, starting at the coastline and marching far back into the hills then on to the distant mountains. The sliver of beach appeared to be coarse white sand. There was a small swell following *Casablanca* as we slowly motored along the shore looking for a good spot to anchor.

Fifteen cruising boats, of various sizes, were anchored at the north end of the bay, tucked behind a series of small rock islets. These small islands deflected the swell that parades in from the open ocean created by far off storms. We noted that these boats seemed to be lying quietly at anchor with little rocking and rolling, so we approached and circled the area looking for just the right spot to drop our hook.

Anchoring became much easier once Sheryl had come aboard than it had been for me when I single-handed across the South Pacific. We'd already established a good routine in which once we decided where we wanted to be, she would take over the wheel as I went forward to prepare the anchor.

When we found a suitable spot Sheryl brought us to a complete stop and announced the depth reading from the instrument. I then lowered the anchor with the appropriate amount of chain. At my signal, she put the boat in a slow reverse and backed up until the 45 lb. plow anchor dug in. Then, I signaled for her to apply full power, while still in reverse, just to make sure we were firmly secured to the sandy bottom.

Once she cut the power, the boat gently drifted up to where I had dropped the hook. The engine was turned off and after the long day of motoring with the engine noise and vibration, we sat, relaxed and relished the silence. We spent the next half hour or so watching points on land to confirm that we weren't drifting and the anchor was holding.

I was sitting on the bow of the boat when Sheryl came up, kissed me on the cheek and handed me the binoculars. We took turns scanning the shoreline looking for anything of interest. Jack soon sauntered up and took station between us as if he were also checking out our new neighborhood.

We saw locals playing in the slight surf off the small palapas, or open-air thatched roof restaurants, that dotted a portion of the beach. There were a number of dinghies from the cruising boats pulled up on the sand at the head of the bay. Then we saw an occupied dinghy appear out of the thick vegetation and motor out through the one area that didn't have any surf breaking.

Pointing, I said, "I bet that's where the jungle cruise starts."

"Rick, do you really think there are crocodiles up that river?" Sheryl asked with a hint of worry in her voice.

"Well, let's take Jack with us and find out," I replied in my usual smart ass way, which earned me a playful slug in the arm.

This jungle cruise was legendary and we'd heard about it way back in San Diego. *Charlie's Charts*, the cruising guide we were using, showed the entrance to the mangrove-lined river. The water way was narrow: barely enough room in spots for two dinghies to pass each other. Its slow moving waters stretched for about a mile before depositing you on another white sand beach with many more palapas on a small hidden bay.

"Tomorrow should be pretty interesting. We can do the jungle cruise in the morning, then hike along the beach later on and have lunch at one of those palapas," Sheryl said with growing excitement.

As the sun was closing in on the western horizon I walked to the port rail and dove into the 80 degree water. Nothing quite like an evening swim to cool off. After I climbed back aboard I showered off with fresh water in the cockpit. Even with the sun below the horizon, it didn't take long for the warm air to dry my skin and suddenly I was very tired.

I awoke the next morning and the smell of breakfast cooking coaxed me out of the berth. I found Sheryl busy and doing her 'galley dance' where she flips eggs with one hand, mixes batter with the other while closing the refrigerator door with a kick of her foot. All the while she's softly humming that mysterious unidentifiable tune that she comes up with when she's quite content.

Jack is near her feet feasting on a concoction of dry kibble mixed with fish oil, and he seems quite content as well.

"You're up early," I said giving Sheryl a peck on the cheek.

"It's the rocking that woke me up. There seems to be some bigger rollers coming in," she explained.

"Now that you mention it we are rocking and rolling a bit more than when we got here yesterday," I replied as I became aware of the difference in the motion.

I popped my head out the hatch where my eyes were assaulted by the already bright sunlight. Squinting, I looked toward the beach and saw two to three foot waves breaking all along the shoreline.

"Yeah, there is a small break happening on shore, but it doesn't look bad and we should still be able to get in no problem," I called down to her.

"Breakfast is ready," was her only response.

After breakfast and cleaning up the dishes, we lowered the dinghy into the water where it bounced wildly alongside *Casablanca* due to the incoming swell. We'd need the outboard on for this excursion, so I hooked the halyard that's used to raise the mainsail to the handle of the engine. That way Sheryl could use the mechanical advantage of the winch to lift the motor from its place on the rail and lower it to my awaiting hands in the pitching dinghy. We always keep the halyard attached until I have the engine secured to the transom of the small boat, lest it slip and fall to the bottom of the sea.

"I'll get some snacks put together while you get the engine going. I can't wait to motor up that river!" Sheryl was just bubbling with anticipation.

"Don't forget the crocodile bait," I said looking at Jack, who was washing himself in the cockpit undoubtedly getting himself ready for another nap in the sun.

"I'm going to pretend I didn't hear that," she responded as she gave Jack a good scratch behind the ears.

Once again, trying to start the cranky outboard was a test of patience. I pulled and pulled and swore and swore. Finally, after about the 10th try, a puff of blue smoke and a momentary cough and sputter indicated there may be hope for the old engine yet. Two more pulls and the reluctant engine sprang to life. It took a full minute for it to quit spewing the blue cloud of exhaust. I just couldn't figure it out. Once it starts, it runs great, but getting it started is another matter.

Sheryl handed me the waterproof bag packed with the snacks, shoes, camera and some pesos for our shore and jungle excursion. Off we went toward the river entrance which was about a half mile away.

The mouth of the river was 150 feet wide and there were some very shallow rocky areas. It was much like going into a pass through the coral in the South Pacific, there were breaking waves on either side as we carefully navigated in.

"Keep a good look out for rocks and sticks," I told my wide-eyed passenger. The river was narrowing down, the foliage was getting quite thick and the sounds of the waves breaking on shore were being replaced with an eerie silence. The humidity was climbing and the air was heavy and pungent with the odors of decaying vegetation.

Soon we were completely swallowed into the jungle, the river narrowing so much that we could almost touch the mangrove trees on either side of *Exit Visa*. The water was thick and brown, leaving to your imagination what might be lurking beneath the surface. There were scatterings of bright color from the flowers lacing the thick vines and noisy birds were darting after the big flying insects.

The plants, trees and vines formed a dense canopy letting almost no sunlight through which caused the temperature to drop noticeably. It was as if we'd entered another world. Minutes later, the river widened, the canopy opened up and we were once again bathed in sunlight.

As the river opened up it became more shallow, causing the outboard propeller to bump the rocky bottom. I tilted the engine up slightly, locked it in place and Sheryl used an oar to help me dodge around big rocks and other obstacles that would appear in our path. She would push off from the sticks and stones and keep us moving in the right direction since the maneuverability of the outboard was much reduced, due to the position it was in.

I was scanning ahead for the best path through the maze, when out of the corner of my eye, I saw Sheryl getting ready to push off from a mostly submerged small tree trunk.

"STOP!" I yelled, breaking the silence.

She quickly turned her head to see what was the matter. Locking on to my stare and following it to the paddle she was holding, she saw that what had appeared to be a tree trunk was moving! And it had eyes and a long snout.

She let out a yelp and nearly levitated across the small boat getting as far away from the basking crocodile as possible. I put the engine in neutral so we could just drift behind its 5 foot long body.

"Oh my God! I almost poked that thing!" she said nearly breathless.

"I can't believe we got that close without seeing it," I responded in a low hoarse whisper.

He looked prehistoric and slow moving, but I had seen enough of the *Crocodile Hunter* on TV to know he was not to be fooled with.

"The river is getting too shallow to go much further, I think maybe we should head back to the beach," I suggested.

"Rick, he went under the water. Let's get out of here before he thinks about biting the dinghy!" Sheryl said with real worry.

I slowly turned us around and we started the 45 minute trip back to the river's mouth.

There wasn't much talking between the two of us as we slipped along the river, both keeping a close eye out for more wildlife. The natural events we'd experienced that week, the pelican, the whale and the crocodile, were things that we'd surely never forget. After offering us up all these amazing experiences, we would soon find out that Mother Nature can also have a nasty sense of humor.

CHAPTER 4
THEY WEREN'T ALL HAPPY DAYS...

"Gravity isn't easy, but it's the law."
—Anonymous

The sound of dishes crashing to the floor cut through my REM sleep. At the same time my brain was trying to incorporate the sounds into my dream, *Casablanca* lurched again and I found myself on the floor, having been tossed off the bed: about a 3 foot fall.

"Rick, are you OK? What happened?" Sheryl asked with groggy concern.

"I think the swell has picked up and we are rocking more side to side." As if punctuating my last statement, the remaining dishes that had been on the countertop in the galley took flight and crashed to the floor. Thank goodness for unbreakable dishes.

"I'll take a look outside," I said, "but don't fall asleep until you hear me safely back down below."

A soft snore indicated I was wasting my breath.

Grabbing a flashlight, I staggered toward the hatch. When I stepped into the cockpit I was staring at an inky black sky crowded with so many stars they gave the illusion of light feathery clouds.

The roar of the waves crashing on shore validated my initial impression that the swell had grown during the night. I walked to the front of *Casablanca* to check the anchor chain and make sure the snubber was still in place. The 10 foot length of heavy duty nylon webbing that I use for an anchor snubber works as sort of a shock absorber. One end is attached to the anchor chain near where it enters the water, with the other end attached to a cleat on the boat. The webbing has more give than the chain so it prevents the chain from putting undo strain on the bow of the boat.

Seeing that everything was in order, I headed back to the cockpit. I decided that the next morning I would put out a stern anchor to keep us from taking the waves on our beam, thus eliminating the side to side rocking motion, which is very unnerving and irritating.

I retreated down below and picked up the dishes and odds and ends that had been flung to the cabin sole. When I returned to bed I put up the canvas lee cloth that I had installed on *Casablanca* to prevent me from rolling off the bed. These simple restraints are attached to the base of a berth and then to the ceiling, forming sort of a cloth crib. Jack quickly assumed a position between my head and the lee cloth, taking full advantage of the security it offered.

The next morning, Sheryl and I discussed the plans for the day over a breakfast of fried Spam and blueberry pancakes. The menus got a lot more creative aboard *Casablanca* once Sheryl joined the crew. When I'm alone I have a tendency to fix cereal or peanut butter sandwiches for nearly every meal. Sheryl also feeds Jack a better quality of food always adding some tasty morsels of cheese or cooked meat to his bowl instead of just tossing him a dead flying fish off the deck as was my habit.

"I can't wait to go walk on that beach!" Sheryl exclaimed. She was God's own beachcomber and could walk for hours picking up shells, beach glass and any other little treasures that were in her path. She would also be happy to sit on a rock or log and dig with her hands, sifting through the sand looking for nature's hidden surprises.

"As soon as I set the stern anchor we can go in," I informed her and I headed out to perform the task.

After I finally got the cranky outboard engine running, I took a small anchor that I keep attached to the stern of the boat and put it in the dinghy and then instructed Sheryl to feed out about 100 feet of anchor line as I motored away from the boat.

I moved slowly toward shore, making sure that when the slack was pulled up that the bow would be facing the open ocean, thus the oncoming swell. When I dropped the anchor, I could barely spot its shape lying in the sand about 25 feet down in the semi cloudy water. The lack of clarity was quite a change from the crystal clear water we'd enjoyed in the Sea of Cortez. Motoring back to *Casablanca*, I climbed on board, pulled the slack out of the anchor line and securely tied it off.

"The swell's not near as bad as it was last night, I'm probably over reacting," I said, but I was glad I'd set the extra anchor just in case those nasty rollers reappeared.

Giddy as ever, Sheryl loaded up a small day bag filled with everything she could possibly imagine needing, or wanting, for our time on the beach. She had sunscreen and sunglasses, a disposable waterproof camera, zip lock bags for her shells and other finds, water and sandwiches and some pesos to buy anything she may have forgotten. She loaded all the supplies into a dry bag, which is a waterproof duffle that seals tight at the opening keeping everything inside safe and dry.

So we were off. The outboard wasn't near as hard to start this time, probably because I'd already used it that morning. I had determined that new spark plugs would remedy the engine's starting problem and I made a mental note to replace them before it became more serious.

"Look," I said pointing to shore, "There's already about six dinghies on the beach. We'll get to meet some of our new neighbors."

"It must be a good place to land the dinghy, since all those people are there. Can you tell what they're doing?" She asked.

Straining to get a better look, I could see there were two inflatable boats ahead of us, and the people on shore had their hands cupped around their mouths and seemed to be yelling instructions out to them.

A large swell lifted *Exit Visa* up about 3 feet and with the better view it became clear as to what everyone was doing. The small boats trying to make it to the beach position themselves outside of the surf line until an incoming wave passes underneath them. They then gun the engine in an attempt to ride in on the back of that roller, before the next swell rises up and overtakes them. My anxiety level was high, as we prepared ourselves for our first lesson in 'Surf Landings 101'.

We hovered just outside the line of breaking waves, watching the two boats ahead of us perform this feat. The first driver chose his timing perfectly. As he motored on the back of a wave toward shore the following incoming wave broke just behind his dinghy and he effortlessly surfed to the beach where all 3 occupants jumped out in knee deep water, tilted up the outboard motor and quickly drug the small boat up the sandy shore. It was so well orchestrated that it was obvious this wasn't their first surf landing. Then we saw what the small group of people on shore were doing, as they raised up cardboard signs with numbers on them. Three 8's and two 9's. They were scoring the performances as if it were an Olympic event. It was obvious these people take their surf landings pretty seriously. The pressure was on.

The next boat, with a single occupant had a smaller engine, so after waiting for the swell in front of him to break, he applied full power. But it appeared that the following wave would be very close to overtaking him with his lack of speed. The people on shore were urging him on with their shouts and I found myself leaning forward as if I could transfer some momentum to his small craft. As the five foot wave reared up and started to crest, the dinghy disappeared behind the cascading wave.

From our vantage point, we could only see white water and feared for the worst, but as the wave dissipated, the boat shot out of the froth seemingly unscathed. The gathering crowd rushed down and pulled the boat out of the surf line. The dinghy was filled with water, but none the worse for wear. He received three 6's a 7 and a 5. Tough judges.

"That was close, what do ya think?" I asked Sheryl, giving her a last chance to abort the mission to shore. The voices in my head were pulling for her to choose to spend the day aboard *Casablanca*.

"Look, we're in no hurry, we can float out here until there's a break in the swell and then go for it!" Sheryl surprised me with her response. After all, we had never attempted such a landing and I really wished the surf was smaller and there wasn't an audience on shore. I was very apprehensive but she seemed gung ho. The voice of reason lost out again.

We putted around the surf line for about 5 minutes, until there seemed to be a longer space between wave sets. Then, with the urging of the shore crew, I gunned the engine. *Exit Visa* lurched forward and immediately started sputtering. Franticly I fumbled with the choke and the accelerator.

"Rick, lets go!" the strain in Sheryl's voice was unmistakable.

"Dammit," was my only reply.

The motor, although running, was acting like a heart in fibrillation. It was working, but without much power. The engine would rev up and we'd go forward a short distance, then it would nearly die and leave us floundering. We could hear the shouts from shore telling us to start rowing, but when I looked back I knew that wasn't an option. A swell that had likely marched thousands of miles, born in a storm in the Pacific was getting ready to crest right over our heads. I gave the motor one more twist of the accelerator hoping for a miracle and was rewarded with a big puff of blue smoke and silence.

Everything started to happen in slow motion. The wave was slowly lifting the stern of the boat, where I was sitting, high into the air. Soon I was looming 6 feet above Sheryl, who was perched near the bow. Her eyes were the size of saucers as everything on the floor of the dinghy, including the fuel tank and dry bag, rushed toward her.

"Jump!" I shouted, but by the time the word had left my mouth, she was gone.

The boat then accelerated down the wave face and just as I thought things could work out, the nose of the boat dug in causing us to cartwheel. I was disoriented and couldn't tell up from down until the pressure of the wave forced me against the coarse sand bottom.

I was struggling for air and thrashing around, afraid to open my eyes because of the sand in the churning surf. Suddenly, a hand grabbed the neck of my tee shirt and lifted my head out of the froth. It was Sheryl and she was laughing uncontrollably as I pulled up my swim trunks and brushed the sand from my face. I was embarrassed when I realized the water, that I'd thought I was going to die in, was only knee deep.

"Are you OK?" I asked with great concern.

"I'm better than you or the boat," she replied, still laughing.

I turned to see where the dinghy had ended up, and saw a couple of fellow cruisers dragging an upside down *Exit Visa* to shore. Just beyond that I saw that the judges had given us three 3's, a 2 and a minus 1 for our score, which I thought was quite generous considering the way we tumbled to the beach.

Another lesson I learned that day is to never turn your back to the sea, for as I struggled to shore in ankle deep water, a breaking wave flattened me without mercy. Sheryl helped me up and we hurried out of the water before another knock down could occur. My knees were skinned and bleeding, I was a little dazed and a great deal embarrassed. Sheryl was clutching the dry bag she'd picked out of the surf, still snickering.

"What happened to you?" I asked as I absently picked sand out of my hair.

"When I thought the boat was going to turn over on us, I bailed out. It looked like you and everything else was going to land on top of me," she said, still grinning wide.

"Well, it probably helped not having your weight up front, but I think our score was lowered by you abandoning ship," I said trying to shift the blame a bit, even though I was thankful she did get out and was alright. Then I added, "Sure wish I'd been quick enough to think of it."

A small parade, or viewing, if you will, filed past Sheryl and me as we sat near the overturned inflatable. Each offered their own "disastrous dinghy landing story" basically encouraging us not to take it too seriously.

"Here comes another dinghy!" came a shout from the water's edge and the self-proclaimed judges scampered back to their respective places on the beach.

A deeply tanned gringo, with wild snow white hair pulled back into a shoulder length ponytail, walked over and introduced himself. Obviously he was not one of the judges or he would have had to get back to work.

"Hi, I'm Butch," he said with a smile as he held out his hand for me to shake. Adding, "My hobby is small engine repair and it looks like you could use some help."

"I'm Rick and this is Sheryl," I replied noticing he was carrying a leather satchel, much like a doctor's medical bag. He was a short, stocky man with faded tattoos on his freckled skin. I guessed his age to be nearing 60.

He looked at Sheryl and said, "that was a great exit from your dinghy. You timed that one just right."

I'm sure he was thinking that Sheryl should have been driving the boat since it appeared my sense of timing wasn't quite as good as hers.

He went on to say, "My wife and I travel down here in our RV from Oceanside, California every year. I help the locals repair their outboards cuz Lois says it keeps me out of trouble. I'd be happy to look at yours if you want."

All three of us turned and stared at the upside down dinghy and watched water dripping out of the engine, which I knew was not a good sign, so I said, "Yeah, I could sure use some help with this one."

Butch and I took the engine off and turned the dinghy right side up. Luckily, the only damage to our little boat was a slight bend in one of the aluminum oars.

"Good thing the engine wasn't running when you flipped. It'll be easier to clean up and get running this way," Butch said. I could tell by the grin on his face that he liked a good challenge, and that this would be one. I also thought it rather ironic that it would be easier to fix the engine since it hadn't been running, whereas if it had been working, we wouldn't even need to be repairing it at that time.

Opening his satchel, Butch withdrew a screwdriver and began dismantling the salt water soaked hunk of metal. When he took off the engine cover a murky, sandy slurry oozed out. I knew that wasn't a good sign for the already iffy engine. I wasn't really surprised at the amount of sand that was found in every nook and cranny of the outboard, as my body was suffering from the same fate.

Sheryl was already wandering down the beach, intently looking at the sand near her feet in her quest for nature's treasures. I was happy to see that despite the calamitous start to our day at the beach, she was able to enjoy herself.

Meanwhile, Butch had propped the engine up on a nearby log. He had removed the sparkplugs, taken the fly wheel off and held some assorted electrical wires in his hand. He certainly looked like he knew what he was doing, I just hoped he really did.

"Hey Rick. Inside my bag is a bottle of vodka. Will you grab it for me?" he called out.

Thinking this wouldn't bode well for my disassembled outboard I hesitantly replied, "Sure." I was worried what would happen if this guy got hammered, but with trepidation I handed him the unopened fifth.

He unscrewed the cap and asked, "You need a bump?" as he handed the bottle back to me.

"No thanks, Butch," I said as I watched him take a swig. He then began to pour the rest of the clear liquid over the exposed engine parts and into the holes where the spark plugs had been. He also doused the wires and exposed terminals, even soaking the pull rope and spring starter mechanism with the vodka.

And without even looking up to see my surprised stare, he said, "The cheap vodka with it's high alcohol content makes this the best stuff for cleaning water soaked parts. It evaporates so quick that it takes the water molecules with it."

I'll certainly have to file that little nugget away for future use, I thought. Especially if I stay in Mexico long with these treacherous surf landings.

After thoroughly scouring the beach, Sheryl wandered back with a clear plastic bag full of colorful shells, bones, beach glass and other miscellaneous finds. She had her head down, still scanning the sand as she approached me. Spotting the empty vodka bottle lying by my feet she glanced up at my face with a puzzled look and said with a hint of sarcasm, "Well, it must be going well, I am surprised you're still standing,"

"Butch used it on the engine to help dry it out," I said by way of explanation. She just gave me a skeptical look that said, "Sure, nice try".

After the parts and pieces had time to dry thoroughly in the hot Mexican sun, Butch began putting the puzzle back together. After an hour's worth of tinkering we put the engine back on the stern of *Exit Visa*.

Pushing the boat into the shallow water, Butch gave the starter cord a jerk and the engine sprang to life.

"Even when it was brand new it never started on the first pull!" I exclaimed. I was astonished that my cranky little motor actually sounded better than it ever had. Considering what it had gone through, I was surprised it was working at all.

"It's the vodka," Butch said with a smile. He then made a minor carburetor adjustment before putting the engine cover back in place.

"That should do it," he said triumphantly as we pulled the dinghy back on to the beach.

"We can't thank you enough, Butch. What do I owe you?" I inquired, hoping I would be able to pay for this small miracle.

"Nothing at all. It's really therapy for me. I enjoy tinkering with these things."

"At least let me replace your vodka," I offered.

"Sure, that's fine, but really, don't worry about it," he mumbled, and I could tell he was a little embarrassed.

"Rick, just be careful going out. Getting past the incoming waves can be even trickier than coming in to shore," he advised as he started walking down the beach with his tool bag clutched in his hand.

"Who was that masked man?" I said under my breath, feeling like one of the lucky souls that benefited by a visit from the Lone Ranger in their hour of need.

"What did ya say, Rick?" Sheryl asked, as she dug in the sand with her toe, still searching for treasures.

"Oh nothing," I replied as I watched Butch disappear behind a sand dune.

With the outboard problem taken care of, we could now enjoy the rest of the afternoon ashore, and headed to a palapa down the beach. As we walked I was amazed at how thick the jungle and its underbrush was where the sand ended and the growth began. The same colorful birds we'd seen on our jungle exploration were here as well. We stopped and watched a small group of Mexican teenagers skillfully surf the incoming swell. Finally reaching the palapa all I could think about was having a cold beer in hopes it would wash away some of the sand that seemed stuck between my teeth. Finding a table in the shade of the thatched roof we sat down, ordered cervezas and fish tacos, then talked with two other cruisers at a nearby table.

"Rough landing, but you both look to be OK," a tall, thin man sporting a floppy woven hat and sunglasses, said by way of conversation.

"Yeah, the old engine conked out at the worst possible time," was my humble reply.

The stranger introduced himself, "My name is Chris. I've had a few landings like that myself, but it doesn't help having those idiots critique you with their obnoxious score signs," as he glanced down the beach to where the judges had stood.

"That's how they get their jollies," added a gravelly voiced woman sitting to our left. In front of her sat an empty plate and she was just finishing off a beer. She was short, with medium length gray hair, and I noticed her arms were quite muscular even though she appeared to be about 15 years older than me.

"Hi, I'm Rick and this is Sheryl. We're off of *Casablanca*," I said as I pointed to our white-hulled boat bobbing lazily in the afternoon swell. When we shook hands, I was surprised at the thick calluses, which were emphasized by her strong grip.

"My name's Marge, off of *Inspiration*. My boat's the green one out in the middle of the bay."

Having originally thought Chris and Marge were a couple, after we'd talked a while I discovered that they were both single-handed sailors, from different boats.

Chris was planning to do the "Puddle Jump" as cruiser's like to call crossing the Pacific. He anticipated leaving from Zihuatanejo that year, just as Sheryl and I were going to do.

Marge, on the other hand, was a Mexican veteran, having been cruising up and down the coast for nearly five years. She'd found it a comfortable life and had no plans to leave the Mexican waters.

Sheryl and Marge easily struck up a conversation, while I reminisced with Chris about my single handed sailing days in the South Pacific.

Talking with Chris, I got the impression that he wasn't having as much fun single handing as he'd hoped he would. He said it was really wearing him down.

"It's toughest sailing alone along the coast," I said, pointing out the obvious. "Too many things to hit," I added. "It gets much better when you set off for the Marquesas. Your watches don't have to be quite as vigilant when you're out in the open ocean, so you get more sleep. Plus, after you're out a few days, you get into a comfortable routine, or rhythm and time passes faster."

We chatted for about an hour, and I told him of my experiences in Tahiti and the Cook Islands. I even talked about losing *Rick's Place* in Fiji.

"Well, I should get back out to *The Swallow*, so I'll say good bye for now. Hope our paths cross again soon." Chris said, giving a little salute as he ducked out of the palapa.

As I finished my tacos, I could hear Sheryl asking Marge numerous questions about single handed sailing from a woman's point of view. It turned out Marge was a licensed delivery captain and had been all over the world on boats of all types and sizes. I could see Sheryl was in awe of the short, salty dynamo.

It was helpful watching the other cruisers leave in their dinghies, because it gave us an idea of what would be in store for us. There seemed to be a pattern where after every 5th or 6th wave there'd be a short period of calm before the rollers would resume their march to shore.

"Timing," I said, as if it was a major discovery, "is everything."

We formulated our plan: We'll get the boat into the water facing out, I'll get the engine started, Sheryl will jump in and off we go. We were ready.

"Looks like plenty of time between wave sets, let's do it!" I said when we were in position and it appeared calm.

We pushed the boat out and I started the engine on the first pull, but when I attempted to lower the motor down into the deepening water, it wouldn't budge. Tilted up like it was, the propeller was very ineffective and we weren't making much head way.

"Rick, what's wrong? We better get going," Sheryl said glancing up and seeing the beginning of another wave group coming toward shore.

"I'm trying. This lock is bent from this morning's crash and the motor is stuck in this position." I said with growing frustration and panic.

I could tell Sheryl was getting pretty nervous and was probably contemplating how long to stay in the boat before jumping again.

"Hand me the oar," I said, then with the paddle in hand, I beat the offending latch into submission and the motor rotated down to its working position.

"Hold on! It's going to be close," I yelled over the noise of the revving engine. Our small dinghy leapt forward and we began to climb the unbroken face of the first wave. Sheryl started to slide back toward me, but quickly found a handhold and stayed in place. With Sheryl about 5 feet over my head I realized that this was just the opposite of the morning's calamity, except she'd also had the outboard motor looming over her. She'd certainly made the right decision to jump when she did.

The face of the wave grew more unstable as it began to break. I was fearing the worst, when at that precise moment we punched through the top and headed down the backside of the roller as white water began to cascade from the crest.

"Geeze, that was close!" I said as relief flooded through me.

"What a rush!" Sheryl exclaimed with that same goofy grin on her face that I'd seen that morning.

Back aboard *Casablanca* we showered off in the cockpit. It felt good to wash away all the sand and dried salt crystals with the cool fresh water. After drying off I applied antibacterial ointment to my numerous scrapes and scratches and dug what I hoped was the last of the sand out of my ear.

Sheryl handed me a cold beer and as I relaxed in the shade of our cozy cockpit, the events of the morning soon became an exciting memory instead of the disaster it had felt like earlier. It's true what they say: the only difference between an ordeal and an adventure is your attitude.

Jack was instantly out on deck as Sheryl spread her bounty of the beach out to dry. He helped her sort through the collection of shells and small bones and his curiosity had him sniffing and chewing on each little item.

I turned to Sheryl and said, "Let's leave tomorrow for Troncones."

"Sounds good," was Sheryl's distracted answer as she continued to examine her assortment of treasures from the beach.

CHAPTER 5
TRONCONES

"Troncones: where the misfits fit in."
—As seen on a bumper sticker

Rather than harbor hop down to Troncones from Tenacatita, we chose to sail the 240 miles non-stop. This would require us to be out to sea at least two nights. We began to question our decision when we were slammed with squalls, thunder and lightening that first night.

Happily, the next day brought partly cloudy skies and benign weather that stayed with us for the remainder of the trip.

On our last morning at sea, sitting in the cockpit having breakfast, Sheryl asked me, "When was the last time you saw Sparky?" as she handed my mug of cocoa to me.

"I guess back in Hawaii, nearly four years ago," I said thinking about it and continued on, "He'd come out of nowhere with some friends to surf the hurricane swell that was formed by Iniki. He didn't have a care in the world and I was terrified of losing my boat, which was all I had."

"How did you first meet up with him?" she asked between sips of her tea.

"What a joke that was! I was getting *Rick's Place* ready to sail to Hawaii, and one day this guy shows up and said he heard I needed crew." Reminiscing I continued, "Then just as suddenly as he appeared, he dropped out of sight. I figured he'd come to his senses after thinking about it, then – boom – he shows up the day before I was leaving with a duffle bag and surfboard!"

"Then, as I recall, the "big cruise" began to fall apart," Sheryl added.

"Yeah, things were OK for the first couple of days until we lost sight of land, then Sparky got so nervous or scared or whatever, that he couldn't come up on deck for a watch. I ended up sailing solo, which wouldn't have been bad, except that I also had to try and take care of surfer boy for the next 8 days." I said smiling.

"What's the big grin about?" she inquired.

I realized I was thinking about what I call "Cosmic Pinball" – where one random action affects another action that's seemingly unrelated.

By way of explanation I answered, "Well, as you know, since Spark was so sick, instead of going directly to Hawaii, we came into San Francisco to get him off the boat. And who should I meet when I got there? Jack the Cat and his flower shop owning mistress," I replied, thinking once again how fortunate I'd been with the turn of events.

Now Sheryl was smiling, "So much for solo sailing.. I'm sure glad things turned out as they did."

"Yeah, it took me forever to figure out how Spark first heard I was headed for the islands. But a while back, Mom mentioned that he was working down here at Troncones and he was getting married. Turns out Sparky's aunt plays bridge with Mom. I always thought Mom must have had something to do with my suddenly having crew, since she wasn't wild about my solo sailing to Hawaii, but I didn't know how on earth she'd ever know someone like Sparky."

We just sat in silence enjoying the tranquility and the shared thoughts of how karma had brought us to this spot together. Then suddenly, a splash and clicking sounds announced that a pod of dolphin would be escorting *Casablanca* for a while.

Jack heard the commotion and climbed the ladder from below and jumped to his favorite dolphin watching perch on the cabin top. Just like his human counterparts, Jack never seemed to tire of watching the acrobats of the sea perform. The remaining miles disappeared quickly as we were transfixed following the antics of the six or so dolphin which were playing in the bow wave as we traveled toward Troncones.

"There's the marker for the bay," I announced as I handed the binoculars to Sheryl to confirm my sighting.

A red buoy marked a dangerous reef on the northern point of the bay. As we rounded the rocky outcropping the water shallowed and the sandy bottom became clear. At the same time, buildings on shore began to form with more detail as we drew closer.

There was about a mile-long stretch of white sand beach arching in a slight crescent shape between the exposed rocks at either end, which formed the bay. This indentation on the coast was more of an open-roadstead anchorage and wouldn't afford the protection we'd enjoyed elsewhere.

Three surfers plied their skills on the southern most point where there appeared to be a natural break producing waves about head high at the time. It was a likely place to find Sparky, I thought.

"It looks like that point will block any big swell from entering the bay, at least from the south," I said more hopeful than actually convinced. I knew this wasn't an ideal anchorage, but we'd been in rolly spots before and I didn't think this would be much worse. After all, we only planned on staying a few days and the weather forecast was promising.

The brightly colored lounge chairs lined up in neat rows along the beach, indicated where the small hotels stood. The buildings themselves were hidden, for the most part, behind the lush vegetation which bordered the sand. In addition to the surfers, there was a smattering of people walking the beach.

"Sheryl, take the wheel. I'll get ready to anchor," I called as I took the boat out of forward gear and *Casablanca* slowed to a crawl.

I moved to the front of the boat and unlashed the anchor from the bow cleat I keep it tied to when traveling. I wouldn't want that to come loose, for I'd heard a story of a guy who was making an ocean passage when the boat's anchor broke free in some rough seas and it banged against the hull doing lots of damage, nearly sinking the boat.

"What's the depth?" I called back

"40, no 35...35...30...31..." was her robotic response.

"That looks good," and with that I let the anchor go, the chain free falling off the windlass. I always feel better anchoring when I can see the hook hit bottom and this was another one of those nice clear spots.

When the chain markers indicated I had 60 feet out, I called back to Sheryl, "put it in reverse now. Slow at first: until the anchor digs in."

As *Casablanca* started to move backward, I continued to let out the chain until I had 120 feet in the water. I could tell by the vibration that was being transmitted up from the anchor that we had not dug into the sandy bottom yet. Just as I thought we'd need to try again, the chain went bar-tight and the boat stopped its backward progression.

"How deep?" I asked.

"40 feet," was Sheryl's reply.

"OK, full throttle back now," I instructed. This would ensure that it was locked in and should hold us if any big wind or waves crop up.

A small puff of smoke from the stern signaled the engine RPM's had increased. For several minutes both of us visually lined up objects on shore to gauge if the boat was dragging or moving in any way.

"I think we're set, hon," I called back to Sheryl.

"Neutral?" was her one word question.

"Yeah."

With that, *Casablanca* slowly drifted forward, pulled by the weight of the chain as it dropped to the seafloor.

Comfortable that we'd done a good job anchoring, I started scanning the beach looking for Sparky's familiar 6'2", slightly hunched frame. I was surprised at how excited I was to meet up with my first sailing partner again. We hadn't had a really great experience together out on the deep blue sea, but despite the problems we'd had, Sparky was a great guy and I was anxious to see how things had turned out for him.

"Does he know we're coming?" Sheryl's lilting voice broke the silence.

"Not sure. I don't think I told Mom that we were headed to Troncones, and that's the only way word could have worked its way down to him."

Turning, I saw Sheryl already untying the dinghy from its storage place upside down on the cabin top, forward of the mast. Getting the dinghy into the water and then lowering and securing the outboard to its stern went quickly and efficiently, since we'd been doing the same procedure numerous times along the way.

All the while, Jack was up on deck and underfoot nearly tripping both Sheryl and myself, very obviously in need of attention.

"Jackie, are you hungry?" Sheryl cooed to him. As if he understood just what she had said, he yelped and ran down below, taking up station near his food bowl.

"I'll feed Jack and get some pesos while you get the outboard started," she instructed.

"Aye aye captain!" I called in reply.

"Rick, don't be a smart ass," she said with a smile, knowing that's like telling the sun not to shine.

When the engine started on the first pull, I silently thanked Butch, knowing that a dependable engine would make any beach landings much better than our last experience.

We pushed off from the mother ship and searched the long beach for a good place to land the dinghy. Sheryl pointed and said, "That looks like a good spot. It's fairly calm over there."

After successfully avoiding some submerged rocks, we motored to within 5 feet of shore and jumped in unison into the shallow water and pulled *Exit Visa* up the fine white sand beach, well out of the tide's influence.

One of the small hotels was right in front of where we'd landed, back about 300 feet from the water's edge. As we neared the buildings we could see a sign that read "Mike's Surf Resort".

"Looks like a good place to start," I offered, stating the obvious.

The well-worn path from shore led past an unused outdoor 'beach bar' with a few small tables and chairs spread around. Palm trees, along with the thatched roof over the tables, provided an abundance of shade from the hot sun and it made me think of *Rick's Place* back on the beach in Fiji.

On the other side of the walk, a dozen lounge chairs were lined up, their bright blue and white striped cushions inviting guests to a comfortable afternoon siesta.

Nearby, there was an outdoor shower set up to rinse off the salt and sand before entering the resort or getting into the beautiful swimming pool which graced the middle of the compound. Surrounded by 9 thatched-roof bungalows, the infinity pool had a rock waterfall with a glistening cascade splashing into the blue-tiled pond. It was quite an oasis.

The bungalows were also quite charming, built of stucco cement, rounded in shape with steep palm frond roofs. Each unit had a outdoor sitting area which was made private by the tropical vegetation that had been planted around it. There was ample room for lounging on the long, cushion-covered cement benches. A hammock, hung between the posts, completed the picture of comfort, offering a lovely place to enjoy a sunset. On several of the porches there were surfboards leaning against the stucco walls, just adding to the ambiance.

Beyond the pool's waterfall, we could see an open-air restaurant. Built with palm tree logs for support, it had a high thatched roof just like the bungalows, only larger. There were a number of tables with chairs scattered around on the cut bamboo floor, with a long bar separating the eating area from the kitchen. A shelf, built into the wall behind the bar, had colorful shells set alongside the liquor bottles adding to the charm of the place.

It wasn't quite lunchtime, so save for one person at a table drinking coffee and reading a book, the place was empty. Housekeepers were busily going in and out of some of the rooms, but not very many tourists were in sight and we assumed they must be out enjoying the beach before the heat of the day.

Sheryl was loving the landscaping, stopping to look at all the plants and smell the flowers surrounding the paths and buildings. Blossoms of all shapes and colors were laced among the greenery giving the feeling of being in the Garden of Eden. Watching her, I wondered if she was missing her flower shop back in San Francisco.

As she lingered in the gardens, I followed the directions on a small sign that said "Check-in at Surf Shop" which had an arrow pointing down the path we were walking.

I soon found myself standing in front of a small office that looked like it must be the guest check-in. Inside was a counter with a telephone that looked straight out of the 1950's and a rack that held sightseeing brochures. Standing behind the counter was a woman. A 'gringo' as the Mexicans call us Americans. She looked to be in her early 30's, about my age, with ashen blonde hair cut to shoulder length. Her head was down and she appeared to be writing something.

As I stepped through the door, she looked up with a big beautiful smile. Her blue eyes sparkled as she asked me, still smiling, "Hi, may I help you?"

"I'm looking for the surf shop," I said glancing around.

"It's behind our office, but no one is there right now. He's giving surf lessons down the beach," she said still beaming.

"Could you tell me the guy's name?" I asked

For just a moment the young woman's smile wavered, as she tried to figure out what I was up to, so I quickly added, "I think I may know him."

Her smile was back full force as she stated, "His name is Sparky."

What luck! I couldn't believe I'd stumbled on to the right place so quickly.

"Sparky and I go back a ways," I started, "We're both from Washington state and he sailed with me to California a few years ago."

With that the woman bounded from behind the counter, shrieking and laughing, and without warning wrapped her arms around me. Her 5'4" body exhibited a lot more strength than I would have expected.

"Rick, I've heard so much about you!" she said, still hugging me uncomfortably close.

Just about that time, Sheryl came through the door, giving me a questioning look. I kind of held up my hands behind the young ladies back with a bit of a shrug, as if to say, "I don't know what's going on here."

Releasing me from the bear hug, she looked up, still grinning from ear to ear, and said, "I'm Tami! Sparky's wife of one month!"

"Tami, I'm so happy to meet you," and gesturing with a nod of my head added, "This is Sheryl."

"Sparky will be so surprised you're here," Tami said looking like she could explode from happiness.

"Well, I'd heard he was down here and that he was getting married, but didn't know when, so we took a shot in the dark and came down," I said by way of apology for missing the wedding.

"That's my fault," Tami confessed, "I mailed the announcement to your mom's address, but it came back. I messed up the PO number. Will you be here long?" she queried moving on to another subject.

"For a bit. Our plan was to find Sparky then set sail for the Marquesas after a short stop in Zihuatanejo for provisioning." I added, "How's the business going?"

"It's great." She replied, still smiling. "Lots of experienced surfers come down here for the good surf and some rent boards if they don't bring their own. Then there's always lots of vacationers that have never surfed that want to take lessons. I even teach a women's class when there's enough interest, but Sparky's busy with lessons five days a week during the peak season." And without taking a breath she continued on saying, "but my main duty is managing the resort. That's how we met. He would come down here to surf off the point, then at the end of the day he'd come up to the bar to have a Margarita."

"The shop is around the side of this building. It's open, go have a look," she offered.

"Great, thanks, we'll take a look and be right back," I said turning to Sheryl.

"Rick, I should call the flower shop and see how my sister is doing, I'll catch up with you in a bit," Sheryl said.

"Use this phone," Tami suggested with the smile returning to her face, "It looks like an antique, but it will get you connected."

"HURRICANE SURF SHOP" proclaimed the boldly lettered sign which hung on the side of the building. A mural of a big breaking wave was painted on the wall below the sign. Again it was a simple thatched roof structure with a wooden door that couldn't keep anybody out that happened to lean on it. I pushed it open and stepped in. A glassless window provided plenty of light as the bright sunshine filled the room. Against one wall there were 8 surfboards stacked on racks, a few were damaged and in various stages of repair. The smell of fiberglass resin filled the air and took me back to my boat building days when I had turned a fiberglass hull into a great cruising boat.

Across from the surfboards was a picture gallery with several framed photos hung side by side and slightly askew. Most showed impossibly huge waves with the same slightly hunched figure riding a surfboard down the face of the behemoths. Names and dates were written under each shot. It was the last three photos in the group that caught my eye. In those pictures you could see several surfers, including Sparky, riding waves that were strewn with all kinds of flotsam and jetsam. I immediately recognized that it was the Mala Wharf area on the island of Maui even before reading the scribbled caption. These photos were taken during hurricane Iniki.

I had been aboard *Rick's Place* at Mala Wharf when Iniki swept through the Hawaiian Islands. It was a terrifying time for me as I watched 8 boats destroyed in that small anchorage in a matter of hours, not knowing if mine would be next. I was standing on shore during the high wind mayhem and shocked when a battered pickup truck skidded to a stop and several surfers hopped out. Sparky was one of the crazies that chose to ride the giant storm generated waves that day.

The last of the hurricane pictures was a real shocker. Sparky was standing near the water, with a board under his muscular arm and talking to some guy. It took me a minute, before I realized that guy in the picture was me.

I was really taken aback because I didn't realize a picture existed of the two of us together, especially one taken at such a critical event in my life. I would have to get a copy of that one.

Even with my back to the door, I could sense that someone had come into the shop. Expecting Sheryl, I said without turning, "Hey, you gotta see this picture."

"I have, plenty of times, "came the reply in a deep male voice.

Spinning around I saw Sparky's lanky body, leaning against the door jamb with a big grin on his face, and his blue eyes twinkling.

"Hey Crazy," was my first response as I headed to him with outstretched hand.

We then shook hands, slapped backs and told each other we both looked good, all the usual male bonding stuff.

Sparky asked, "You here for awhile?" Posed as more of a statement than a question.

"Yeah, for awhile. Then we're off to the Marquesas," I stated, not knowing if Sparky had ever heard of those South Pacific islands.

At that time Tami came into the room, followed closely by Sheryl.

Tami gave Sparky a peck on the cheek and said, "Sparky, this is Sheryl, Rick's friend."

Extending his hand he greeted her with, "Hi Gayle."

"No Sparky: Sheryl," Tami said enunciating carefully while raising her voice in volume.

This brought to mind a major problem Sparky and I had in our adventure down the coast. He has a severe hearing impairment, and I didn't realize the problem it could be until we set out from the coast of Washington. Misunderstanding someone's name is no big deal, but not hearing a warning or some important instructions out at sea could be disastrous.

"Oh, sorry Sheryl," he said a little sheepishly, "surfer's ear," he continued as he pointed to his head. He'd explained to me before that his deafness was caused by an infection, like swimmer's ear. Seems it had developed when he was young and was spending all his free time out in the water on a surfboard.

Sheryl smiled and shook hands with Sparky, but I could tell she was distracted, like something was bothering her.

"I've got to get back to the class," he told us as he picked up a surf board fin off the work bench, "a knucklehead broke one of these off in the first 10 minutes. Dinner, here tonight." And then he was gone.

Turning to Tami, with a smile, I said, "He hasn't changed a bit."

Before she could reply, the ringing of a telephone had her heading out the door of the shop and back to the office.

"Let's walk the beach a bit then go back out to *Casablanca*," was my suggestion.

"Sure," was Sheryl's soft reply.

The course, warm sand felt great on the soles of our feet as we walked away from the resort in silence.

"I can't wait to take you to the South Pacific," I said reaching for Sheryl's hand and continuing, "no more dangerous surf landings, great snorkeling – it's just a bigger adventure."

When she didn't respond I asked, "Everything all right?"

"Yeah, it's my sister, Joni. You know how she and her husband have been trying to have a baby?" she said slowly.

"Sure, is something wrong?" I queried.

"No, nothing's wrong. She just told me on the phone she thinks she's pregnant." She replied, sounding a bit choked up.

"That's great!" I said as I turned and gave Sheryl a big hug, relieved that there wasn't some horrible health issue that had cropped up.

It was then that I noticed a tear leaving a faint moist trail down her cheek, as she said, "Rick, I'm so happy for Joni, but I am worried that this will mess up our plans for leaving." Then she wiped her eyes with the back of her hand and continued, "She's going to the doctor tomorrow. I'll need to call again to see what he has to say."

The silence was deafening as we continued our walk, both thinking about how this bit of news could affect our lives. When we reached the end of the short beach, we turned and retraced our steps back to where we had landed the dinghy.

"So what's the worst that could happen?" I inquired, finally breaking the agonizingly long silence.

"Well, I would need to get back to my flower shop and figure out what I want to do. I'll have to get someone else to manage it, because Joni won't be able to work once the baby is born. Or maybe I should just sell the business.

I just hadn't given it any thought because things had been going along so well."

Then her lip started quivering slightly as she added, "I just don't know how long it will take to figure it out and get things taken care of. And it's already time to start heading south."

"Listen," I said, "let's not worry about it today. Wait until you talk with Joni tomorrow. We should just have a good time tonight and try to forget about it for now."

"You know I love what we're doing," she said as we hugged.

As we rowed *Exit Visa* back to *Casablanca*, we were surprised to see a couple more boats anchored near us, where none had been before. Since this spot wasn't listed in the guidebooks we'd expected to have the anchorage to ourselves. It's funny how boats will flock to a spot, just because they see another boat there and they assume it must be a good place to anchor.

That night, at dinner with Sparky and Tami, a lot of reminiscing dominated the conversation. We talked about how I had come to meet Sparky, how Tami had come to meet Sparky, and on and on.

"You tried to kill us!" Sparky said between mouthfuls of the savory lobster salad the restaurant had prepared for us.

"You should have taken a look at a globe before you signed on to sail to Hawaii with me," I said laughing, "you had no clue, did you, that we were going to be out of sight of land on that trip?"

"I knew, I just didn't think about it until it was too late," he confessed.

So how did you and Sheryl meet?" Tami asked in her soft voice.

"Well, we have Sparky to thank for that," I said smiling at Sheryl, and added, "After we decided to go into San Francisco, so he could get back on land, I ended up at a marina in Emeryville. There I actually met Sheryl's cat first. I was sleeping in the cockpit and when I opened my eyes, there was this big, fat cat sleeping near my head."

Sheryl picked it up from there, "Jack is a very friendly cat and prone to wander, looking for company. We lived aboard my boat on the next dock over and Jack quickly befriended Rick. Whenever I couldn't find him I would look on *Rick's Place* and that's where he'd be. So when Rick resumed his solo journey to Hawaii, Jack stowed away by accident and didn't show himself until they were well on their way. That cat ended up sailing thousands of miles before I was able to fly to Fiji and bring him back home."

"So what happened to *Rick's Place*? How'd you end up with this other boat?," asked Sparky.

"While I was in Fiji, a freak storm whipped up and I lost the boat on the rocks," was my simple reply. It surprised me how painful the memory of that fateful night still was.

"I'd heard from some surfing friends about a popular barefoot bar called *Rick's Place* and asked my aunt about it. She said it was yours but she didn't know how it all came about," he offered.

"Well, I'm surprised word got this far, though it seemed to be popular in Fiji. Tourists would stop by and have a beer. It was pretty unique having the boat cut in half and made into a bar," I said by way of explanation. "And ya know, I do remember meeting up with some surfers that were passing through on their way to a surf camp on Kandavu. That's probably who told you about it. It's such a small world."

"Where will you go after Troncones?" asked Tami.

An awkward silence followed as I worked through just what would happen next, then I said, "The plan is to sail to the Marquesas and Tuamotus: places I missed on the first go round."

"You guys oughta have a blast," was Sparky's observation.

After dinner, the ride back to *Casablanca* was devoid of the frivolity that had highlighted most of the evening.

Sheryl finally broke the silence with, "They sure seem happy together."

"Yeah, she's the best thing to happen to Sparky; keeps him grounded," I added.

"Rick, things are going to work out. I'm not sure how, but I just know," she said as she grabbed my hand and gave it a gentle squeeze.

That night we both slept fitfully, neither of us getting any rest. The hours were punctuated with lots of tossing and turning, so Jack actually chose to sleep elsewhere, rather than risk being rolled on.

The next morning we were both up at sunrise. The warm smells from breakfast lingered in *Casablanca's* cozy galley. Sheryl was working a crossword puzzle as I tried to tune in Voice of America on the high-seas radio. Anything to distract our minds from the phone call Sheryl would make later that could change our plans drastically.

I was startled by what sounded like a knock on the side of the boat. "What the heck is that? I sure didn't hear an outboard," I said looking out of a porthole.

"Hey man, it's me out here." came a yell.

"It's Sparky. He paddled out," I informed Sheryl as I climbed out into the cockpit, where I could see his head just sticking up above the railing.

"I'm just on my way to work," he said smiling, as if to say: how cool is this going to work on a surfboard. "I've got a class in an hour, but thought I'd get some early hang time in. Still on for this afternoon, huh, Rick?"

"Sure Sparky," I called as he started to paddle away, confirming I was still planning on joining him for a surf lesson later that day.

Then, looking back, he said, "Hey, I almost forgot. Your sister called and talked to Tami. Said you should call her back."

I thought I heard Sheryl, who was standing behind me, utter a curse word under her breath. Then she said, "Let me get ready and we'll go in," and disappeared into the aft cabin.

I didn't want to listen as Sheryl talked with her sister on the telephone in Tami's office, so I wandered into the surf shop. Perusing the pictures on the wall, I was drawn back to the one of Sparky and me talking at the water's edge during hurricane Iniki on Maui. I realized I was envious of Sparky and Tami. Not because of how they got along, Sheryl and I had a great relationship that way, too. It had to do with being married, which seemed to take away some of the unknowns or uncertainties in life.

Suddenly an arm, then a second, wrapped around me as Sheryl held me tight from behind. She was silent, but I could feel the slight spasms of her body as she tried to control her gentle sobs.

"The doctor told Joni to get plenty of rest. Rick, she has to quit taking care of my flower shop right away, because there is a real concern about another miscarriage," she said choking on the words.

I turned and faced her, seeing that she once again had tiny tear tracks down her tanned cheeks. We held each other tightly as she told me that Tami was busy making plane reservations for her: she'd have to fly out the next day.

There was a long pause and then she added, "Rick, I want you to go to French Polynesia anyway. I'll fly down and catch up with you after I get things straightened out with the business back home."

"Sure," I responded with the best smile I could muster considering the knot that was forming in my stomach. I remembered only too well how hard it was for us to get together last time I sailed away aboard *Rick's Place*. Every time we made plans, hurricanes, the shop, her mom's health, all resulted in missed opportunities for more than a year.

That night it was decided that Jack would sail with me aboard *Casablanca*, which felt like a guarantee that Sheryl would be returning. That was a small comfort. He had always been great company when I had to sail solo before, so I'd be happy to have him along.

The next morning, after cooing over Jack and making me promise not to be abusive to her four-legged friend, we threw the duffle she'd packed the night before into the dinghy and motored to shore.

Tami had arranged for a shuttle to take us to the airport. After hugs and goodbyes all around, we climbed into the battered van for the hour long "cannon ball run" to the Zihautanejo/Ixtapa airport. We were white-knuckled most of the way and I was seriously concerned that we would end up as road kill in a big fireball of an accident. I didn't want us to become one of those short "two line stories" you read in your local paper telling of some disastrous fate in a far off country.

Sheryl tried to carry on a conversation with me, but I could not sustain a string of thoughts to keep it going. There would be a huge void in my life and I felt completely unprepared for this sudden change.

The airport was small, but busy. It was packed with tourists: some with sunburns, some with hangovers and all dressed in their tropical wear. Everyone just milled around shopping in the little storefronts for last minute gifts or buying Tequila in the duty free shop, as they awaited the plane that would take them back to the 'real world'.

We waited in the long line and obtained Sheryl's ticket and boarding pass.

"You'd better hurry, the plane is already boarding," the smiling ticket agent said.

We rushed over to the security line where there were about a half dozen people in front of us. That gave us a little time before we reached the point which separates those with tickets from those without. Sheryl turned and hugged me tight, saying, "Well Rick, this is it. I'm going to miss you."

"You need to get on that plane or you'll regret it, maybe not now...." I started to quote the ending of my favorite movie, *Casablanca*, sort of my usual defense, trying to make a joke of everything.

"Very funny," she said, beginning to tear up.

A quick kiss as she was urged on through the security and x-ray line. There was a large glass partition separating us by just a few inches, and when she turned for a final look at me, I was pressed to the glass waving her over. Nervously she looked to the open door of the tarmac, knowing she was probably the last one needing to board. I could see the ticket agent saying something to her, obviously telling her to get moving.

I waved her over one more time and when she got close, I mouthed the words, "Will you marry me?"

It took a second for her to comprehend what I'd said, then her eyes got big and just as she started to say something, the ticket agent gently took hold of her elbow and started to escort Sheryl to the open door. She managed a quick look back. Then she was gone.

This time I had to wipe a tear from my eye.

CHAPTER 6
OLD FRIENDS

"Life is made up of sobs, sniffles and smiles, with sniffles predominating."
—O. Henry (1862-1910)

A week after the emotional airport goodbye with Sheryl, I was again having to say goodbye with deep sadness. Since Sheryl's departure, Spark and Tami had gone out of their way to keep me company and buoy my spirits. They'd invited me over for home cooked dinners nearly every night. I, in turn had them out to *Casablanca* for spaghetti, complete with my signature drink: Kealakekua Bay punch. That is a concoction I first threw together for a cruiser's pot luck while sailing in Hawaii. At the time, all I could find to mix with rum was Tang and limes, but it was a big hit, all the same. After all, if Tang was good enough for a voyage to the moon, it was good enough for rum.

Tami instantly fell in love with Jack and he took advantage of the situation, spending the entire evening on her lap. She was especially intrigued by the way he used the toilet.

"Nothing better than a cat that doesn't need a litter box," she said.

After dancing around the subject, Tami finally asked me, "You've talked with Sheryl on the phone a couple times now, what did she say about..... you know..... the proposal?"

I knew I should have kept that one to myself. Oh well. After a bit of silence I answered her, "She says we both need time to think about it: say a month. She thinks I'm too emotional right now and may have made the decision in haste." What, me emotional I thought to myself, suppressing the urge to scream.

"So basically she said yes," Tami pushed on.

"She said she would get back to me," I countered.

"Well, when you two decide to tie the knot, you can count on Sparky and me to be there," she said with her infectious smile.

"Yeah, I'll keep that in mind. Well, I'd better get going. I need to stop in Zihuatanejo for fuel and fresh veggies before Jack and I hit the road," I said wanting to change the subject that I was finding uncomfortable to talk about.

Sparky shook my hand saying, "Rick, man, you did good learning to ride."

"Well, thanks for the lessons Sparky. And thanks again for the surfboard. I'll make good use out of it." Turning to Tami I added, "And thank you for all the fantastic dinners," as I gave her a big hug.

"Rick, you know Sheryl loves you," she was saying.

I wished Tami would just drop it. It was hard enough saying goodbye as it was, but throwing in all the emotions of missing Sheryl, it was getting to be too much.

"Yeah, I know," I finally answered looking down at my feet.

I then pushed *Exit Visa* into knee deep water, jumped on board and was relieved when the outboard started obediently on the first try. I turned and gave a final wave to my friends, once again, a little choked up.

Jack met me at the rail of the boat in a rather agitated state. I guess he was having issues with Sheryl's departure as well. Instead of having her lovingly fussing over him, he just had me. And, instead of always having a full food bowl, he'd constantly have to remind me to fill it up. When we'd traveled together several years ago, he had an annoying habit of biting me, even though he should know you don't bite the hand that feeds you. With Sheryl onboard, the biting was less frequent, but once she left he lapsed back into that nasty habit. It's his way of saying "You're not Sheryl," I thought as I rubbed the fresh wounds on my hand. Another way he chose to express his displeasure was about every other day he'd use the sink instead of the toilet to relive himself. Now that's emotional.

It was a short trip along the rugged Mexican coast from Troncones to Ztown (as the cruisers affectionately call Zihuatanejo) and we were there in just a few hours. We rounded the point about midday and I was surprised to see so many boats in the large anchorage. I counted 30 sailboats in addition to a massive, 900-foot-long, cruise ship that was plopped right in the middle of the bay. Several bright orange shuttle boats were bussing back and forth from the long, concrete public wharf to the gigantic ship, ferrying passengers to and from town. Add in the local pangas, which are the 20 foot-long open fiberglass boats with oversized outboards, zipping about making it a very busy scene, indeed.

The view was picturesque. The gray sand beach in front of the town was crowded with pangas, their fishing nets spread out to dry in the sun. The older, original buildings of Zihuatanejo were built on the flat just behind the shoreline. Steep cliffs rose to the south and were covered with newer hotels and condominiums.

All the other cruising boats were congregated in a nook of the bay between the town and the condos, so I followed suit and dropped the hook setting it in the soft sand. It was the first time in quite awhile I'd had to anchor single handed and as I ran back and forth between the bow and cockpit, I realized how much easier it was with Sheryl on board. At least I'd been able to tow the dinghy the short distance, so I wouldn't have to worry about launching it by myself.

I could see where the other cruiser's had left their dinghies on shore, just to the right of all the pangas. I again followed 'herd mentality' and landed *Exit Visa* alongside the rest. I tied a line to a beach-side palm tree to prevent the dinghy from floating away should the tide come up.

Then I wandered on to the neat and tidy little sidewalk that bordered the bay. Scores of vendors had set up booths on both sides of the walk and there was a large crowd of people milling around: presumably off the cruise ship. For them, it was like running a gauntlet to get through the maze of silver jewelry, brightly painted pottery and food carts of mouth-watering Mexican cuisine.

I used a few pesos I had in my pocket to purchase a fish taco and proceeded to a nearby bench to sit and watch the scene in front of me. As I savored my treat I enjoyed observing the interaction between the tourists and the Mexican merchants. It was 'people watching' at its best.

Then I heard a laugh that rose above the din, catching my attention with its familiarity. Turning to the source my eyes fell upon a face from my past. My mind was racing trying to place the petite brunette, when she happened to look my way. Suddenly stopping her conversation, she yelled, "Rick!! Is that really you?"

With outstretched arms she started toward me and I stood up to catch her embrace. Over her shoulder I saw her tall, thin companion and thankfully I was able to put names to the familiar faces.

"Liz, Tom! What are you guys doing in Mexico?"

"We're on that ship," she replied pointing to the behemoth of a cruise ship that took up a large portion of the harbor.

"Are you here on *Rick's Place*? How's Jack? Did you sail around the world? Do you still hear voices in your head?" she asked, her brown eyes peering at me from behind her stylish wire rimmed glasses, then she paused to take a breath.

Tom, her husband, knew this was his chance to get a word in and said, "Do you have time for lunch?" in his usual, nonchalant manner. The two were a perfect pair since their personalities balanced each others so well. She being animated and excitable, while he always seemed calm and reserved. It had been some years, but they looked much as I remembered them save for a bit more gray around the temples in Tom's dark brown hair.

As we walked the mile to La Ropa beach, where they'd been headed when they ran into me, thoughts of how we'd met in Maui years earlier flooded my mind. Jack and I had been alone and stranded on shore in the midst of hurricane Iniki, watching the surf pummel the boats in the anchorage. *Rick's Place* was one of those boats. Liz had come along and taken pity on us, and took us in to share their home on that terrifying night.

Reaching La Ropa beach, we found a quaint shore-side restaurant called *Elvira's*. We sat at one of the dozen or so plastic tables under the shade of it's large, colorful beach umbrella with our feet in the sand and ordered a round of Margaritas and continued reminiscing.

"So, what's it been, 2 or 3 years since I rescued you and Jack from the hurricane?" Liz wondered out loud.

"Yeah, something like that, but I think its closer to 4," I answered, shocked to realize how long it had been, then continuing, "What's really weird is that guy that started sailing with me from Washington is living up the road about an hour north of here. Remember, he was there surfing near your condo the day Iniki hit the islands? Small world, isn't it?"

"Oh, I remember you talking about him," Tom chimed in, "he had a nick name of some kind.... Moondoggy or something...."

Laughing, I said, "Sparky."

We then relived how Jack and I were taken off *Rick's Place* where it was anchored near Mala Wharf on Maui, just before the wind-generated swell started destroying boats in the open roadstead anchorage. That was one fitful night wondering if I'd have a boat to go back to in the morning.

After recounting the highlights of my adventures across the Pacific once we left Hawaii, I then explained about the demise of *Rick's Place* in a freak storm in Fiji. They really enjoyed hearing how I'd turned the wrecked hull of the boat into a barefoot bar. I went on to explain that I eventually sold the bar and bought another cruising boat, *Casablanca,* and had set out again, this time with a girlfriend and the same old cat.

"So where is Jack? And the mystery girlfriend?" Liz inquired.

"Jack is here. He's out on the boat. As far as my girlfriend, Sheryl, you just missed her. She had to fly back to San Francisco last week to take care of some business." With that sentence I just about summed up my life since I'd last seen them.

They brought me up to speed on their lives, too. Tom had retired early, having had a very successful career as an architect. They still had their condo in Hawaii, but spent most of their time traveling the world. Liz explained how they'd always wanted to see Mexico by boat, so this was their first time on a cruise ship. Since we were all travelers, though in vastly different modes, we talked of the possibility of meeting up again in some exotic place.

"Oh, and I had a book published, if you're interested," I added.

"Are you kidding me? What's the name?" Liz asked.

"*Adventures Aboard Rick's Place,*" I informed her wishing I had a copy with me to give them.

I'll order one just as soon as we get home! I can't wait to read that!" She exclaimed.

"Rick, what was it you used to call this kind of coincidence?" Tom pondered, thinking back and then said, "Cosmic pinball."

"Yeah, that's right," I replied as I thought about how weird it all was to run into them, especially so soon after leaving Sparky up at Troncones.

A whistle from the ship indicating it was time for them to get back aboard had us up and rushing, hastily exchanging new addresses and phone numbers. We each promised to do a better job of staying in touch and then they were off, waving at me from the window of a taxi that would take them back to the wharf.

Once again I was left alone with my thoughts. Seeing Liz and Tom had somehow made me miss Sheryl even more. I guess maybe I am pretty emotional......no way.

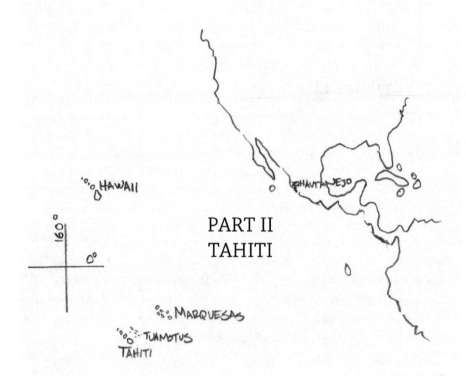

PART II
TAHITI

CHAPTER 7
FLYING FISH AND LIGHTENING BOLTS

"Let a smile be your umbrella, because you're going to get soaked anyway."
—Anonymous

One week out of Z-town, the seas were still turbulent. *Casablanca* had left at the end of a gale and the winds had dropped to the normal 15 – 20 knots, down from the 30 – 35 that had thrashed the coast for the better part of a week. Though I'd timed the wind right, I had miscalculated the sea state. Rollers coming from the northwest collided with the residual storm swell from the south, creating steep, pyramid-shaped waves, making for a very uncomfortable ride. With the amount of spray dousing the boat in the turbulent seas, it felt like I was in the middle of a washing machine minus the fabric softener.

I was, however, getting my sea legs and adapting to the constant movement. Jack, who had been listless for the first few days, had regained his usual voracious appetite and even managed to devour a flying fish that I had found on deck that morning.

The excitement mixed with all the busy activities involved in preparing for another offshore passage had kept me from dwelling on my love life, or lack there of. I did know that once the routine of the voyage set in, dreams of Sheryl would fill my short sleep periods and renew the feelings of loneliness.

The longer we were out, the more the days began to blur together. Catching a fish, being visited by dolphin, spotting a whale and avoiding squalls became my ocean yardstick of our progress to the Marquesas. The one big obstacle between me and my landfall was the Inter Tropical Convergence Zone, or ITCZ as it's commonly called. This is the area on the ocean, near the equator, where the trade winds of the northern hemisphere and the trade winds of the southern hemisphere come together. This meeting creates some very unstable conditions that can stretch from 100 to 500 miles in width. This band of crazy weather, everything from dead calm to gusty, contrary winds and frequent squalls, grows and shrinks and moves around, almost seeming alive at times.

The best strategy for crossing the infamous ITCZ is to determine the narrowest point on this ever changing mass and then cross it as quickly as you can. With its constant undulations and the sometimes hard to pick up weather reports, it can be kind of difficult to know exactly where this point might be. But this time I had an ace up my sleeve.

Before leaving on my first offshore cruise to Hawaii, I became friends with an honest to goodness alien from outer space, or so I thought at the time since he seemed to possess powers stronger than those of mortal men. Alien Allen had just returned from a cruise through the South Pacific as I was preparing to set off in *Rick's Place*, and since the South Pacific was where I was headed I began to buddy up with this guy. He had a wealth of information stowed in his completely hairless round head and was a wizard at fixing anything on board, from computers to toilets. We spent many hours together going over charts of South Pacific landfalls and he gave me lots of tips on where to go, and more importantly where not to go.

We had both lived on the same dock back in Gig Harbor, and often, at night, I would see his slight stature hunched over a high powered telescope scanning the sky. I always imagined he was checking up on his old neighborhood, somewhere in the Andromeda galaxy, perhaps? But the thing that really had me convinced that he was an alien was the weird feeling that would overpower me whenever he came into close proximity, whether I saw him or not. Every hair on my body would start to twitch like he was emitting some sort of static pulse. As long as there was no alien probing involved, I could tolerate the tingly sensation.

Back in San Diego, as I was planning my trip to the Marquesas, I'd contacted Alien Allen with some questions concerning the ITCZ and the route I should take. He, in turn, offered his help as a weather prognosticator and I was intrigued with his simple plan. He would use all the resources he had at his disposal via the internet to collect the latest real time data for my position. Then, using the Single Side Band radio at predetermined times each day, he would relay to me anything of significance. Hopefully his plan would get *Casablanca* through the unsettled weather zone without major incident.

When I was about 600 miles from the equator I thought, "Sailing just doesn't get much better than this". The trade winds stayed consistent at 10 to 15 knots with a gentle following sea, pushing *Casablanca* across the ocean comfortably at 6 knots. But I'd begun to see lightening far off in the distance at night so I knew that the dreaded zone was fast approaching.

Jack, of course, was fully acclimated at that point and was spending a lot of time out in the cockpit and even climbing up on the dodger, which was making me quite nervous. So I dug out his harness and tether, which just made him mad when I attempted to put it on him, even though I tried to explain it was for his own good – and mine. I had a feeling if I showed up without Jack at the end of this cruise, Sheryl wouldn't be very pleased with me. Several nips to my hand later, the harness was finally on the disgruntled cat and I was satisfied he wouldn't end up as fish food; just yet.

Turning in for a short nap I was thinking we might get lucky and not hit any real adverse weather while crossing the ITCZ. Content, I drifted off to sleep ignoring the little voice that was trying to warn me that it might be a false sense of security.

Four hours later I awoke to the main sail flapping back and forth on a windless sea. A dirty gray cloud cover had replaced the intense blue sky.

"Well, Jack, so much for missing the doldrums," I muttered, eliciting a lazy yawn from my big gray tabby.

There were still several hours before the scheduled radio contact (or sked in cruiser's lingo) with Allen back in Gig Harbor. I hadn't had any luck touching bases with him for several days. Propagation, or simply the distance that radio waves carry in the atmosphere, is always unpredictable and sort of hit or miss. Radio reception is affected by sun spots, local interference or just bad juju as far as I can tell. It seems any number of things can keep a High Frequency radio from receiving or transmitting a good signal.

At the appointed time and frequency, I sent out a call to Allen and waited, listening intently through the static trying to pick out any sort of response. Nothing heard. After several more unsuccessful tries, I just put out a call that gave my latitude and longitude in hopes that my alien friend could hear me, even though I wasn't hearing him. I also passed on that I would be trying the radio again in 3 hours time. Static was the only answer I received.

Climbing back on deck I could see what was causing at least some of the interference: lightening.

"Man, I HATE lightening," I said to the sky as I studied the clouds trying to judge the distance and direction the disturbance was moving. It didn't appear the dark mass would cross my track, though it would be close.

A couple minutes later, the wind picked up and we started to move again quite briskly. But the problem was it was sending us toward the big ugly cloud that was spewing the bolts of lightening. No matter what tack I sailed we seemed to be drawn towards the giant black mass as if it were some kind of boat magnet.

The bright flashes of light streaked across the sky as I removed all of the instruments I could easily disconnect and placed them in the oven for protection. That seems to be the standard cruiser's practice, the thought being that if you happen to take a direct hit your electronics won't be fried. I kind of think that if we take a strike it will light up the oven and melt everything inside, but I do it anyway.

Three hours later an alarm reminded me it was time for my next attempt at communicating with my weather/space man, Allen. Since the squall had pretty much paralleled our course for about an hour, I figured the interference it created would prevent him from getting any word through to Casablanca. Plus, I didn't even know if Allen had heard my earlier "shot-in-the-dark" message asking to try our radio sked again at the later hour.

Right on time I turned on the radio and was met with loud static punctuated by even louder static when the nearby disturbance would discharge a bolt of electricity.

Then, as if God himself was talking to me, Allen's voice boomed in, crystal clear, "Casablanca, this is the Star Ship Enterprise." (I made that part up)

What he actually said was, "*Casablanca*, this is *Veeger* calling. Rick, you can probably hear me, but might not be able to get through the static to reply." How did he know that?

He continued on, "You need to sail to longitude 125 W and turn due south. Don't be tempted to turn sooner, you need to be very precise. This is *Veeger* clear."

I looked at the note I had just scribbled down and compared the instructions to my present position and determined I would be making the big turn in about an hour. What I didn't understand is where he was getting that information, because as far as I could see, the sky was heavily overcast with squalls and lightening in the direction he was telling me to go. It appeared to me that it would be better to continue my course which was running parallel to the worst of the ugly weather.

I kept a close watch on the GPS for the next hour, totally convinced that Allen had misjudged what was happening out here. I feared that if I followed his instructions, *Casablanca* would be headed into some very bad weather.

When the GPS read 124.98 W I was bracing myself to head into the blackness and I tried, unsuccessfully, to reach Allen on the radio one last time. So, at a few minutes before midnight when the GPS told me I was at 125 W, I disengaged the auto pilot, turned due south and said a prayer as the mainsail noisily slapped to the other side of the boat. I held my breath and refused to look beyond the bow, just waiting to get slammed by an ugly squall. Five minutes stretched to thirty and soon an hour had passed without problem. Suddenly a bright light that was more than just a flash of lightening caused me to turn and look behind me. And what to my wondering eyes should appear, but a big full moon, complete with stars and clear sky!

It seemed *Casablanca* was traveling down a cloudless corridor about 5 miles wide, with squalls and lightening clearly visible on either side. It was as if the clouds had parted for me, just as the seas had parted for Moses for his safe crossing of the Red Sea. How Alien Allen had known (or caused....) this to happen will always be a mystery. Like I said, he definitely has powers greater than those of mortal men.

From that point on the winds remained constant and the seas flattened out. We were closing in on the equator and within a week Jack and I would be in the mysterious Marquesas.

CHAPTER 8
THE MARQUESAS

"Sometimes you have to get lost to find yourself."
—Unknown

Twenty-three days after leaving Zihuatanejo, dawn revealed a dramatic volcanic island on the horizon. As we sailed closer, I had an eerie feeling as I looked at the misty clouds hanging on the rough, jungle covered cliffs. A shiver ran down my spine as I realized it reminded me of Skull Island, the island of King Kong lore. That movie had so terrified me as a young child it caused me to have nightmares for years. Even in the sunlight, it looked dark and foreboding.

Looking in closer with my binoculars, I was able to spot silvery, glistening waterfalls threading their way down the rocky faces of steep cliffs. Jutting out of the dense jungle, sharp rocky spires, devoid of vegetation, shot up to the sky. Rainbows began to appear as the heavy mist lifted, changing the effect of the island from one of menace to fascination.

Jack had joined me on deck, probably being drawn out of his sleep state by the delightful fragrances wafting across the water to the boat. The fresh, sweet scents of the lush tropical foliage were a nice change from the somewhat locker room smell that was permeating *Casablanca* after weeks at sea.

I'd set Tahuku Bay on Hiva Oa as our destination since it was near one of the Marquesan Ports of Entry: Atuona. As my trusty GPS told me we were nearing the waypoint for entering the bay, I began to worry. It appeared, to me, that if I followed the course it was recommending, I would be driving *Casablanca* right up on shore. I continued to scan the area with binoculars, but could see nothing other than the large South Pacific swell breaking with effervescence against the tall cliffs. When I was within a quarter mile of the supposed anchorage my heart was racing and beads of perspiration were running down my forehead. Why couldn't I see the entrance? What had I missed?

"Damn," I said out loud, thinking I must have entered the coordinates wrong. I didn't have time to re-check my data entry as we were basically in a box and if I didn't act quickly I wouldn't be able to make a U-turn in time to retrace my way out of this blind corner. *Casablanca* was starting to feel the swell as the water shallowed beneath her keel. We were lifted slowly as the rollers passed under the boat then crashed violently ashore. I was afraid one of these waves would get hold of us and drag us to rocks, as well.

"I am outta here," my brain screamed as I spun the wheel to make an about face for deeper water to re-evaluate the situation. As I turned my eye caught a glimpse of something moving along the shoreline. A small boat appeared to be coming out of a slight fold in the land right in the direction the GPS had wanted me to go.

When I lined my bow to head toward the opening, which still was not very apparent, it put us broadside to the deep swell, and the boat, without sails up, rocked hard from side to side. Things down below that hadn't been dislodged in 23 days of ocean sailing were flying and crashing about. It sounded like a war zone downstairs. Jack, freaked out by the noise, ran from the cockpit up to the bow of the boat.

"You're on your own, buddy!" I yelled, adding, "Don't fall in cuz I'm not coming back!" Yeah, tough guy.

I slowly guided *Casablanca* forward; still not convinced the harbor was there, all the time nervously watching Jack on the bow. Finally I saw the small cleft of land gradually opening to reveal about a dozen sailboats anchored in the hidden bay. Relieved to know I was headed in the right direction, I increased my speed to cover the distance as quickly as possible. It's always scary to turn toward land when entering an unknown port, but it's especially bad if the entrance is completely obscured from view until you're right in front of it.

Once we entered the bay, the swell gave way to flat water and I easily maneuvered *Casablanca* to what appeared to be a good spot to drop the hook. When I went up front to lower the anchor, Jack rolled on his back, quite smugly, looking for a belly rub.

"You were lucky that time, Jack Cat, not falling in," I scolded as I obliged him with a brush of my hand on his sun warmed fur. Little did I know then that Jack's luck had just about run out.

The bay, which ran roughly north to south, was about a half mile long and a quarter mile wide, rimmed with black rock cliffs topped with lush greenery and a scattering of homes built on the western slope. The town was not visible from the anchorage.

After setting the anchor, I picked up my binoculars and checked out the dozen or so boats that were anchored in the small bay. This brought to mind that cruising is one of the only endeavors where it is perfectly permissible to spy on your neighbors with binoculars. I recognized a few boats that I had seen in Mexico, including Chris's boat, *The Swallow*. There were also flags from many other countries present, including Germany, Switzerland, and, of course, France. In Mexico, for the most part, all the boats seemed to be from either Canada or the US, with the occasional Australian yacht thrown in, but here it was really more a melting pot from around the world.

Even though exhaustion was catching up to me, I quickly went about pumping up the dinghy. I wanted to get to shore to check in with the gendarme, since I know the French can be real sticklers for protocol. I figured I could rest up once I got that out of the way.

An hour after anchoring, I made the short row to the small, cement boat launch, which was on the east side of the bay, where I'd seen other dinghies pulled up on shore. Once there, I stumbled on wobbly legs as I stepped onto the first solid surface I'd touched in nearly a month. My sea-legs weren't turning back to land-legs quickly enough and I promptly did a nose dive onto the water washed concrete slab. Embarrassed, I picked myself up and glanced around to see if there were any witnesses to my header. Seeing no one laughing at my blunder I brushed myself off and drug *Exit Visa* to the top of the ramp to join the other tenders.

As I walked along the road that would take me to town, the lyrics, "What do you do with a drunken sailor," kept running through my head, for surely I was staggering like a sailor on the sauce.

The humidity was high as I walked through the small town in search of the Gendarmerie. Heavy clouds, threatening rain, hung over the steep, jungle clad mountains that the village was cradled beneath. The buildings looked to be 1950's era, very well kept and tidy with fresh paint and swept walks.

The Gendarme was, as I'd remembered from the last time I made a visit to French Polynesia, very official and not very friendly. It didn't seem he knew a word of English, for when I'd get stuck on a word or phrase in the check-in process, a blank stare would greet my inquiries. At that point I'd pull out my French/English dictionary and try to piece it out. I know it's not their responsibility to learn my language, I'd just like a smile or look of understanding as I struggle to use theirs.

The one question I did understand was concerning whether there were any pets on board, to which I answered NO. That was a mistake, I did have a pet, and I had the proper paperwork to make Jack legal, but..... Well, I just sort of froze up and denied his existence as I'd had to do on my first trip with him, when he was a stow-a-way and I didn't have the necessary documentation for him. Old habits die hard.

My second stop was the Post Office where they had public pay phones, so I could call the States.

"Hello, this is the Flower Pot, Sheryl speaking," came the lilting voice on the other end.

Then, in a loud, fast talking manner, I pronounced," This is KPIG radio and if you can identify this hours song for lonely sailors, YOU WIN!"

"Rick! You goof!" Sheryl said through a gaggle of giggles. "Where are you guys?"

I did a quick rundown of the trip and brought her up to date and assured her Jack was doing great. I knew from past experience I'd have to keep the call as short as possible, or I would severely drain the cruising kitty. We talked of missing each other, but I did leave the question of her joining us unasked.

"Even with the bad economy, the shop's still doing well. But the best news is that there's a developer looking at maybe buying up the whole block, including my shop. We'll know in about 30 days."

That was a bit discouraging to me, since it really meant that I probably wouldn't be seeing her for at least another month.

"Another piece of news," she added with great excitement, and taking a deep breath she said, "Joni's having twins!"

"Wow! That's great," I exclaimed, truly happy for her. "Maybe Jack & Rick should be a consideration for boy's names," I suggested.

"Yeah, I don't really see that happening," she said dismissing my great idea.

After another minute or so, we said our good byes and I promised to call again in a few days. Boy, it was hard to hang up that phone.

Before heading back to the boat I found a small store to pick up some fresh provisions, including my favorite treat on these islands – the 3 foot long, crusty and inexpensive baguette.

I don't necessarily agree with much of anything the French have imposed on these friendly island people, but I'm certainly thankful they brought over the bread recipe. Since it's also one of the subsidized foods, it is cheap enough that anybody can afford it—and you can't say that about much else around there. Baked fresh every morning, your mouth just waters as you pass by the bakeries and inhale that warm "bread-in-the-oven" smell. The baguettes are a real treat and sustained me well on my previous visit to French Polynesia, so I was happy to find them in the Marquesas, as well.

It was another two days before I made it back in to shore. There had been lots of cleaning to do, repairs to make and some much needed sleep to catch up on. Once fully rested, I went in and did some longer distance hiking, discovering some outstanding viewpoints overlooking the bays and valleys of Hiva Oa.

I found Paul Gauguin's grave in the cemetery above Atuona. I'm not a big fan of graveyards, I still feel the need to hold my breath as I pass one as dictated by our childhood superstitions. But, it seemed like a "must do" while in the neighborhood, so I hiked up the hill, through the picket fence encircled burial plots and gazed upon his headstone. His final resting place had a commanding view of the Pacific Ocean, but the graveyard itself was overgrown with long grass and showed signs of neglect. I didn't stay long. I was nearly out of breath.

Along the road there were a few stands selling various fruits and vegetables. There were the standards, like cucumbers and tomatoes, but some were unidentifiable, at least to me. I'd become accustomed to taro and breadfruit in my last venture into the South Pacific Isles, but some of these fruits just didn't look real to me. I'd later find out that the huge green orbs which were 8 to 10 inches in diameter and looked like limes on steroids, were really a giant, sweet grapefruit called pompamouse, and they are just about as delicious as the baguettes. They also grew a very tasty sweet green orange, which is really kind of an oxymoron to me. Shouldn't they just call them greens?

The other surprise I found on that, and other walks, was the friendliness of the Marquesan people. The men were strong and powerful looking with tattoos on their bodies and even on their faces. At first I found them very intimidating, but, when they'd learn I was from the U.S., they would warm up and ask lots of questions. My favorite question being whether I knew Brad Pitt.

Back in the anchorage, the cruisers had set up a net on VHF channel 22: a hold over from Mexico, I believe. This informal radio program helped cruisers with local assistance, information and was also a way to find out where old cruising friends might be. They'd also announce any events that were being planned. It was through this net, about a week after my arrival, that I heard there would be a dinghy raft-up in the anchorage the following afternoon: sort of a floating potluck. Everyone was encouraged to join in, meet your neighbors and bring a snack to share.

At the appointed time the next day, once the morning rain shower gave way to fluffy white clouds, ten dinghies were loosely tied together forming a floating island that looked a bit like something out of Kevin Costner's *Waterworld*. I reacquainted with old friends from Mexico, and met new ones who had just come through the Panama Canal.

There were dinghies of all sizes and even a couple kayaks. We were free-floating through the anchorage and when the mass would drift toward one of the anchored boats, someone would give a gentle shove and the strange flotilla would slowly drift in another direction.

Things were going along just great, with everyone trying to outdo each other's storm stories while a variety of delicious snacks were passed from dinghy to dinghy. Then, without warning, a 32 foot blue-hulled sailboat that had been anchored on the outer perimeter of the fleet started to slowly make its way toward the rest of the anchored boats.

"MY GOD! That's our boat," yelled a middle-aged couple in shock and disbelief, just two dinghies down from me.

"You must be dragging anchor," came another shout.

Then all Hell broke loose. The blue-hulled boat began to pick up speed and was about to T-bone a nearby vessel. Everyone was scrambling to get untied from the raft-up so they could get to their own boats and defend them from the run-away sailboat.

The most puzzling thing was that there was no one on board *SeaHawk*, the wandering boat. It was like a ghost ship being moved by an unseen hand. There was no wind, or big swell to propel it along and the anchor chain was stretched out in front of its bow, so it obviously wasn't dragging anchor. All the same, *SeaHawk* was pin-balling off its third hull when it set a course for *Casablanca*.

The first boat that was hit, ended up with a big blue stripe down the entire 40 feet of its hull when the errant vessel scraped along its side before the owners could push the blue demon away.

After that, *SeaHawk*, minus some blue paint, grazed the stern of its next victim, damaging the windvane that is used to steer the boat during ocean passages. It, too, received a blue tattoo.

I had climbed aboard *Casablanca* and was trying to get the engine started, thinking that I could at least swing out of the way of the approaching battering ram. So far the damage inflicted by the blue hulled boat was fairly light: at least not critical. But, if it came head on into the side of my boat as it appeared it was lining up to do, the outcome could be disastrous.

When the engine failed to start, I gave up and ran to the bow, grabbing a boat hook that I hoped would help me deflect the 11,000 pound mass heading toward us. Then, just as suddenly as she had started her rampage of terror, *SeaHawk* stopped. She was a mere five feet from impact with *Casablanca*, bow sprit pointing for a direct hit. I was praying she wasn't just gearing up for the final charge.

In an instant, Scott, a wiry built sport diver from the boat *Scott Free* was in the water with his facemask and fins. He quickly disappeared into the murkiness as he effortlessly pulled himself down *SeaHawk's* anchor chain. His bubbles indicated his progress as he followed the chain down into the depths in front of *SeaHawk*, just to the right of *Casablanca*. Meanwhile, *SeaHawk's* baffled and frightened owners had finally managed to climb aboard their errant boat.

We were all beginning to worry about Scott, since it seemed he'd been down too long. Then, much to our relief, he burst to the surface with a big gasp.

"A manta ray!" he shouted, "a huge bloody manta ray has the anchor rode wrapped around his right mandible. Give me some slack on the chain and I'll go back down and try to untangle him. He's lying on the bottom now, exhausted."

I couldn't believe what I was hearing. How could this be? Now would I have to worry about being taken from my anchorage in the middle of the night by some unseen monster in addition to all the other worries of anchor dragging? It made me think of the time when Sheryl and I were frightened by the crash of a pelican on our deck. I felt sorry for the poor Manta Ray having to cope with man invading its territory.

SeaHawk's owners were on the bow of their boat letting out some more anchor chain. You could see the relief in their faces since the mystery of the moving boat was finally solved.

Scott made another 21 foot dive and, again, he was down so long I was getting ready to go in after him, when he rocketed to the surface with a flourish.

"He's loose and starting to move away," he announced, eliciting a cheer from the anchorage. There was also a lot of cruiser's chatter about the unlikely event and how horrible it would have been if something like that had happened at night when everyone was asleep.

Later, after *SeaHawk* had re-anchored and things had settled down, I took some beer over to Scott's boat to have a chat. His wife, Monica, greeted me and welcomed me aboard while Scott finished changing his clothes.

"So how big was that thing?" I queried once Scott had joined us in the cockpit.

"About 12 feet across, I think. Kinda hard to tell with the water being so murky. But, he wasn't the biggest Manta Ray I've ever seen," he told me.

"I can't imagine a ray bigger than that," I replied, totally in awe.

"Yeah, it wasn't far from here, either. Monica and I were taking some guests out on a dive charter and we came on one that was about 18 feet across and musta weighed close to a ton," he informed me.

"No thank you!" was my response.

"Oh, they're really harmless, gentle creatures. They just eat plankton and very small fish. No stingers or anything, either," he added.

After that terrific rescue, Scott was a hero amongst the cruisers and never had to buy his own beer again.

The day after the big Manta Ray incident I picked up my anchor to go explore the other side of the island and headed for a bay called Hanamenu. Traveling northwest along the sheer black cliffs of Hiva Oa, I stayed several miles offshore as the charts had not been updated since the turn of the century and there were many uncharted areas noted along that 10 mile coast.

Since the water wasn't good for snorkeling in the Marquesas, I came to enjoy what the land had to offer. In Hanamenu, wild pigs would venture down to the shore around sunset and I found it fascinating to watch them from afar. I don't think I would have liked to come upon one of those in the brush anymore than I wanted to be face-to-face with a shark in these waters.

I spent one rocky night in Hanamenu before making a short day sail to the quiet bay of Hanaiapa. The heavy flowery fragrances wafting out to the boat were so enticing I was drawn to shore, despite the dicey surf landing that needed to be made. And I thought I'd seen the last of those when I left Mexico. There was a small, tidy village that stretched about a half mile inland through the lush jungle. The villagers had beautiful gardens surrounding their homes filled with very exotic flowers.

Jack and I spent several days traveling around Hiva Oa by boat. Most of the anchorages were rolly from sea swell and not the best visibility for snorkeling. I wasn't very keen on the notion that the islands shark population could see me before I could see them, so I didn't spend much time at all in the water. For as lovely as all these areas I'd visited had been, the frequent rain showers, the dangerous surf landings, not wanting to swim in the murky water and the nasty little gnat-like bugs called no-nos had me ready to move on. So Jack and I set off for another of the seven Marquesan Islands, Nuka Hiva. We were in search of greener pastures, or in my case, clearer waters.

It was 83 miles to Baie Taioa on Nuka Hiva, so we'd had to travel through the night. Upon our arrival, I was disappointed to find the same dishwater visibility that I had found on Hiva Oa. It looked like my snorkeling gear would get a longer rest.

Once I got the dinghy inflated, I rowed to shore to visit a couple who were legends in the cruising world: Daniel and his wife Antoinette. Now in their 70's, they had been welcoming cruisers to what has been dubbed "Daniel's Bay" for over 30 years. They lived simply in a small open-air house that sat neatly between the jungle and the beach. It was a very traditional thatch roofed building with mat screens that could be rolled down to protect them in nasty weather conditions.

When I reached the beach, Daniel hobbled down to where I was tying up the dinghy. A small man, with dark mahogany skin, he was somewhat frail and evoked images of ET, the extra terrestrial, of Steven Spielberg fame. He greeted me with a big, nearly toothless smile and in broken English he welcomed me and invited me to sign his guest log book. I'd heard about his book; actually "books" since he'd been doing it for so long. I was anxious to take a look at the names of those that had traveled through this way and I felt honored to be asked to put my name right alongside the others.

Before getting to the log, I reached into my backpack to pull out the small gifts I'd brought in for Daniel and his wife. Antoinette wasn't there as she was off visiting relatives, so I didn't get a chance to meet her. I'd heard through the coconut telegraph that canned meat, fish hooks, pencils, medicines or any other items would be greatly appreciated. I gave him my small offering and he seemed delighted with the T-shirt and cans of Spam and was very happy with the tube of antibacterial ointment. He, in turn, took me into his house and gave me a cup of some sort of hot tea drink. Laid out on the table in front of us were the guest books and I leafed through the different years. There were boat and crew names going back well before GPS was even invented. I spotted names of many of the legends of the cruising community that I'd read about in magazines and books. I also saw some boats I had met during my first cruise on *Rick's Place*. When I commented on one of the names I recognized as a bit of a cruising guru, Daniel chuckled and told me he was a very nice man and had visited many times. But Daniel found it humorous that he seemed to have a new wife whenever he came.

When I finished perusing the logs, I added Jack's and my names to the current book. Daniel then pointed to a buoy anchored off of his beach and explained that a water hose ran out to the float. Offering fresh water to fill their tanks was his gift to the cruisers who came to visit. I would find before

I left that it was just one of the gifts he gave as he also insisted I take plenty of fresh limes and pompamouse with me.

As I was getting ready to leave, he also told me about a beautiful waterfall that was a short hike away. He said it was one of the most beautiful places on earth and I must go see it. I loaded my gifts into *Exit Visa* and Daniel led me to the trail head and off I trudged.

The path was well marked; at least in the beginning. But after about an hour, I found myself surrounded by heavy vegetation and just hoping I was still on the right track, because the trail certainly wasn't very evident. In addition to the coconut palms and the thick foliage I was in amongst the dreaded no-nos. They are so small you barely notice them (thus their other name: no-see-ums) until their bite leaves you with a mind numbing itch that can drive you mad. These horrible little devil bugs live in the grasses and low shrubs and can easily make a mess of your exposed legs as you walk naively along. You don't feel the bite as it happens, it seems to take about an hour before the welts appear and the itching begins.

It was a full two hours before I reached the waterfall, though I had heard its roar from about a half mile away. What a site to behold. Daniel was right, it was one of the most beautiful scenes and I couldn't believe my eyes. The cascade of water appeared to be coming right out of a cloud that was hanging at the top of a 2000 foot sheer cliff. It fell with deafening thunder into a bowl-shaped pond that was a couple hundred feet in diameter. A small creek spilled out of one edge of the pool and ran down to the valley below. I shouted at the top of my lungs to see if I could even be heard over the din of the crashing water.

When I sat on a rock at the shore of the pond, I counted at least 50 bites on my legs and they were just starting to itch so I decided to retreat into the water for some relief. The effect of the cool liquid on my limbs was almost immediate and the bites, for the time being, had calmed down.

I immersed my whole body into the clear pool and floating there on my back I found the concussion of the falling water hitting the pond very hypnotic. My eyes were closed and I was slowly being drawn toward the rhythmic pounding. A voice in my head was trying to tell me that it would be unwise to get any closer, but none the less I drifted slowly as if in a trance....

Suddenly, the sensible side of my brain came back to life and I opened my eyes to see that I was within a mere 10 feet of the impact point of the crashing waterfall. I knew the voices were right (as they always are) and I needed to stay away from the skull-crushing cascade. But, Mother Nature had her own program going and I found I was being sucked toward the squash point by an unseen current that was probably a result of the upwelling. I was being drug to what could be a very unpleasant situation.

I immediately turned toward shore and started stroking and kicking hard as the adrenaline began to course through my body. I could feel the water that was just outside the main fall stinging my back like buck shot and it seemed like an eternity before I got clear of the currents tug.

I staggered ashore and sat down to catch my breath. As the sun slowly dried my skin, I stared, mesmerized at the power and beauty of this wonder of nature. Without warning, a jumble of rocks tumbled down mixed in with the falling water, crashing to the point I'd just struggled away from. I was lucky to have gotten out of there when I did.

Sitting near the shore I continued to watch the waterfall. Truly in awe of its power, my mind started to wander (as it usually does).

What was Sheryl doing at that moment?

Did she miss me?

Would she marry me?

Or did I scare her off with my sudden proposal?

I knew one thing: I missed sharing adventures such as Daniel and the waterfall with her. Her wide eyed wonderment was a true delight and made the experiences all the more special. But it was the flowers more than anything that got to me. They were a reminder both of her and of the reason for the distance between us. They were everywhere and just a hint of fragrance from the brilliant and exotic blossoms made me miss Sheryl all the more.

A crawling sensation on my ankle snapped me back to reality, where I was horrified to see more than a dozen tiny black bugs having lunch, courtesy of the flesh on my ankle.

I jumped up and waded back into the cool water, both to get rid of the recent interlopers, as well as to soothe the previous irritations. It was going to be an uncomfortable walk back to the bay.

Along the way, I got to thinking about Daniel. His skin, though wrinkled, displayed absolutely no bug bites. How could he be immune to the nasty little creatures?

Daniel was waiting for me as I emerged from the jungle path, and with his toothless smile said, "Thank you for your coming."

"It was a pleasure to meet you, Daniel. Please say hello to Antoinette," I enunciated a bit too slowly, as if talking to a child, and immediately felt the flush of embarrassment.

At that point, I looked down and the sand around my feet was alive with the vicious black biting bastards, but Daniel was still untouched.

My obvious question to him was, "Why don't these bugs bother you?"

"Because they are my friends and I talk to them," he replied, the smile leaving his face.

At that exact moment, a cloud crossed in front of the sun, suddenly bringing the air temperature down several degrees and casting a shadow over the beach. A slight chill ran down my spine and I was a little spooked.

I pushed *Exit Visa* out into the water and climbed aboard. As I looked back, Daniel was waving his arm in a slow goodbye. I could see his lips moving as if he were mumbling something to his black bug army. In my heart, I knew no ankle would ever be safe on that beach.

CHAPTER 9
MAKEMO ATOLL

"Life is not measured by the number of breaths we take,
but by the moments that take our breath away.
—Anonymous

Roughly 250 bug bites later, Jack and I checked out of the Marquesas. Well, actually, Jack was never officially there, so I was the only one that needed to check out. We headed for the Tuamotus, which we had heard are the polar opposite of their neighboring Marquesas. It's been said you explore the Marquesas by land and the Tuamotus by sea and I was looking forward to getting back into the water.

Although only 600 miles southwest of the Marquesas, those 5 days seemed like one of the longest passages I'd ever done. In my travels I'd come to find that the short passages are usually the hardest because the first three days are always difficult as you try to adapt to the constantly moving boat coupled with short sleep cycles. After the initial break in period you get into a comfortable routine and the days pass quickly and start to blend together.

We had great wind for the first day. It blew 15 – 20 knots from just behind the beam with gentle following seas, which makes for very fine sailing, indeed. Then, as if a switch was thrown, the wind died and I was forced to start the motor if I wanted to continue my forward progress. Once again, I had trouble starting the thing. What is it with me and boat motors and where's Butch when I need him? They seem to be the bane of my existence on this trip.

The engine would turn over OK, but then take an inordinate amount of time to kick off and start running smoothly, all the while belching out lots of black smoke. It was uncomfortably reminiscent of the problems I'd had back in Mexico with my cranky outboard. Since there was nothing I could do about it at that time, I just put it to the back of my mind. After all, *Casablanca* is a sailboat and I could always sail. Well, except when there is no wind. I planned to take a serious look at the engine when I got to Tahiti.

My cruising guide research revealed that there were over 70 islands within the boundaries of the Tuamotus spread over some 1000 miles of ocean. All but two are coral atolls which makes them very hard to spot from any distance. Since the palm trees are the highest point on the land, you don't see the atoll until you're about 8 miles away. My only other experience with finding one of these low lying islands was when I made my first foreign landfall, aboard *Rick's Place*, on Fanning Island.

Thank goodness for GPS. Until the advent of Global Positioning Systems, this dangerous archipelago was usually bypassed and most certainly wouldn't have been on my route. The area is rife with strong currents and swift moving squalls that can quickly get the most diligent of navigators off course. Since there are many miles of coral lying just below the surface of the water there is little margin for error in crossing these areas. By the time you see waves crashing on a fringing reef, it could already be too late to avoid it. Many unsuspecting ships and yachts met their fate in these treacherous waters and their rusting hulks, lying aground, seemingly miles from the nearest land, serve as an eerie reminder to stay ever vigilant.

Casablanca had 3 different GPS units onboard, so I was confident that keeping knowledge of my position wouldn't be the tricky part. The problem I was most concerned with had to do with entering the lagoons. Most of the passes a boat goes through to get into the protected lagoon have a significant out-flowing current. When this out-flowing current meets with an incoming tide, it makes for some pretty rough conditions, often creating a horror called a 'standing wave' which can build to 8 feet or more. That makes for a very dangerous entrance, to say the least.

Even though you can look at tide tables to see when the tidal current will be flowing in or out of the pass (and you want to go in with the tide), it can be hard to predict the outflow that is created when rough seas throw unusual amounts of water over the reef and into the lagoon. The excess water needs to "drain" out through the passes, and especially with a narrow pass, it can flow quite forcefully. Mix this strong outflow with an out going tide and you can have currents of 8 or 9 knots: too much for most boats to motor against. So you look for the incoming tide and hope to hell there isn't a wall of water fighting against it to get out at the time you want to go in.

From the guidebook, I'd picked out a few atolls whose passes were relatively obstruction free and fairly wide, thus, hopefully, pretty easy to enter. The other criteria was that they had to be in the general direction of Tahiti, and Makemo atoll seemed to fit the bill and would be our first stop.

On the sixth day out of Nuka Hiva, I spotted palm trees right where the trusty GPS said the island should be. As *Casablanca* drew closer, the sun-bleached white coral beach became more evident, as did the surf beating down on it.

When I was about a mile out, peering through my binoculars, I could just make out the narrow pass. The guide said it was 150 feet across on the ocean side, but from my perspective it looked too small for my 11 foot wide boat, especially with the big South Pacific waves breaking on either side in an explosive display of white water.

There was still an hour before "slack tide", which is that magical time in between the ebb and flow when there seems to be no tidal movement at all. I knew that the slack tide would offer the calmest conditions I could hope for in transiting this pass and I would wait outside until the time was right.

While I bobbed out in the open ocean, I took the opportunity to check the engine making sure nothing obvious was out of order. I couldn't risk having the old Iron Genny giving me trouble once I started through the pass. It would be difficult to rely on sails alone to make the transit into the anchorage against any outflow, plus the narrow channel didn't leave much room for tacking.

Bobbing around a mile offshore, I had to fight the urge to turn in and commence the trek through the pass and put an end to the anxiety of waiting. I knew that patience in giving the waters plenty of time to achieve their celestial influenced calm was the smart thing to do.

Finally, 15 minutes beyond the official predicted slack tide, I lined up *Casablanca's* bow to what appeared to be the center of the channel and increased the engine's RPM. In protest to the sudden increase in work load, the motor shot out a plume of black, sooty smoke.

As I drew closer to the pass I could see, not really what I would consider a standing wave, but a series of deep troughs that I would have to push through. With a knot in my stomach and a prayer that the engine would keep going, I plunged in to the channel.

Casablanca went from a fairly stable platform to an out of control roller coaster ride. The 4 foot waves were stacked closely together and had us "hobby horsing", where the bow rises on the wave and then quickly crashes down the other side over and over again giving the feeling of being on a bucking bronco. Luckily, our progress remained constant at 5 knots even though there was a strong current running against us. The surf breaking on the reef on both sides of my small boat was rather unnerving, especially when I saw the engine still puffing out the dark cloud of exhaust.

As we got further into the pass the boat speed began to drop slowly due to the increased effect of the current, so we were only moving forward at about 3.5 knots. That was a little worrisome, but no real cause for concern because the engine was still running, though it sounded a bit rough. The waves I'd encountered at the entrance were gone and now the current was creating swirling whirlpools as the water tried to rush out the pass.

When the speed dropped to 2 knots I did begin to fret that the current was going to bring me to a complete stop. I dared not try a u-turn for fear of losing control in the tempestuous waters. One misstep and *Casablanca* could end up on the sharp reefs which were clearly visible on either side of the boat. Plus, I'd just gotten through the waves at the entrance and didn't want to repeat that nerve-wracking feat.

A glance behind told me that the black engine smoke had intensified so I began to suspect that the current wasn't as strong as the engine was weak. I was straining to hear any anomaly in the engines vibration or pitch.

Casablanca was then half way through the pass into the lagoon and like a giant funnel the pass was narrowing as I progressed in and soon it was only 25 feet across. Working hard at the wheel to keep us on a steady course and keeping an eye out for any rocks or obstructions that would impede our progress, we pressed on.

After what seemed like hours, but had actually only been 40 minutes, our speed over ground was gradually increasing as the narrowest point of the pass gave way to the vast lagoon.

I slowed the engine RPM's so I could scope out where my first anchorage in the Tuamotus would be. I had been warned that traveling through these lagoons took vigilance and patience because of the coral spirals that rise up from the 50 to 100 foot depths to just below the surface, making for a dangerous obstacle course.

I saw no other boats which would indicate where the good anchorage was, but I did spot the old concrete wharf that the guide book identified as a reference point. As I passed close by the wharf that is used for the inter-island tramp steamer, I saw children of all ages jumping and diving into the turquoise water. They were laughing and playing as they climbed up the sides of the worn concrete structure waving enthusiastically to me.

As *Casablanca* slowly motored to what appeared a likely spot to drop the hook, the kids started yelling louder and waving more franticly, some even swimming out toward the boat.

Of course I couldn't understand what they were saying because of the language barrier, but I assumed they were just happy to see me. Wrong.

When I turned away from the greeting party and back to the business at hand, the depth sounder shrieked a low water warning and the slow moving *Casablanca* became the no moving *Casablanca*. Oh, so that's what the kids were yelling about. I'd finally learned to listen to the little voices in my head about impending doom, I realized then that I should listen to the voices around me, as well.

The relief was that it wasn't the hard crunching, hull gashing grounding if I'd hit coral, but the slow stopping of a soft sand landing. I was glad there weren't other boats in there to witness my faux pas.

By that time, five of the older teenage boys had reached *Casablanca* and were attempting to communicate with me. Finally, from amongst all of the voices yammering at the same time, I managed to hear a few words of English.

I needed to back the boat up to get out of the predicament I gotten myself into, but I couldn't put it in gear until the young swimmers were out of the way.

"English," I called out, "who speaks English?"

"I will." came a voice from the center of the pack of kids.

"OK, come up on the boat," I instructed the thin young man.

With that, five lanky, yet muscular, boys scrambled up the life lines on to the deck, some running up to the bow and the rest crowding around me in the cockpit.

The one that had spoken to me in English was the tallest of the lot: nearly six feet tall, I would guess. He pointed to a large rock off to my port side and told me, "Go there. Other side of rock."

I shifted into reverse and increased the RPMs, but we didn't move, just kicked up great clouds of sand. As skinny as they were, the added weight of the group of kids was keeping us aground.

My English speaking buddy suddenly started chattering to his compadres in their native tongue, and in unison all of the deeply tanned bodies ran to the stern of *Casablanca*. Before I could grasp what they were up to, they all ran back to the bow, then back again to the stern. They were laughing like it was great sport, and I finally caught on that they were rocking the boat to dislodge it from the sandbar's grasp. On their third return to the stern of the boat, we slowly began to move in reverse and soon I was back into 10 feet of crystal clear water, where I stopped our motion.

"My name is Rick," I said pointing to myself.

"My name is John Paul," was the young man's response.

"John Paul, where can I anchor safely?" I asked my new friend. There's nothing as valuable as local knowledge.

He pointed to a spot, not far from where we were. The other boys, now bored with the whole operation, jumped in the water and swam toward the wharf.

I shifted into forward and slowly followed John Paul's directions to the spot he deemed best. I set the anchor approximately one quarter mile from shore in 24 feet of transparent, turquoise water. As the anchor plunged down, I could plainly see a variety of brightly colored fish scatter in all directions. What a change from the murky Marquesas.

Back in the cockpit, I found Jack sitting in the lap of the shy young man. John Paul was stroking the cat's back, much to the feline's delight. It was nice to see someone doting on him the way Sheryl would be, had she been there.

After shutting down the engine, I went below and took my last two cans of Coke out of the refrigerator. I'd been saving them for my landfall celebration and was glad I'd kept more than one.

Handing a soda to John Paul, he politely thanked me and asked if I needed a guide around town because he would be happy to show me his village, Pouheva.

I told him that I was tired from many days of sailing and needed a good sleep, but would be most grateful for a tour in the morning.

"I meet you there," he stated, pointing off the stern of the boat to a small patch of grass near the shore. Then he gracefully dove into the water and was gone.

The next morning I felt refreshed after enjoying a long, deep sleep, and quickly got to the chores at hand. I inflated the dinghy, put the outboard on and then motored the short distance to shore. John Paul was already waiting for me.

As I clambered out of the small boat he waded into the water, and helped me drag it up to a safe spot on the beach.

"I need to see the Gendarme," I told him.

He eyed me quizzically, so I added, "To check in. I need to let him know I have arrived here from the Marquesas.

"We will go," he said as we started off for the village.

He led me down a well-packed road made of crushed coral, past cinder block houses, some with thatched roofs and others with the familiar wavy pattern of corrugated metal, both providing shelter from the elements. The homes and yards were immaculate and well tended with small fences or plants marking off each property. I didn't see any cars along the way, or in any of the yards, but supposed there must be a pick-up or two around to haul supplies to the small stores when the inter-island ship comes in.

Walking quietly along for sometime, I relished in all the sights, sounds and smells of this new place.

Then John Paul broke the silence with, "Rick, you like Marquesas?"

"It's very beautiful there. Lots of mountains and rain," I replied.

"I go there once with my dad," he told me. "Not good – too wet – very hot."

"And too many bugs," I countered, absently scratching the last of my healing bites.

"Yes, yes! No-Nos very bad," he agreed enthusiastically.

"So where did you learn such good English," I asked my friendly tour guide.

"My older sister leaves in Hawaii. She teach me," he answered proudly.

We came to a stop in front of a white washed one-level building with a neat little garden edging the entrance walk. A large French flag fluttered in the light trade wind breeze from the top of a tall flagpole in the center of the small courtyard.

"Here is your check-in," he said a bit nervously, adding, "I will meet you again here," and he strolled away. I remembered being his age and making it a point not to hang around the authorities, lest they think of something I may or may not have done that I should be reprimanded for.

Since I hadn't left French Polynesia, and was just traveling from one island to another, the checking in to Makemo was just a formality, with no new paperwork, just a fresh stamp in my passport. The gendarme was very cordial and friendly, not like my previous experience on Hiva Oa. It occurred to me that the official's moods were greatly affected by the amount of paperwork that they had to complete.

Mission accomplished, I stepped outside into the bright sunlight, but John Paul was nowhere to be found, so I continued along the road we had been walking. I was admiring all the nice gardens with bright flowers in the front yards when I noticed that many of them had headstones in them. They weren't just gardens, they were graves.

Boy, I thought, that's really keeping the family together. I wondered what would happen should the family decide to move? Do they dig up and take Grandma along, or leave her to join a new family? They were very creative with the decorating of the gravesites, as well, lining the perimeter with nice stones or shells, and in some cases beer bottles. I don't know if that was a comment on the deceased person's lifestyle, or they just thought it was a good look.

Many of the islanders were out tending their yards as I passed, sweeping the walks with brooms or the more traditional palm fronds. I was always greeted with a big smile and a nod of the head.

"Rick!" came John Paul's voice, but I couldn't identify from which direction.

"Here Rick," he called again and I got a sense of where he was and headed down a small path that led off the main road. He was standing by a shed near the water. I recognized the place, having seen it as I came in through the pass the day before.

Approaching the small building, I could see through the large open window, that there was a long table that ran the length of the room. Three locals sat behind large magnifying glasses, the type you'd see in a jewelry store. The well-lit magnifiers were each attached to an articulating arm that was in turn, clamped to the table's edge.

As I drew closer to John Paul, he smiled and proudly held out his hand. In his palm were five perfectly formed, black shiny orbs that were the size of large peas. This was my first close-up look at Tahitian Black Pearls, and I was mesmerized by their rich beauty.

"My uncle grows the pearl farm," John Paul said beaming with pride.

"What are these people doing?" I asked nodding toward the woman and two men obviously hard at work at the table.

"Come, I show," and he signaled for me to follow him into the hut.

He led me in behind the people at the table and I looked over the shoulder of the seated woman, while John Paul spoke rapidly in Tahitian, eliciting a smile from each of the workers. I wasn't sure what he said, but I guessed the joke was at my expense. It seemed I was once again providing entertainment for the local residents, but not knowing the language, I didn't know why.

They kept busy at their tasks. The woman would grab a large oyster shell from a 5 gallon plastic bucket sitting beside her chair. With the skill of a surgeon, she would gently pry the bivalve open with a odd looking tool that looked like pliers, but worked in reverse. She would lock the shell open with the same tool, and then with great care she'd reach into the fleshy part of the oyster with a long handled instrument and extract a pearl, placing it in a cloth-lined dish in front of her. Then very quickly, with the same scooping tool, she would pick up a perfectly round light colored ball and place it in the shell where the pearl had been. I noticed that one of the men was performing the same steps as the woman and they were accumulating a lot of pearls. The third worker was doing something different at the far end of the table.

As if sensing what I was going to ask, John Paul said, "The seed they put in the oyster to grow the pearl comes from your America. It is made from a mussel shell in the Mississippi river."

"How many times can the oyster make a pearl," I inquired as I stood watching the amazing process.

"I think about three times. It takes two years for the pearl to grow and the oyster cannot make a pearl until it has been living two years," he informed me.

With that, one of the men picked up a bucket that had been filled with newly seeded oysters and took it out the door, down to a small boat on the beach.

John Paul told me that the boat would take the shells back out to the lagoon where they had buoys with lines attached that hold the pearl oysters in twenty to thirty feet of water. There is a small hole drilled into the side of the shell so it can be tied to the line. The oysters are tended to with great care and moved when needed to keep them in the proper water temperature for the best growth.

He then led me to where the third worker was seated so I could see what he was doing, and explained that this is where the pearls got sorted. Only about 1 in 10 of the harvested pearls would be perfect enough to bear the name of Tahitian Black Pearl. The rest would be slightly misshaped or scarred and wouldn't make it to market. Here in the reject pile would be pear shaped pearls, some with deep ridges and a few that just looked like inkblots to me. I found the imperfect gems as beautiful as the prized pieces. John Paul spoke again in his rapid Tahitian to the older man who was wearing white gloves while working at the sorting. The man nodded and John Paul reached into a small bowl that held what appeared to be very small pearl colored cornflakes and handed them to me.

"Rick, take this. They are not really pearls, but the scraps of pearl that form around the lips of the oyster," my young friend explained.

I was slightly embarrassed, but gladly accepted the offered gift. I said thank you and good bye to the workers as we left the pearl shed and headed back to the wharf.

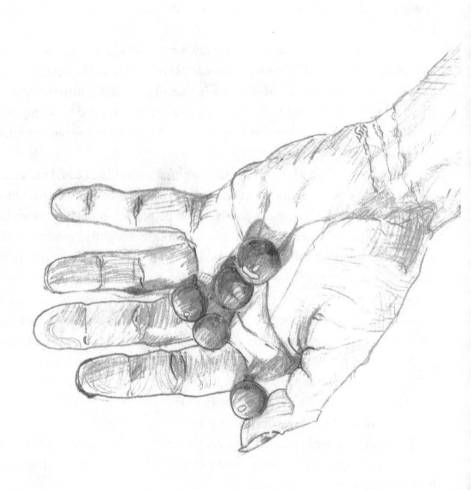

CHAPTER 10
ON THE WHARF

"It's easier to stay out than to get out."
—Mark Twain

I stood on the wharf staring out at the tranquil lagoon, taking in all the different hues of blue green that clearly defined the varying water depths. From that vantage point it was easy to spot the sandbar that I had run up on the day before. That's the reason many cruising boats will have someone climb the mast to act as a lookout when moving through an unfamiliar lagoon. Since my only crew member was a fat, lazy cat, I didn't have that option.

The same kids that swam out to *Casablanca* when I had run aground were playing soccer in the field across the street and I thought what a wonderful place to grow up. It wouldn't be long before they would want to leave this island for the bright lights and fast life of a bigger city such as Papeete or even Honolulu, but for now they didn't know how lucky they were to be able to play so freely; safe in this beautiful tropical paradise.

John Paul was exchanging some words with his compadres, and by the tone I gathered, he was getting some good natured ribbing about hanging out with the American. Grateful for his introduction to the island, I asked for more information, "How often does Makemo get supplies?"

"The *Touloa* comes every 6 weeks. It come in 3 days," he said with a smile. I knew from past experience that when the supply ship came into a remote island it was a very big event for it was their lifeline to the outside world.

"I'm going back out to the boat. Thanks so much for showing me around. You can go hang out with your friends now and I'll see you tomorrow, OK?" I said to relieve him of the responsibility of being my guide.

Walking back down the beach to *Exit Visa* I noticed there was absolutely no wind blowing. The normally steady trade winds had dissipated while I was in town and the water in the lagoon was like glass. This made me uneasy and the voices in my head began to talk amongst themselves. Three years ago, the very same conditions had morphed into an out of season cyclone while I was anchored in a bay called Ruku Ruku in Fiji. As a result, I lost *Rick's Place* on a reef that suddenly became a lee shore when the wind grew strong and clocked around to the wrong direction in the middle of the night.

Pushing off in my dinghy, I gave a last wave back toward John Paul and the rest of the kids who had finished their game and had gone down to the water to cool off. I, on the other hand, didn't feel so carefree any longer and was thinking about what I could do if the wind did come up strong and put *Casablanca* in a dangerous position.

Jack scolded me when I opened the door that had him confined down below. He was pacing around and rubbing against me; acting strangely for my normally placid cat. I think he sensed something in the air, too. He's always been sensitive to the approach of stormy weather but unfortunately I'd never picked up on the reason for his anxiety till after the fact. This time I would heed his warning.

I scratched Jack's head and said, "Yeah, don't worry little guy, we will be prepared this time."

I knew what was bothering Jack, because it was very much on my mind as well: this felt so much like the weather before our ship wreck. My mind wandered back to that night and how quickly the quiet little anchorage was transformed into a nightmarish maelstrom. A simple change in wind direction brought huge swells into the previously smooth waters of Ruku Ruku. When *Rick's Place* turned to face the incoming wind and waves, its new position brought us dangerously close to a sharp coral reef.

I remember being terrified seeing the reef as it was illuminated in the pitch dark night by the flashes of lightening that accompanied the nasty storm. Just a couple feet off of *Rick's* stern, the coral head appeared to be getting closer by the minute as the boat bucked wildly in the seething seas. Due to the severe pounding the boat was taking, something in the anchoring system broke under the enormous strain. Within seconds, Jack and I were in the surf struggling to reach the safety of shore. I felt I had prepared the boat and myself that night, but apparently not well enough. I would not make the same mistakes again and have *Casablanca* fall to the same fate.

I set about checking *Casablanca's* anchor and our position in relation to rocks and reefs. When I felt the first stirrings of wind, I looked up and saw the tell tale clouds indicating a change in weather off in the distance. The eerie stillness we had experienced was indeed the "calm before the storm" as I had feared. As usual, these events always chose to raise their ugly heads in the dark of the night. Why couldn't it happen in the bright of day when it would be so much easier to deal with?

Before the sun was gone, I formulated a plan to keep *Casablanca* safe through the approaching storm. I didn't feel that moving to another spot would be any more advantageous than staying put. After all, I didn't know anything about Makemo's lagoon beyond where I was presently anchored. Who knew where there might be uncharted coral heads lurking below the surface? One thing I did know was that my anchor had set well in this spot because I dove on it the day I came in. While in the water, I'd also inspected every inch of the 90 feet of chain attached to the hook.

One further precaution I took was to pull out a 40 pound lead weight I had been carrying around for just such an occasion. This lead unit, often called a sentinel, has a roller attached to one end which is hooked to the anchor rode so it can roll down the length of the chain until it hits the seafloor. There is a rope attached to the weight, which is used for lowering and retrieving the sentinel. The idea is the added pounds will keep the anchor from pulling out of the sand if the wind and waves get to be extreme.

After setting the sentinel, I was surprised when the VHF radio came alive. There normally isn't any radio traffic when there aren't other boats around since the transmission and reception is pretty much line of sight. The conversation was broken and full of static, but it was in English and I was able to pick out little spats of information. I gathered it was a conversation between two boats about 20 miles away on a nearby atoll. Apparently strong wind gusts had just hit them catching them completely off guard. I heard the number 45 which sent chills down my spine. I hoped that they were talking about the depth where they were anchored, but I knew in my heart it was the strength of the wind. This prompted me into quick action.

Racing down the companionway, I double checked the front hatch and the port lights to make sure they were dogged down tight. All cabinets were closed and latched and I stowed everything away as securely as I could. As I climbed the stairs to go out on deck, I took one last look to make sure Jack was snug in his hiding place between the sails and I grabbed the key to start the engine.

Soon there was a moaning from the boat's shrouds as the wind increased just as the sun began to set. I fumbled with the key, trying to get it into the ignition as the twilight was fading fast. Finally turning the key, I got the customary turning over of the engine, but it would not fire.

The wind was building and I knew by the sound it was the start of something unpleasant.

"Come on you stupid engine START!" I pleaded with the lifeless machine.

The boat was slowly turning into the wind, and this new direction had the stern of the boat pointing to shore, which now seemed much closer than I had thought.

Again I turned the ignition switch to start the stubborn engine, knowing that if it didn't start I would have to quit trying. I didn't want to draw the batteries completely flat. Then, thankfully, I felt the distinct vibration that comes just before the cranky thing starts, just as the wind hit 25 knots.

The engine chugged to life with its usual veil of black smoke, which momentarily blocked out the scattering of lights that were shining on shore.

I shoved the transmission into forward about the same instant the wind instrument read 40 knots.

My plan was to use the slow forward motion of the boat to take the strain off of the anchor chain as the wind increased. I could see that this would take constant vigilance, so that if the wind had a lull I wouldn't over run the anchor and inadvertently un-set it. That would not bode well.

All the noise had Jack's curiosity up and he was starting to climb the stairs. I grabbed a bottle of water and uncapped it, getting ready to douse the cat to keep him down below and out of harms way.

Turns out I didn't need to worry, because the waves had now caught up with the wind and the boat started to go crazy. These wind-generated waves were traveling across the 10 miles of lagoon and when they hit the shallow waters where I was anchored it made for some very steep, close together, unpleasant walls of water. After beating in to *Casablanca*, the waves would then crash to shore with an unnerving thunderous clap.

The bow would plunge down into the dark on-coming waves, scooping up gallons of water, then rise up and point to the sky, the dreaded-hobby-horse-effect, sending a cascade of water down the decks and off the stern. I closed the main hatch.

"Don't worry, Jack," I said more to calm myself than the cat.

Before I knew it the wind gauge was registering gusts of 45 knots and I increased the engine's RPM's to battle the onslaught the best I could. Minutes dragged on. Shining a light below at the ship's clock, I was disappointed that only an hour had gone by since the start of the gale. I feared it would be a very long night.

My head and eyes were feeling the strain of having to watch the wind instrument so closely. The four inch square face of the gauge has a stenciled outline of a boat with the bow pointing up, and there's an arrow that shows the direction of the wind relative to the boat. My goal was to keep *Casablanca* headed directly into the wind, for if she got turned sideways and a gust hit amidships, the strain on the anchoring system could have unpleasant results.

In the center of the instrument there's an LED readout that shows the wind speed. For some time, it would read 47 knots then drop down to 44, the higher speeds gave me a stomach ache, the lower speeds gave me hope.

Another hour passed before my prayers were answered and the wind began to drop. When a steady 42 knots appeared on the screen for several minutes, I began to see the light at the end of the tunnel. It was a mere 3 knot difference, but it was in the right direction.

After another two hours, I felt I could finally shut down the engine. The wind speed was down to 15 knots and had swung to a direction that took *Casablanca* out of danger of the lee shore. Totally exhausted, I laid my head down in the cockpit for just a second.

Hours later, the rising sun coupled with Jack crying at the door to come outside, was my wake-up call. My neck was stiff from sleeping in an awkward position in the hard cockpit and I had a pounding headache. When I opened the door for Jack, he immediately pounced into my lap, and for the first time in quite a while seemed pleased with me.

"Dodged that bullet, eh Jack?" I said with a sense of relief, and a bit of pride, knowing I had kept us safe through the dangerous blow that could have turned out quite badly had I not been so prepared.

He responded with his typical bite to my hand.

Around mid-morning, John Paul swam out to *Casablanca*. He climbed into the cockpit with his usual ease, then with a big wide toothy grin asked, "Rick and Jack good last night?"

"It was rough," I replied, "too much wind."

"I watch your boat, it was........" he was gesturing with his arms in a back and forth motion.

"Swinging," I said helping him with the word he was searching for, adding, "yes, it was swinging a lot."

I was surprised that John Paul had even noticed that the weather had created an uncomfortable situation for me because most often, people on shore are totally unaware of the effects of strong winds on an anchored boat.

Changing the subject, I asked John Paul where there was a good place to go snorkeling, though I suspected that almost any place in this lagoon was filled with colorful fish, just going by what I'd seen around the boat.

"Go there, to motu on the left," he said pointing to the far side of the lagoon.

I followed his outstretched arm with my eyes and peered in the direction he indicated. In the distance I could just make out a couple of small patches of land rising off of the fringing reef, maybe three miles away.

"It's very good, Rick, on this motu. Good sand for your anchor. Nice coral nearby with big fish. No one lives there. You'll like," he said and then added, "Rick, be careful of the corals when you go there. They are plenty and just under the water. Don't want to hurt *Casa Boata*."

I chuckled at John Paul's name for *Casablanca* and assured him I would keep a vigilant eye out as I didn't want to hurt *Casa Boata*, either.

John Paul wished me well and said he had to get back to shore. He wanted to guide me out to the motu, but he couldn't miss school and had to stay in the village. I remembered, too, that the supply ship would be coming in soon, and imagined that he wouldn't want to miss that, either. After I assured him I'd see him when I returned this way before leaving Makemo, he dove over the side and swam gracefully away.

I knew from past experience that to traverse a coral-studded lagoon, the sun should be directly above or, even better, slightly behind you so the coral obstructions are illuminated clearly. So at noon, local time, I pulled anchor after finally getting the engine started.

I moved slowly, weaving my way around the coral spires that stood just below the surface. With the water smooth and the sun high in the sky, it was easy to distinguish the different shades of blue and green which indicated the depth of the water, but I still had to be vigilant.

The water was absolutely crystal clear, and when I wasn't straining to navigate the path in front of me I would sneak a peek over the side and marvel at the variety of fish teeming around the coral heads I was passing. At one point a large manta ray glided by, its sleek black and white body effortlessly slicing through the water.

Two hours later I dropped the anchor, just off "the motu on the left", and finally had a chance to take in the natural splendor of my surroundings. The small island, or motu, which was slightly larger than a football field, was picture perfect with its white sand beach and coconut palms. I dubbed it *Gilligan's Island* and couldn't wait to get to shore to explore it and the reef beyond. Huge Pacific swells relentlessly crashed on the ocean side of the half mile wide reef, while the turquoise water surrounding *Casablanca* was still and mirror like. The trade winds were gently blowing through the palm trees, adding a pleasant rustling sound to the salty air. This was a place of beauty for all my senses.

I rowed to shore to check out my new backyard. Stepping ashore I enjoyed the feel of the coarse sand, which was a mix of crushed shells and coral, beneath my feet. Once in amongst the vegetation of the small island, I discovered it wasn't really uninhabited as John Paul had said, for it held a large population of hermit crabs, some with shells the size of baseballs. They were underfoot everywhere and even climbing up the trees, crawling slowly; seemingly burdened with the great weight of the homes they must drag with them everywhere.

The little motu itself looked like something you'd see on a beer commercial on TV. All it needed was a hammock strung between a couple of the trees and it would be the perfect picture of paradise.

Moving out to the ocean side of the land, I was struck by the starkness of the fringing reef. It was completely washed of sand and shells due to the constant pounding of the sea, just a long barren strand of rugged old dead coral which acts as a big fence keeping the ocean at bay. Of course, upon closer inspection, there was much life there, too, just as a desert first appears to be void of living things when, in fact it is quite alive. I discovered birds nesting among the rocks and small eels and brightly colored crabs moving through the tidal pools.

I was totally spent by the time I returned to the boat. It had been a big day and not having slept much the night before, I was out like a light shortly after sunset and didn't awaken till sunrise.

Stumbling around the next morning, I put the kettle on for hot water and, through sleepy eyes, opened a can of cat food. As I bent to put it in Jack's dish, I was surprised not only that there was still food in his bowl from last night (maybe he didn't like the flavor of what the label so proudly called beef heart or tongue or something), but more surprising was that Jack wasn't sitting at my feet awaiting his new treat.

"Jack, buddy.... Are you sick?" I called out, looking around for the big fur ball. No answer. Not really a surprise.

I checked all his favorite haunts, but he was nowhere to be found. He'd used the toilet, I observed, and then I noticed the port hole in the head was open. Normally there was no way for the cat to escape out of it due to it's height above the floor, but last night, before retiring, I'd stashed a sail bag in the room and it was right below that window.

I went out on deck, expecting him to be stretched out enjoying the morning sun, but he wasn't in sight. I called some more and looked around, but he definitely wasn't outside so I went below to start the whole search process again. This time even more thoroughly as there are a lot of cat-sized hidey holes on a 35 foot boat.

Dread was starting to wrench at my stomach. If I'd lost her cat, Sheryl would be devastated and it wouldn't be a big plus in our relationship. And, to be quite honest, I would miss my ornery little companion just as much as she would.

Frustrated by the fruitless search, I went back out on deck, hoping he'd be sitting there staring at me like he couldn't understand what I was up to. I seem to get a lot of looks like that from him. Finding the cockpit empty, I felt certain that he must have gone over the side of the boat in the night while I was in my deep, "dead to the world" sleep. I certainly didn't hear any commotion.

Jumping into *Exit Visa* and madly paddling to shore, I was hoping beyond hope that Jack had been able to swim the short distance to the motu. Had he gone the other direction, out into the lagoon, he wouldn't have reached land for miles. Most of all I hoped he hadn't become chum for some shark.

I hopped out of the dinghy before it even reached shore, and waded through the shallows, pulling the small boat by its anchor line.

"Jack! Jack! Here boy!" I called out and whistled, all the while going over in my mind how I would start the awkward conversation with my girlfriend concerning her castaway cat.

I scanned the beach in both directions. I couldn't see anything out of the ordinary from the water's edge up twenty-five feet to the low brush and palm trees. Hurrying away from the water towards the center of the motu, I continued to call his name. The palms were situated rather far apart, so I could get a good look at the surrounding ground without having to move a great deal.

During my frantic search, I recalled that Jack had fallen overboard once before, several years ago, while we were anchored in the Cook Islands. At that time he was able to climb back aboard *Rick's Place*, though I was never quite sure how he'd accomplished that feat.

As each minute of my search went on, I felt more dread building. Then a slight movement caught my eye, about thirty feet to my right, at the base of a palm tree. Thinking it was probably just one of the giant hermit crabs, but hoping for the best, I hurried over to investigate. Stepping around the base of the tree, I saw a tuft of fur.

"Jack, for God's sake," I said with tears beginning to well in my eyes.

He looked up momentarily, and then went back to what he was doing: watching a hermit crab lumber along. His fur was matted with sand and stiff with salt making it spiky and unkempt, but other than that he appeared none the worse for wear. He didn't even seem surprised to see me and acted like this was a perfectly ordinary activity.

I picked him up, telling him, "You just used up another of your nine lives, buddy. Then I took him, and the small crab he'd befriended, and rowed them back out to *Casablanca*.

For the next couple days I just relaxed in this little piece of paradise. I'd spend my days snorkeling around the coral heads, or boomies, as the Australians call them. These large spirals grow up from the deep depths of the lagoon to about 3 or 4 feet from the surface and they can be hundreds of feet in diameter. I would tie the dinghy to one of the outcroppings and then snorkel around the perimeter. The eco systems there were an explosion of bright colors from the fish and plants to the many types of coral. Eels would poke their evil heads out of a dark hole, just like a frightening Jack-in-the-box, then just as quickly pull back into their little cave: a good reminder not to go sticking my hand into any crevasses as I explore the underwater wonderlands.

But, the real attention getters for me, as always, were the sharks. I'd been schooled by the indigenous people of different tropical islands as to which sharks are the so called "good sharks" and which are not so good. But if you ask me, black tip, white tip, gray, White, Basking, Hammerhead or Nerf, they are all SHARKS and therefore, they all get my undivided attention.

When I went snorkeling I always made it a point not to stay in the water if I saw a shark right off the bat. No good can come of that, I thought.

The more time I spent in the water near The Motu on the Left, the more I got in tune with the local shark population. I still wouldn't call any shark "good", but I did become more comfortable with them. Most of the time, I could be in the water for half an hour to 45 minutes before I would glimpse the lifeless, black marbles that they have for eyes, staring at me. Oh, they thought I wouldn't see them and just as I'd look in their direction, they would turn and swim away acting like they weren't interested in chewing on my leg. Then pretty soon, another shark buddy would stop by and then I'd be outnumbered so I'd head for the dinghy. Without any splashing or fanfare I'd climb out of the water and call it a day.

Generally when you see a shark, you see their tag-a-long friend, the Remora. I disliked the Remoras as much as the sharks, even though they are harmless. These creepy little fish can be anywhere from six inches to a foot long and they have a suction-cup like appendage on their head to attach themselves to the shark's body. These aquatic hitchhikers have been known to glom onto swimmers and divers as well, so I just didn't like to be around them.

My time in Makemo went by in a blur, because time certainly does fly when you're having fun. I did stop back by the village, as promised, to say good bye to John Paul and do some provisioning before setting out to sea.

I also got a chance to trade for some black pearls. In exchange for a small boom box and some Beach Boy's CD's I received three really nice pearls, though not "perfect" by Tahitian standards. They also threw in a very interesting misshaped glob that seemed the result of a rebel oyster playing a joke on its keeper.

There was one dark cloud hanging over *Casablanca*, however. My once reliable 3 cylinder diesel engine was quickly becoming the bane of my existence. It had refused to start when it was time to leave Motu on the Left, and I'd had to sail back to my original anchorage near the town. I'd tried every trick I knew to coax the stubborn thing to start, but I could tell something was seriously wrong deep inside the engine. Crankshaft, rings, valves, pistons.... who knew? Not me, for sure.

After much consultation with the cautioning voices, we made a change in plans. I would need to postpone visiting any of the other atolls in the Tuamotus that I'd had on my itinerary. I couldn't take a chance entering a pass and having the engine suddenly go gunny sack on me at a critical moment. I decided to sail straight to Tahiti to have the necessary repairs done, then I could return to see the other islands. My mind started wandering to the thought that perhaps Sheryl could even fly in and enjoy this beautiful paradise with me.....

When I explained this plan to my feline traveling companion, he promptly jumped into the sink next to the toilet and did his cat duty. I didn't know if this was a comment on my plan, but I knew it wasn't good that he'd taken to using the sink and I explained to him that just as the world is not my oyster, the sink is not his toilet. I really need to get Sheryl back on the boat with us.

CHAPTER 11
TAHITI

"Tis sometimes the height of wisdom to feign stupidity."
—Cato the Elder

Tahiti, ahhhh.... Just saying the name conjures up images of swaying palm trees and beautiful bronze skinned Polynesians adorned with fragrant tropical flowers. These are my thoughts as I clean up Jack's indiscretion in the sink.

Getting *Casablanca* out of the swiftly flowing narrow pass on Makemo was also right up there in my mind's eye. The plan was to wait for the slack tide, pull up the main sail, bring up the anchor and simply sail out. I would wait until the wind and the current are both moving in the same direction, pushing me out to the open ocean.

It sounded so easy saying it out loud. In my mind I repeatedly practiced the maneuvers I would need to make to safely exit the lagoon. I also walked to where I could observe the pass in order to get the timing right for the slack tide. Finally the day arrived when I felt I was as prepared as I could be and the weather forecast was positive. I decided to get the show on the road.

My biggest concern was losing the wind, which in turn, could cause me to lose control, then, well, you know.

Jack came out of the cockpit just as I was hoisting up the sail. In his mouth, he was carrying his new playmate, the crab. It was the same crab I had picked up on the motu the day Jack had jumped ship and gone ashore. I figured I could never have too many crewmembers, so I selected an appropriate Tupperware container that could serve as his new surroundings and we had welcomed him aboard *Casablanca*.

At first Jack would just sit and stare at the "shell that had legs" trying to figure it out. Then, ever so gently, he would paw at our new guest. After a couple days of that, he decided to show the crab who was boss and would pick the shell up in his mouth and move it to the floor or the table or the cockpit and watch it try to escape. Whenever Jack got bored I would see him carrying Crabby around. It was nice for Jack to have some entertainment onboard again. He had had another 'live toy' back on *Rick's Place*. I'd brought a couple geckos on board to keep the bug population down and one of them had grown to a very large size and I'd dubbed him Godzilla. Jack would spend hours just staring at the wall hoping the great big gecko would make an appearance, and then he'd fruitlessly fling himself at the wall once the lizard did appear. It was good harmless fun for Jack and great entertainment for me.

It was not a good time for Jack to be on deck, however. The sail was up and the anchor nearly broken free from the sandy bottom and there I was having to chase down a cat with a hermit crab in his mouth. I couldn't let him mess up my carefully made departure plans by falling overboard.

Once around the deck and then Jack climbed under the dinghy which is stowed upside down on the bow of the boat.

"Jack, dammit, come here!" I yelled, but to no avail. I was on my hands and knees peeking under the overturned inflatable and I could see Jack with the large shell firmly grasped in his mouth, but he was just out of my reach.

A sudden gust of wind and *Casablanca* lurched awkwardly. I knew that the sandy bottom had released its grip on the anchor so I had to get moving fast. I quickly pulled up the rest of the chain and anchor as *Casablanca* started to drift. Luckily we were being pushed toward the center of the lagoon.

I hurried back and adjusted the main sail, turning the steering wheel all the way to its stops in an attempt to get the boat headed in the right direction. We slowly began to build some momentum, and, with that, some steerage. I carefully avoided the sandbar I had hit some weeks earlier while coming into the lagoon. The wind was lighter than I'd hoped, so our progress was agonizingly slow toward the lagoon side of the pass.

Then I spotted Jack coming out of his hiding place.

"Remember what happened at the motu!" I yelled, trying to jog his memory of falling overboard. There I was trying to reason with a cat: another sign that I was in need of human contact on board.

As if it suddenly hit him (or maybe it was the sudden change in boat speed) he made a mad dash to the cockpit then clambered down the stairs, the whole while holding his crab friend in his mouth.

I promptly shut the doors to keep him down below and out of harm's way.

The out flowing current now had *Casablanca* firmly in its grasp. The boat speed was up, but the steering control was mushy, due in part to the wind dying off. Like a leaf going down a gutter in a heavy rain, the current was now my sole source of propulsion. I just had to concentrate on keeping us going straight, for if we got sideways, the control I presently had, would be lost.

By the time we were half way through the channel my heart was pounding so hard in my chest I felt light headed.

A yell from shore broke my concentration, and I turned to see John Paul waving to me from the pearl shack. I returned the wave and yelled a big "Whoop!" to him then focused back on the situation at hand.

When I reached the end of the pass, the turbulence of the water caused the mainsail boom to crash from one side of the boat to the other, since it had no wind to fill it. I was beginning to feel the effects of the ocean swell and the first big trough seemed more like a cliff. The bow of the boat nosed down and then immediately started to climb the five foot wall of water in front of it. With the dying momentum of the current pushing us, we struggled to the top of the wave when the boom, along with its full sail, loudly crashed back over to the port side and we finally started to move under sail power. The wind which had been blocked by the island, was now unobstructed and filled the sails.

Casablanca pushed through several more waves and continued to pick up speed. My heart rate was starting to level off and the beads of sweat on my forehead were quickly evaporating in the warm breeze. Once clear of Makemo, I entered the coordinates for Papeete, Tahiti into my trusty GPS and we were on our way.

Thankfully, the 4 day cruise to Tahiti was uneventful. The trade winds remained steady with light blue skies and big white cotton ball clouds. The fishing was quite good on this short passage and I was able to land a tuna which Jack and I feasted on for most of the trip. Jack had his fill of fresh flying fish, as well.

Really, the only problem I encountered on our way to Papeete, was that whenever I would lay down to get some sleep, I'd hear a weird noise I couldn't identify. This was going on even after I'd subdued all the usual noisemakers aboard, such as dishes and cans in the cupboards. Unable to sleep, I would get up to search out the disturbance, but once I arose, the sound would stop and all would seem normal. For two days, during every rest period, a scraping noise would have my mind racing through all of the possible causes.

Finally, Jack gave away what was going on. Apparently, soon after I'd lie down, he'd get bored and take Crabby, the crab, out of his Tupperware confines and place him on the floor so they could play. When Jack would tire of the game and go off to sleep, Crabby would then drag himself and his heavy shell-house around making the mysterious scraping noise that was driving me nuts.

On the morning of my fourth day at sea, I spotted the majestic Island of Tahiti. By noon I was passing the lighthouse at Point Venus on the north side of the island where I started to make preparations for landfall.

The entrance to the harbor in Papeete, Tahiti's largest city, was wide and without obstructions. I short-tacked in and set anchor in a spot that gave me plenty of room for engine-less maneuvering. I was quite pleased with my entry and anchoring, but unfortunately the authorities weren't as impressed. As I was flaking, or folding, the mainsail with a long afternoon nap on my short agenda, a small runabout pulled alongside of *Casablanca*. My limited French was enough to help me read the "Port Captain" stenciled in big letters on the side of the vessel, and I figured this wasn't a social call.

"Monsieur, you cannot anchor here," was what I could make out from the clipped English coming from the gentleman onboard. Squinting in the bright sun, I saw the uniformed European man standing at the helm and he looked all business.

"My boat is broken, I have engine problems," I called back using my best pantomime gestures to accompany my words.

"I am sorry, but this is a restricted zone. No anchoring," he stated firmly, with much emphasis on the NO. "You will need to move to the other yachts," he informed me as he pointed to the collection of boats anchored about 300 yards away.

"I cannot use my engine, I need a tow," I pleaded my case, knowing that there was no way I could sail and drop anchor in amongst the crowded fleet.

Right about that time, Jack, with Crabby in hand (or mouth as the case may be) was heading up the stairs. This was making me pretty nervous since I knew the quarantine rules of French Polynesia were very strict and could involve long periods of isolation: for me and the cat. Additionally, the cost would be high. And since, according to the paperwork from my check-in, I didn't have any animals on board, it would make for a rather awkward situation should Jack show up on deck along with his crabby friend while I was talking to this government official.

So, as nonchalantly as possible, I used my foot to close the door on Jack's progress, hopefully averting an international incident.

I also then lapsed into my tried and true method of dealing with officials: acting dumb. Fortunately, that's a pretty easy act for me and most times it's not even an act. So as the official was repeating for the 100th time that I needed to move my bateau, I would repeat the words, "I need a tow," and then stare at him with open mouth.

Forty minutes later I was resetting my anchor in the "proper zone" after wearing down the officialdom of Papeete and getting him to tow *Casablanca* to the area he wanted us to anchor.

All the boats in the anchorage area were med tied, that is their anchor was set in about 30 feet of water in the usual fashion, but then a line was led from the stern of the boat to the base of one of the palm trees on shore. This arrangement keeps the boats all facing the same way, no matter the wind direction or tide. It also allows a great many boats to be squeezed into a small space since there is no chance of swinging and bumping into each other.

I was getting the dinghy ready to put into the water, when I heard the whine of an outboard motor coming in my direction. Looking up I was pleasantly surprised to see Chris from the boat *The Swallow*, whom I had first met in Tenacatita after the great surf landing fiasco. We'd briefly crossed paths when I arrived in Atuona, but he was heading out the day I arrived.

"I'll take your line ashore for a beer," he quipped.

"It's a deal," I replied, handing him the end of a coil of rope. As Chris motored to shore I slowly fed out 100 feet of line, making sure it didn't get tangled into a big knotted ball. Once the rope was securely tied to a tree, I pulled in the slack, tied it to a cleat and *Casablanca's* stern immediately swung into orderly formation, mirroring her neighboring boats.

Chris motored back to *Casablanca* and climbed aboard carrying a small cooler.

"I lied, Chris, I don't have any beer – I just got here from Makemo." I confessed.

"Yeah, I saw you sail in then get towed over here," he said, handing me the cooler, "help yourself."

When I opened the cooler I was delighted to find a six pack of Hinano, the local brew, surrounded by sparkling chunks of crystal clear ice. Then, with cold beers in hand, we toasted our Tahitian landfall.

We sat, drank and caught up with each other's travels, while absorbing the ambiance of Papeete. I explained that I was single-handed again for a while, since Sheryl had to fly home to take care of her shop.

The shore near the anchorage was covered with brightly colored outrigger canoes, while in the other direction sat the colossal cruise ship, *The Paul Gauguin*. Chris and I were both struck by the noise of the heavily trafficked main road running right along the shore line, as neither of us had been in a big city in quite some time.

"Sorry about the engine, if you need help, give me a holler, between the two of us, we should be able to screw it up even more," he joked.

Then looking down at Jack, who had taken position on his lap sometime during the travelogue, Chris remarked, "This cat reminds me of a dog. He's been drooling just like a Saint Bernard the whole time I've been petting him," as he wiped the moisture off his hand.

"Yeah, I've thought that before, too. It's not just the drooling, he also runs to the door to greet me whenever I come back to the boat. He doesn't act as indifferent as most cats I've been around," I noted.

The sun was in its final throes of the day as we finished the last of the beer. We'd also gotten pretty well caught up on each other's travels and my body was telling me it was time to catch up on some much needed sleep.

As Chris got up to leave, I said while stifling a yawn, "Hey, thanks for the refreshments and the help, I'll see ya tomorrow."

"No problem, we single handers have to stick together. See ya later," he called back as he motored off.

The next morning, after officially checking in, I set off to find a local boat yard that would be able to pull *Casablanca* out of the water. On my way to Tahiti I decided it might be a good time to have the bottom painted. It had been over two years since I'd had it done and when I dove on the boat in Makemo, I could tell the paint had lost its effectiveness and was not keeping the growth of barnacles and scum off the hull as well as it should. I could have the bottom done at the same time I had the engine worked on.

Following the directions to the industrial part of Papeete, I traversed the heart of the city. Papeete looked like any other big city, except for the absence of high rise buildings. There was a mix of new construction with big storefronts and gleaming glass right along with dilapidated, run down buildings with faded paint and broken windows.

But it was the traffic – buses, cars, trucks, scooters – that assaulted my senses. I think each vehicle had at least two horns and both were used at all times and the exhaust fumes burned my nostrils. There had to be more cars than people in this city and they were all crowded onto the main street of Papeete at the same time. It was like a slowly moving traffic jam stretching from one end of the city to the other. After being at sea and away from such hustle and bustle for the past several months, the fast pace was at first overwhelming.

Finally arriving at the marina haul out yard, I proceeded to the customer service counter behind which were stationed several desks. The people sitting at these desks were all talking on their phones, very rapidly in French. Every now and then, someone would walk by me carrying papers and looking extremely busy.

After I'd waited at the counter for 15 minutes, without so much as a glance from any of the busy workers, I decided to take matters into my own hands. Spotting a door that led out to the yard I made my move. As I put my hand on the doorknob, I got the response I'd been hoping for. Two people, whose phone calls suddenly became not so important, jumped up saying something very fast in French. I guessed it meant something like "No Admittance" by their quick actions.

A heavy set man with a sheen of sweat on his face, came over to me looking like he'd drawn the short straw.

"Est-ce que je peux vous aider?" he inquired.

Not knowing for sure what he asked, I thought I should just state what I wanted and said, "Yes, I would like to take my boat out of the water."

The Frenchman just stared.

No English here, I realized and picked up a brochure that showed a boat on a travel lift and pointed to it saying, "This, pull boat, paint bottom." Once again using my most descriptive arm gestures.

This seemed to get through to him a bit and he started speaking quite rapidly in French for about two minutes and then he stopped.

Not having understood a word of it, I decided to try the old play dumb routine; after all, it worked great in getting *Casablanca* a tow.

So I repeated, "Pick up boat, paint bottom."

The guy just stared at me with open mouth. I guess the playing dumb routine had no borders.

As the two of us stood facing each other, our mouths agape and bewildered looks on our faces, an older, part Asian gentleman came along.

He looked at me and said, "He's saying he is booked up for a month."

I was shocked at the near perfect English coming from this Pat Moriata look alike, but managed to reply, "Oh hey, thanks for that, I just got in and I'm not quite up to speed yet." I didn't want to confess that I may never be up to speed when it came to French. They speak way too fast for me.

"My name is George," he said, holding out his hand.

"George, I'm Rick. Thanks again for interpreting for me," I said, shaking his hand.

"So, you need a place to take your boat out?" George inquired.

I spent the next 15 minutes explaining my engine problems and the need for new bottom paint.

"I know of a nice marina with a haul out near Tahiti Iti. They may have room," he informed me.

That was encouraging so I asked him for directions and if I could get there by bus.

"No need for that. You are a guest here and I will take you, Rick," he offered.

"Please, you don't need to go to all that trouble," I answered.

"No trouble Rick, my truck is right outside," he said and motioned for me to follow.

He led me to a newer SUV with knobby tires and shiny rims: a pretty nice ride indeed. When we jumped into the truck, George turned on the air conditioning, a luxury I hadn't experienced in quite some time.

For the next hour as we drove through and then out of the city, George asked questions about sailing from the U.S., about me, my background and I did the same in return. It turned out George was a retired airline pilot, who had a sailboat anchored near the city. He seemed fascinated by my travels. He confessed he'd always wanted to long distance cruise, but a reluctant spouse was keeping him in Tahiti. Not a bad place to be stuck, I thought.

Leaving the city behind, we also left the thick slug of traffic. The road narrowed and wound around the island never far from the sea. In places the steep, mountain slopes edged the blacktop road so closely, the thick jungle growth would brush the side of George's SUV. At the same time, on the other side of the car the road was wide open to the endless ocean. It was quite a startling contrast.

Looking out to the water, the fringing reef that surrounds the island was quite evident. No swell made it to the narrow sandy beach, as all of the sea's energy was expelled when the powerful waves crashed relentlessly upon the coral reef located about a quarter mile from shore.

When we passed a sign that said Port du Phaeton, George let me know we were almost to the marina. A mile later we slowed and turned on to a gravel road that took us to a dusty unpaved parking lot. Off to one side sat a white-washed cement block building with blue trim. A faded sign hung above large screen covered glass windows.

Beyond the building I could see the marina with maybe a dozen boats stern-tied to the short quay, tugging gently at their mooring lines. It was the first time I'd seen a marina with no docks. In the haul out area, which was across a narrow waterway from the moored yachts, sat eight boats high and dry, supported by adjustable stands on both sides. A couple of these boats were being worked on, while the rest looked closed up with no ladders next to their hulls.

George and I walked into the block building and I was surprised at how many boat supplies were crammed into what had appeared to be a small space from the outside. Rows of dusty shelves displayed cans of paint and tubes of caulking that looked as though they'd been sitting there a very long time. I'd definitely check the expiration dates before making any purchases, but it appeared to be a well-stocked chandlery, all in all.

A thin, nearly gaunt, dark-haired man, whom I assumed was French, since he definitely wasn't Tahitian, sat in a small office to the side, looking at some papers.

George strung together several sentences in French, which brought the gentleman to his feet and he sauntered our way.

George again spoke rapidly in French and was spoken to in kind. I was feeling great relief to have a translator with me on this venture.

Then the Frenchman turned to me, introducing himself as Alain, the manager of the yard, and said, "Yes, we can pull your boat out of the water." He sounded just like Jacques Cousteau.

"Soon?" was my first question.

"How deep does the keel draw?"

"5 ½ to 6 feet," I answered.

He paused for a moment and I could tell he must be converting the feet to meters – better him than me, I thought.

"The tides are good for the next week," he said, looking at a local tide book, and adding, "after that, no good for another week or so."

"Great! I can be here tomorrow," I offered, though I was wondering just how I would be accomplishing that feat.

He grabbed a piece of paper and wrote down my name and a description of my boat then said, "Yes, yes. Just anchor out and call on the VHF channel 12. We will guide you in."

Before we got back into the SUV, I took a little self guided tour of the boat yard. Even though the yard was quite small, it was clean and meticulously kept and I knew it would be a good place to bring *Casablanca*.

As George and I were wheeling back to the big city, I sat quietly in deep thought over what I needed to do in order to get the boat to the marina by tomorrow.

Then George broke the silence with, "It's cheaper hauling out at Phaeton Marina than in the city. And they are very good workers," he assured me.

As he pulled off the road to let me out near the anchorage, I thanked him profusely for all his help and tried to pay him for gas, but he would have none of it. What a great guy.

"I'll stop by and see you, Rick," he shouted as he eased back into the heavy traffic, where he promptly came to an accident-snarled stop.

After an anxiety induced fitful night's sleep, I upped anchor at first light to give me plenty of daylight hours for the short passage. Thankfully the trade winds were steady and I easily sailed out of the wide pass into the open ocean. I was quite happy with the sailing skills I had developed since the engine went down and I made a mental note to use less engine and more sail once the damn thing got fixed.

Staying three miles off shore I comfortably covered the 25 miles to the entrance of Port Phaeton in a mere five hours. Coasting along the jungle-covered mountains, it was easy to slip back in time in my mind, and imagine how Capt. Cook and his men felt sailing these same waters, gazing upon the same landscape.

CHAPTER 12
BITING BUGS AND BROKEN ENGINES

"Do what you can, with what you have, where you are."
—Theodore Roosevelt

The heart of French Polynesia, Tahiti is an hourglass shaped island, formed by two extinct volcanoes, the northern larger lobe being Tahiti and the smaller Tahiti Iti (Iti, of course, meaning small). The two are connected by a thin strip of land called the Isthmus of Taravao. Tahiti's highest peak is roughly 7,300 feet high with deep green valleys, and Tahiti Iti's mountain is nearly as tall at 5,000 feet. The entire island is surrounded by a barrier reef with many passes through the coral to peaceful anchorages. Phaeton Marina was located at the Isthmus of Taravao.

Once through the well-marked passé de Teputo, I followed the beacons to the calm waters of the bay of Port Phaeton. I slowly coaxed *Casablanca* in the light wind to the center of the bay where I dropped my anchor. Once secured, I grabbed my binoculars and looked toward the spot where my charts indicated I'd find the marina entrance. The jungle was so dense at the water's edge, that the moored boats I'd seen the day before were hidden from view.

I called on the VHF as instructed and 10 minutes later a small boat with an oversized engine came out to greet me. The two Tahitians manning the skiff carefully maneuvered along side *Casablanca*. Working quickly, with few words spoken, they side tied their boat to mine. I raised the anchor and we motored down the estuary to the boat yard.

In less than an hour, *Casablanca* was positioned on the haul out trailer and pulled out of the murky waters of Port Phaeton and placed near the perimeter of the yard. Six jack stands, three on each side, supported my 35' boat, with the keel resting on the solid ground.

One of the yard workers that had helped bring us in to the marina, a young man in his 20's, brought over a ladder for access to the boat since its cockpit now sat about ten feet off the ground.

"I am Kim, I will be working on your boat," the skinny, deeply tanned Tahitian told me.

"I'm Rick," I said extending my hand and added, "Your English is very good."

"I was in school in Pago Pago, Samoa," he informed me.

Then without another word he went about the business of pressure washing the hull's bottom. This created such a racket inside the boat, I saw Jack, who had just ventured to the edge of the boat looking down the ladder, turn tail and run back down to the safety of his hiding spot, fearful of the water and noise.

I couldn't put it off any longer. It was time to dig into the engine. I climbed the shaky ladder with a great deal of dread. Going below and taking off the engine access panels, I took a 5 gallon bucket, turned it over and sat down on it, assuming the position of The Thinker. For the next 45 minutes I just sat and stared at the non-functioning piece of iron. Occasionally I would swat at a mosquito or some other flying insect, but for the most part I was in a deep trance. I didn't really know what I was looking for, but I had my tools spread out, the portable light strung and the "how to" books opened up to diesel repair.

I had discovered on my way to Papeete from Makemo that the engine was now frozen and it would not turn over. This was made very evident when, one day while at sea, I turned the ignition key and immediately acrid blue smoke enveloped the engine room wafting out of the vents. That was quite alarming. Having your boat burn out from under you while out at sea would really wreck your day, so that's why I chose not to attempt to start it after that.

Back to the task at hand, I took off the air cleaner and found that the filter was damp and moisture had found its way into the engine. Even I knew that was not a good thing. That explained the frozen pistons.

Breaking the pistons free should be easy enough, I thought, and I selected a socket wrench that fit the large nut on the crank shaft. I climbed back down the ladder and scrounged around the boat yard finding a short piece of pipe that would fit over the wrench's handle to extend it a bit for more leverage.

Back in the engine room, I put the wrench with my newly acquired 'cheater pipe' on the nut and tried to turn it with all of my might. Unable to coax any movement out of the frozen pistons, my initial optimism quickly faded.

Next I took out the fuel injectors and used a syringe to fill the cylinders with a concoction of WD 40 and diesel fuel. I was hoping that, given a few hours, the penetrating oil would seep in and release the pistons from their corrosion induced bondage.

While waiting for the magic potion to do its trick, I walked over to the office where I'd seen a payphone hung on the outside of the building. It was covered with thick dust, so I wasn't even sure it would work, but I was relieved when I picked it up and heard a dial tone. I wanted to call Sheryl and bring her up to date on the happenings of the last month.

She sounded as excited to hear from me as I was in hearing her voice again.

"How's Jack?" she inquired. That's always her first question and sort of puts me in my place.

"Oh, he's fine, never better," I say. I had decided long ago not to tell her about Jack's midnight swim to shore at Makemo. No sense worrying her needlessly.

"Yeah, we're both great, but I've got engine problems that I have to deal with here before I can move on," I explained and went on to tell her where I was and that the boat was already hauled out of the water.

"How serious is the problem?" she asked with concern in her voice.

"I'm not really sure yet, I'm still working on freeing up the frozen pistons, I'll know in about an hour if that works out," I told her, and added, "if that doesn't do the trick, it will be pretty major."

I then detailed what my options in the worst case scenario would be:

A. Rebuild the engine

B. Replace the engine

C. Go without an engine (remember there are no bad ideas when you're brainstorming)

D. My personal favorite – turn *Casablanca* into a barefoot bar ala *Rick's Place*

We talked about missing each other and how she was expecting to hear something soon concerning the sale of her flower shop. Again it was evident that this wouldn't be the stop where she would get to fly in and join us as I'd hoped.

After 15 minutes, and $75, we said our goodbyes. As expensive as the call was it was worth every penny hearing her voice and talking to someone, other than Jack, about my problems. It really helped put everything into focus for me.

With renewed energy, I walked back to the boat feeling confident that I could get the engine running. And, if I couldn't do it, Alain, the marina manager, knew a diesel mechanic who could come and take a look at it.

I climbed the ladder to the cockpit ready to go to war, armed with my cheater pipe and socket wrench. I placed the socket on the crankshaft nut, lining it up so that I could stand on it with all my weight. Gingerly I placed my right foot on the extension and gave it a little bounce. Nothing. So it was time for more weight. I held on to a cabinet for balance and placed my left foot on the extension. I was now perched on the pipe like a bird on a limb, but still no movement. I gave it a bounce and before you could say, "hit me in the groin with a pipe" the wrench snapped, sending me awkwardly to the floor, followed closely by the cheater pipe.

I picked myself up, climbed down the ladder and limped over to the marina office to find out about the mechanic. After I answered his questions about the blood trickling down my shin, Alain called the Yanmar dealer in Papeete. Once he had connected with someone that spoke English, he handed me the phone.

"The mechanic is very busy in the shop and your marina is very far away. Maybe tomorrow," was the service manager's reply to my inquiry.

I might add here, that not far from where *Casablanca* sat on the hard was perhaps the largest mosquito breeding ground in the Southern Hemisphere. Life on the boat, out of the water, was one of high humidity and swarms of blood-sucking mosquitoes so the thought of even waiting one extra day to get to the bottom of my problem was pretty discouraging, but what else could I do?

I called the service manager every day for three days. I finally broke his will (or incurred his sympathy to my plight) and he acquiesced. A mechanic would be there the next morning, he assured me.

"Now we're getting somewhere," I told Jack when I got back to the boat. He gave no reply, as usual, making me wish I could call Sheryl again, but many calls like that and I wouldn't have the money for the engine repairs.

The next day, the mechanic's truck skidded to a halt on the dusty marina driveway and a 300 pound Tahitian slid out of the driver's seat.

I quickly learned that he knew about five words of English, which could be a real problem since my Tahitian language skills consisted of "hello" and "does this bus go to town". Thus the engine problem got even more complex at that point. Alain offered to interpret, but he was French and only spoke rudimentary Tahitian, not quite the vocabulary to discuss the mechanics of a diesel engine. So he called on Kim, the Tahitian yard worker to try to aid in the understanding.

So up the shaky ladder the odd parade went. With the four of us (well, it was really more like five, when you considered the size of the mechanic) squeezed unto the main salon of *Casablanca*, the closed up space quickly became hot and very uncomfortable. The slightest movement made the boat rock, causing me to hold my breath in fear that the precariously perched boat would fall off its stands. The mosquitoes, sensing new blood, quickly joined our little gathering.

The mechanic, my last hope, studied the hunk of iron thoughtfully. He mumbled something that, of course, I couldn't understand and proceeded to climb out of the boat and clamber down the ladder, shaking the boat with every step.

He returned shortly with a socket and wrench in hand, maneuvering down into the salon as he swatted at flying bugs. I prayed he would succeed where I had failed.

He placed the wrench and with a mighty 300 pound push he got.... nothing. There was then a flurry of conversation amongst all of the interpreters and the mechanic.

When there was a lull in the babble, I asked, "What did he say?"

"That the bugs are bothering him," replied Kim.

"I mean about the engine," I prodded, as I absently scratched my arm.

More discussion, then he informed me, "He say the pistons are frozen."

"Yes, thanks for that, but what can be done about it?" I begged.

The three of them launched into another rapid fire conversation and then appeared to come to some sort of an agreement.

Kim then announced, "Burn a coil or candles, that will get rid of them."

"I mean about the frozen pistons," I said a bit strained as I felt my face begin to flush.

A little more talking, some nodding and then the pronouncement, "He say the engine must come to Papeete."

The mechanic turned and clumped down the ladder, once again quaking *Casablanca* in the process. I quickly followed.

When he reached his truck he pulled out a can of bug repellant and started spraying his arms and neck. By the time I caught up to him, there was a fog of DDT encircling the large Tahitian. He then pointed at *Casablanca* and began talking rapidly. When he finished he stared at me as if waiting for a response.

So I gave him my best, "Does this bus go to town?"

He gave me a look, maybe somewhat annoyed, but mostly like he understood that I was as lost as an Easter egg in these conversations but there was nothing he could do to help me out. He shrugged his shoulders, climbed into his truck and left the marina in a cloud of dust and flying gravel.

The next day, with the help of the marina manager, I made arrangements for a large truck with a lifting boom to come down from Papeete to remove the engine from my high and dry boat. It would be here in one or three days, I was told.

I set about stripping the remaining parts off of the dead engine and disconnecting all of the wiring and hoses in preparation for the removal. I used a small block and tackle to drag the engine out of its confines.

The galley was as far as I was able to maneuver the 600 pound piece of iron, so that's where it sat for three days until the crane truck finally arrived to lift it out. On the upside, throwing a blanket over the old engine instantly gave me more counter space.

The huge old motor just barely fit out of the hatch, taking three of us to turn and guide it, as not to mar the teak trim along the way. Once out of the boat, the dead beast was lowered on to the truck's bed and was soon headed to Sin-Tung-Hing Marine in Papeete, the South Pacific distributor for Yanmar engines.

A week later I made the same trip to Papeete, but I went on the local bus called "Le Truck". I'd quite successfully asked "Does this bus go to town?" I knew that phrase would come in handy one day. I really did need to learn more of the language, though.

After the two hour bus ride, I walked the final three blocks to the marine store, then up the long flight of stairs to the service manager's office. I would soon find out if I'd be selling beers out of "Café Casablanca" or continuing my travels through the South Pacific.

As I entered his office, the manager, Jean-Marc, was sitting behind his desk and didn't even look up from the folder he was studying. His face offered no clues as to what the prognosis had been. I stood nervously for a few moments before he offered me a seat.

"I'm afraid the engine needs to be redone," he spoke clear English with a very slight French accent.

"How much?" I got right to the point.

"$8500 US dollars," he stated matter-of-fact, then added, "and it maybe will take six months to do it."

I felt bile rise in my throat while the voices in my head pleaded with me to breathe slowly.

Then Jean-Marc offered, "You may wish to consider a new engine." That suggestion caused the blood to drain from my head and just as I was going to put my head between my knees, he handed me the spec sheet he had been reviewing when I came in. I was pleasantly surprised to learn that the cost of a new engine was actually less than the rebuild, and my lightheadedness began to subside. Obviously noticing my distress, John-Marc handed me a glass of water, as he went on to explain that there wouldn't be any import or sales tax because of my temporary status on the island.

The more I read, the better it got, thus the better I felt. The new engine would be smaller, lighter and have more horse power than the original.

"There are several new engines in transit to us at this time and it will only be two to three weeks until the ship arrives," he assured me.

I thanked Jean-Marc and told him I needed to think about it and I would get back to him tomorrow.

I found the nearest phone booth and called Sheryl to bring her up to speed and use her for a sounding board as I worked out my thoughts.

"Rick, how can a hamburger cost $20 in Papeete, but you can buy a new engine there for less than you could in Seattle?" she asked.

"Beats me, but it may be a blessing in disguise to have to take care of it here. I knew I'd need to replace it someday, but expected to do it back home. Since the engine is dead and it's cheaper here, I don't think I really have a choice. It's gonna keep us here an extra month, but Jack and I will still be able to move on before cyclone season," I stated, having already made up my mind.

After the phone call, I hurried right back to Jean-Marc's office hoping to sign some sort of contract. I was afraid he'd discover later that he'd made a pricing error so I wanted a signed document stating the price. Plus, I wanted to get the ball rolling, the sooner I could get *Casablanca* back in the water, the better.

Jean-Marc was surprised at my quick return and I explained that I had made my decision to buy the new engine and was ready to sign the papers to make it happen.

"Oh, no need to sign" was Jean-Marc's reply, "the motor is on its way."

Well, I thought, this is it. And so I left the marine store feeling a bit like I had just taken a step off a tall cliff in my old hang glider: a mix of excitement and terror as to how it would all turn out in the end.

The following three weeks as I awaited the arrival of the new engine, I was busy, dividing my time between: working on engine mounts for the new motor sight seeing around the island continuing my war on bugs

Jean-Marc had given me the spec sheet for the new engine and since the replacement Yanmar was smaller and lighter, the old mounts were in the wrong position to support it. I once again scrounged around the boatyard and came up with some small pieces of angle iron that I could use to make up a jig. This jig would represent the new engine's "foot print" so I would be able to fit the new motor into the engine compartment without really having the engine in hand.

George did stop by, as promised, to see how things were going for me and to find out what was in store for *Casablanca*. After hearing my tale, he suggested we take a drive to a popular surf spot about 30 minutes away, to give me a break from the humidity and mosquitoes of the boat yard. Turned out to be a great way to spend the afternoon just sitting in the shade of the palm frond covered beach bar watching the surfers carving through the faces of the large waves.

On another occasion, George drove me up to the lighthouse at Point Venus. He was a wealth of historical information on his island and these trips were educational as well as refreshing.

He explained to me how Captain Cook made several visits to Tahiti, including one visit to witness the transit of the planet Venus in 1769, thus the name Point Venus.

He also took me to a spot, that legend claimed, captain Bligh came to shore to get breadfruit for his infamous ship, *The Bounty*. On the return from that excursion, George took me up to the top of the mountain on Tahiti Iti and we marveled at the view of the vast Pacific and the island itself.

Meanwhile, back at the boatyard, the heat of the day and the collection of flying, crawling and biting bugs made life nearly unbearable. Jack was even being affected by the heat and chose to go out at night, which was an open invitation to the mosquitoes. No amount of burning coils or candles kept those guys from being absolute pests.

A week before the engine was due to arrive I began calling Jean-Marc to see if he knew anything. Everyday he would politely say, "Maybe tomorrow." I was anxious to get this underway, to say the least.

On my end, all was set on *Casablanca* for the big transplant. I had purchased new hoses, wiring, nuts and bolts: everything I could anticipate needing for the project. I wanted to be sure I wouldn't have to stop and make a day long trip to Papeete for a missing or forgotten item, thus delaying my work.

Early one morning, Kim, the helpful yard worker, came knocking on *Casablanca's* hull.

"Rick! Rick! Engine here now!" he called up to me.

Poking my head through the mosquito netting that covered the cockpit, I saw the same boom truck that had come and hauled away the old engine bouncing down the gravel road. On the deck of the truck, securely fastened down with bright yellow straps, was a crate that must be holding my new Yanmar engine. Hurray!

The truck pulled up along side the boat's elevated hull. The box was opened and there sat a spotless, shiny silver, 3 cylinder diesel engine. It looked beautiful.

Soon a crowd had formed around *Casablanca*, checking out the nice new piece of machinery. A lifting strap was placed on the engine and it was raised high up over my head, and then lowered carefully down through the main hatch, coming to rest on the galley floor.

With a borrowed come-a-long and Kim's help, I was able to pull the engine back into the engine compartment. With the smaller size and weight it was much easier to move than the old beast had been, and my back was very thankful for that.

After a little jostling and adjusting of position, the engine kind of fell on to the new mounts, as if it knew where it was meant to be. What a relief that the jig had done its job and helped me get everything positioned properly.

I then drilled holes to attach the motor mounts and I took the opportunity to run new exhaust and cooling hoses. I spent the next day hooking up the wiring and installing the instrument panel with its switches and fuses. After two long, 12 hour days, all seemed set to go.

Jean-Marc sent a mechanic (not the heavy Tahitian this time) out to bleed the injectors and prime the fuel lines. A garden hose was attached to the engine for cooling water, since *Casablanca* was still up on the hard.

"Ok," was the mechanics way of telling me to turn the key.

Without any hesitation what-so-ever, the engine started right up, sending a sharp vibration through the entire boat.

The yard workers, other cruisers and the marina manager all broke into spontaneous applause. I was elated, and relieved.

The marina expedited our transition from a shaky, on-the-hard mosquito haven, back to the cruising boat that had brought Jack and me safely this far. Unbelievable how different a boat feels when it's in the water where it belongs, it's like you can feel it breathing again, as if it's been restored to life.

My euphoria, however, was short lived. After *Casablanca* was safely tied up in the small marina, several of my 'Engine Support Group' members and I decided to meet at the nearby restaurant to celebrate the successful re-powering of my boat.

Upon returning to *Casablanca*, around 11 that night, I fed Jack, and then promptly flopped into bed. Before drifting off in a beer induced slumber, I caught the sound of a dripping faucet. Checking both of the sinks, I found nothing but dry bowls—no leaks there, so I convinced myself the sound was coming from something outside the boat and I laid back down.

About five minutes later, I again heard the drip, drip, drip of a slow leak, so I drug myself back out of bed and went directly to the engine room access door and opened it up. When I turned on the small overhead light in the confined space, the reflection off of the new, shiny, silver engine immediately brightened the room. Not seeing anything out of the ordinary, I was reaching to turn off the light when I noticed a small puddle of water, about the size of a dinner plate, on the fiberglass floor pan beneath the engine.

Thinking that there must be a loose water hose connection, I grabbed a screw driver and tightened the appropriate hose clamps. Satisfied that it was nothing major, I again reached to shut off the overhead light, when out of the air intake of my brand new, just arrived from Japan, expensive, newly installed diesel engine, came a small stream of water. Not good.

I knew very quickly I had a major problem, because in order for water to be coming out of the air intake, the cylinders must be filled with water. I also knew from my days working with machinery in Joe Perry's yard, that even a few drops of water in a diesel engine can destroy it.

To prevent this from happening, a siphon break is installed in the cooling water intake hose. As the name infers, it keeps the ocean from siphoning back into the engine when it is shut off. To work, this siphon break has to be above the boat's water line, and due to a miscalculation on my part, I hadn't placed the device high enough. So, after I launched *Casablanca* and motored to the marina, tied her up and went out drinking, the motor started siphoning the water in.

I immediately shut off the cooling water seacock, which stopped the incoming flow. Next, I needed to get every drop of water out of the cylinders, so I took out the three fuel injectors and using the starter motor, I spun the engine. With the injectors removed, the engine couldn't start, but the movement of the pistons would force the water out. As I'd hoped, water was pushed out of the cylinders through the injector holes. Heavy at first, it sprayed over me and the entire engine room, but before long, the water was reduced to a fine mist until eventually nothing but air was coming out. After replacing the injectors, I changed the motor oil, just to be sure no water had contaminated the lubricant.

About 3 AM, after bleeding the injectors, it was the moment of truth. If I hadn't gotten all the water out of the cylinders and I started the engine, the trapped water would blow a hole in the pistons, because water can't compress.

Hoping that my sleep deprived mind hadn't overlooked anything, and holding my breath, I reached for the starter key. It was several minutes before I finally got up the nerve to turn it.

The motor started right up and I let it run for sometime, waking up all my neighbors with the sound of a rumbling diesel disturbing the quiet night, then I shut it down and immediately closed off the water intake, before it could start siphoning again.

By noon the next day, I had repositioned the siphon break and my faux pas was remedied.

During my time in the boat yard, I had come to what I jokingly called a 'Life Decision'. Neither Jack nor I were very happy without Sheryl's company, so after a long discussion with the voices in my head (I find they converse better than Jack, but just barely), it was decided that if she couldn't come to us, then we would sail to her.

I fully understood the complexities of her life, what with her flower shop being up for sale, her sister, Joni, about to give birth to twins and the matter of the marriage proposal on the table from moi. The last thing I wanted to do was put undo pressure on her to meet up with Jack and me half way around the world, so I proclaimed to Jack (and the voices), "It's settled. *Casablanca* is headed for Hawaii, and then, if necessary, back to California." Ta da.

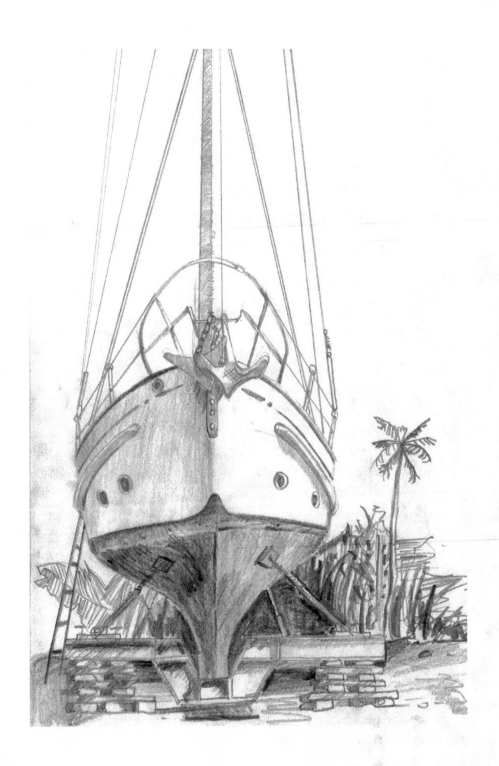

CHAPTER 13
RETURN TO THE TUAMOTUS

"If you wait, all that happens is that you get older."
—Mario Andretti

With the new itinerary in place, one thing was clear and that was *Casablanca* needed to get on her way to Hawaii before, and I stress BEFORE, hurricane season begins in the North Pacific. June is the 'official' start of the season when the hurricanes that form around Mexico start their march across the Pacific on a path that usually runs south of the Hawaiian chain but north of the equator. We had about a month before any serious storms would be spawning off the warm waters of the Mexican Coast, but the trip would take around 20 days, so it was time to move.

Jack and I had dealt with a monster called hurricane Iniki early in our cruising career. Now I can't speak for Jack, but I really didn't want a repeat performance of that. It was nasty, nasty, nasty.

I needed to get a bit east of Tahiti to have a better angle of sail for the long trip to Hawaii. To accomplish this, I would first head back to the Tuamotus. George had talked highly of an atoll called Fakarava, an easy two day sail from Papeete. It is said to have the most spectacular snorkeling in the Tuamotus and he'd given me a chart of the atoll marked with the best anchorages. Having snorkeled in Makemo with its awe inspiring coral pinnacles, I wanted to see if there really was something out there that could top what I'd already seen. It was hard to imagine.

The guidebook I'd been using told me Fakarava is the second largest atoll of the 70 or so in the Tuamotus. It's roughly rectangular in shape, 32 miles long and 15 miles wide. There was a decent size village, so it would be a good stop to pick up some fresh provisions, including crusty baguettes, before pushing on to Hawaii.

While still in Tahiti, Sheryl and I had several long, and expensive, conversations on the phone. I explained to her in simple terms that I loved her and wanted to be near her even if it meant I would take time out from sailing for a while. At first she objected, saying she would feel guilty cutting my cruise short. I pointed out to her that it had been "our cruise" and besides, I was tired of her disgruntled cat always biting me. I was sure Jack blamed me for Sheryl not being there.

"Rick, he loves you. That's why he bites. It's just his way of showing you affection," she reassured me. Then I could hear over the scratchy, 3000 mile telephone connection, a light sob as she added, "I love you, too, Rick."

So Jack and I soon found ourselves crashing through the South Pacific swell on our way to a place with a name that sounded like a word you wouldn't use in mixed company. We were as happy as clams.

Speaking of clams, we did have to say good bye to our littlest crewmate, Crabby, the hermit crab. We left him to make a new home on a beach amongst some palm trees and knew he would make friends there, since we'd seen other hermit crabs nearby. I figured the officials in Hawaii wouldn't take kindly to my bringing live, foreign crabs into the islands. It was going to be a big enough hassle with my vaccinated, domesticated and documented cat.

On the afternoon of our second day out of Tahiti, *Casablanca* poked her bow into the northern pass of Fakarava. Since this was such a large, wide pass the current was negligible and seemed more like entering a bay back home in Puget Sound than the white-knuckle pass entrances I'd endured before. This one was a piece of cake.

We motored past the village as we headed for the south end of the atoll where the spectacular snorkeling and diving was said to be found. I planned to stop back by town on the way out, to get some supplies and hopefully find a phone to call Sheryl.

Heading south through the long lagoon I observed that the east side of the atoll was composed of a long sandy beach with palm trees and islets, where as the west side showed little evidence of dry land, and the fringing reef was only made evident by the crashing Pacific swell.

Traveling slowly, I was being mindful of the hundreds of pearl oyster buoys strung together across the lagoon. They were scattered everywhere, some riding high in the water while others would hover, half sunk, just below the surface. It was a dangerous maze and I was ever vigilant because I didn't want to have to explain to an angry pearl farmer that I had his life's work wrapped up in my propeller.

I dropped anchor near the south pass of Fakarava just as the sun touched the horizon. I paused and watched, hoping to glimpse the legendary green flash, but some far off clouds interfered with the celestial fireworks that evening.

Casablanca gently swung in the light, 10 knot trade winds as the stars began to come on stage for their nightly performance. Jack came up on deck and actually snuggled against me, as if he knew I was taking him back to his mistress with her constant pampering. It was his way of thanking me.

I knew how he felt, because I, too, was more relaxed than I had been in a very long time. It was nice to finally have a plan in place that included Sheryl. I was also pleased with the new engine's performance, even though we'd only needed to use it for a short period while we navigated the large lagoon. I was astounded at how smooth and quiet it ran and thrilled with the way it would start right away with no ugly cloud of black smoke to pollute the air around me. Everything was coming up Rick.

The next morning dawned with nary a cloud in the sky, which is really a rare event in the South Pacific. There is usually some varying degree of overcast with a squall or two in the distance, but this day opened with a vast blue sky. There weren't even any fluffy clouds dotting the horizon.

Around mid-morning, a 45 foot charter dive boat motored by *Casablanca*. It had bright red and white dive flags painted on its sides and a row of lime green dive tanks lined the starboard side, secured in stainless steel racks. There was a sturdy ladder folded up on the six foot wide swim platform on the stern of the boat which could deploy into the water giving easy access for the divers.

The boat dropped its anchor about 300 feet from us and I counted 8 people milling around on deck, checking tanks and regulators and putting wet suits on. Within an hour all but two of the people onboard were in the water, and I suspected those remaining were crew members. I could trace the line of bubbles as the divers made their way to the nearby southern pass that connects the lagoon to the open ocean.

I was anxious to get into the water as well, but first I had some work to do. I spent the rest of that morning re-checking the new engine's alignment, something that couldn't be done until the boat was in the water. It was a tedious job and I had overlooked this procedure in my haste to get going. It involved taking numerous measurements with a feeler gauge and using that information I had to adjust one or maybe all four of the motor mounts to ensure there was as straight a line as possible from the transmission shaft to the propeller shaft. I had done the procedure while still on the hard, but it was necessary to repeat it as it could change once the boat was afloat.

Being in the classical pretzel position in the engine room as I attempted to reach the different mounts, brought to mind the old adage, "cruising is just working on your boat in exotic places". And, as usual, once I was down in the engine compartment all balled up without a free hand, Jack came along, walked across my head and rubbed against my face, seemingly pleased at being such a nuisance.

Once the alignment was to my satisfaction, I ate lunch and prepared to go snorkeling. I saw that the divers were all back on the charter boat and appeared to be resting. They'd completed the morning dive and would probably go out again in the afternoon.

I launched the dinghy and put the motor on its stern. I gathered my fins, mask and a knife and threw them into *Exit Visa*. Before leaving *Casablanca* I shut all the hatches to make sure sleeping Jack would stay put. He was out like a light having worn himself out "helping" me with the engine project.

I motored the short distance to the pass. When I shut down the outboard, the dinghy started a slow drift through the channel. I've always thought the best snorkeling is done through lagoon passes aided by the current. This would be perfect, I thought, as I donned my mask and fins and tied the sheathed knife to a long lanyard. Though I'd never had to use a knife while snorkeling, I always thought it might come in handy some day, and carried it for my own safety.

Once in the water I would hold on to a line secured to my small craft and just let the moving water take me through the pass, out toward the ocean. I was mesmerized watching the watery show flow by underneath me. When

I'd get to the ocean side of the pass, I would hop into *Exit Visa*, start the motor and speed back to the start of the drift and do it all over again, never tiring of the underwater wonderland. Simply being a few feet right or left of my previous track, provided a whole new vista, so there was always something interesting to see. I really prefer to do this drifting when the current is running the other way and takes me from the outer entrance into the lagoon, but that day the seas were relatively calm and the current light, so I felt safe floating out toward the sea.

George, as well as my own guidebook were both right in their assessment of the snorkeling in Fakarava. As I drifted on the outgoing current, I saw not only the schools of bright colored fish I had seen before, but the big difference was that mixed in with the reef fish were ocean species venturing into the pass.

A school of long slender, cigar-shaped Wahoo swam within several yards of me. When they turned suddenly, in unison, I could clearly see their triangular shaped teeth as they headed back out to sea. A giant manta ray, bigger than my inflatable, came so close I could have touched it if I hadn't been so startled by its appearance. It was plain to see how that boat back in the Marquesas had gotten pulled around by one of those big creatures.

Some fish, like a big orange grouper I watched for some time, would just tread water in one place, letting the current bring food to them. And of course there were a couple sharks, the smaller "good" sharks that would slink by acting as if they could take me or leave me. I just hoped their open ocean cousins would stay out at sea where they belonged.

The most impressive part of the whole experience was the sheer variety of fish that were all crowded together in this one narrow corridor. It was like a fantastic aquarium designed by Mr. Walt Disney himself, for one of his spectacular rides.

I drifted through the pass several times, and as the sun began to descend in the sky I decided I'd better end my water fun so I would have some time to explore the beach before sunset.

I landed *Exit Visa* near an old, abandoned fish camp which had been built a hundred feet back from the water on the crushed coral beach. There were two structures, built lean-to style out of palm fronds and both were showing their age. The simple construction of these huts consisted of three sidewalls with open fronts facing each other with a fire pit rimmed with large coral chunks in between.

Approaching the shacks, it appeared they hadn't been used for some time, maybe years. When I poked my head into one of the lean-tos, I spotted a make-shift altar with a cross made from drift wood. At the base of the cross there were about a hundred Cowry shells of all sizes and colors, artfully arranged in a magnificent mosaic. It was a sobering sight.

As I walked back to the dinghy, I tried to visualize the men who had occupied these huts and what life was like for them. Were they nomads, traveling from atoll to atoll catching fish to take back to their village? Did they ply these waters in outrigger canoes? Maybe they were long ago sailors?

Time had passed quickly as I stood pondering the lives of those who had occupied the camp, and I had to race back to *Casablanca* to get home before the sun set. I noticed that some clouds had moved into the previously clear sky.

I was surprised to see the dive boat still anchored, for charter boats usually go back to a town or village at the end of the day as they aren't set up for overnight guests. A loud voice boomed out from the boat and I could see they were trying to get my attention, waving me over in their direction in the fading light.

I made a u-turn and came along side the dive boat, killed the engine and stood up, holding on to its rail to steady myself. Several people with concerned looks on their faces peered down at me. I was afraid this might have something to do with Jack.

A man who identified himself as the captain of the boat spoke to me in a heavy Australian accent, and asked, "Did you happen to see a couple of our people when you were on shore?"

"No, I didn't see anyone," I replied.

"It seems we have a bit of a situation here," he continued, his voice sounding strained, "A couple of our divers got separated from the group, and we haven't been able to locate them."

With twilight in full swing and two people still in the water, combined with an out-going current, the whole thing just didn't feel good.

"What can I do to help?" I volunteered.

"Well, we are putting an inflatable in the water and going into the pass to where they were last seen. We've called the French authorities and alerted them we may have two missing divers," he informed me.

"I'll go get a couple of flashlights and help with the search," I offered, then set off for *Casablanca*.

On my way back to my boat, I could just imagine the terror of being swept out to sea and struggling to get back to shore with night closing in. It sent a cold shiver down my spine.

We searched for four hours that night, until it was deemed to be too dangerous to continue. Visibility in the inky black night had worsened when a steady rain had begun to fall. The local gendarme, who was 20 miles away, informed the charter captain that they had a boat that would join the search the next morning.

Not being able to sleep, I got up and sat in the cockpit after the rain shower had subsided. I could see the beam of a search light originating at the dive boat, sweeping the placid waters of the quiet lagoon. Back and forth went the light. Obviously, they were hoping beyond hope the two wayward divers would be spotted, or at the very least, the beacon would guide them back to the safety of the boat.

Well before sunrise, the lights on the dive boat were burning bright, casting ghostly shadows of the people milling around, anxious to resume the search. I'm sure there was little, if any, sleeping on board the previous night. It had been a fitful night for me, as well, but I was ready to go lend any assistance I could.

The French vessel would be leaving the village at sunrise, and should reach the pass an hour after that. It was determined that the dive boat's bigger, more powerful inflatable would be best suited to go out into the ocean to search, and I would stay in the lagoon and check along the shoreline. It was plain on the faces of the charter boat's crew and guests what a heavy weight they were burdened with. I was starting to feel pessimistic about a safe return for the missing divers.

As we headed out on our search, I turned on my hand held VHF radio so that if something happened or the people were found, I would hear about it.

Forty minutes into my search of the beaches near the pass, an excited voice came over the radio. Since they were speaking rapid French, I didn't really know what they were saying, but I guessed it to be the gendarmes talking from their boat back to their base on shore. Looking in the direction that they would be coming from, I spotted a high powered sport boat throwing out a huge bow wake, heading our way at full speed.

I turned *Exit Visa* and motored to the dive boat. Ten minutes later the French speedboat slowed and pulled along side the charter vessel. A man and a woman in black wet suits with towels around their shoulders, looking weak, their faces caked with salt, were helped out of the police cruiser and up into the dive boat. Amongst the back slapping and cheers, the two, on unsteady legs, told their story.

After becoming separated from the larger group, they had turned to swim back to the mother ship. Unaware that the tide had also turned, they were caught in an eddy of the fast flowing underwater river and swept into the middle of the lagoon. Exhausted and with no air left in their tanks, they jettisoned the tanks as well as their weight belts, blew up their floatation vests and drifted, tied together so they wouldn't be separated. Sunset found them several miles from the safety of their boat and farther still from shore. All night they just floated on their backs and kept each other awake.

Just after sunrise, the two divers again attempted to paddle in the direction of the charter boat. At the same time, the gendarmes were speeding down the lagoon to join in the search. On board the French boat, a sharp eyed observer spotted the lost divers waving frantically from about a half mile away. During their 14 hour absence they had drifted nearly 7 miles from their starting point. What a terrifying night that had been. More so for the searchers than for the lost divers, because they knew they were all right, but the rest of us could only imagine the worst.

I would have liked to spend several more days in Fakarava, but I had to begin the leg to Hawaii, as the number of days for a safe, 'hurricane free' passage were dwindling. On my provisioning stop at the village, I found their only public telephone. Over a less than perfect connection, Sheryl and I made a date to meet in Honolulu.

While I was in town, *The Swallow* had come in and anchored near *Casablanca*, so I stopped by to talk to Chris. His plans now had him setting sail for Hawaii as well, since he'd been offered a job with a charter company on Maui. Like me, he was stocking up on provisions for the three week trip north.

Anxious to get started, I rowed back to *Casablanca*, knowing things were working out very nicely indeed. A new engine, good weather, another boat to travel with and most of all, getting to see Sheryl in a couple weeks... what could be better? What could go wrong?

oo   HAWAIIN
Honoluw °o°o   ISLANDS

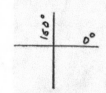

PART III
HAWAII

160°

0°

°°° MARQUESAS

°°°° TUAMOTUS

TAHITI

CHAPTER 14
THRASHED

"It wasn't raining when Noah built the Ark."
—Unknown

There's an old cruiser's adage that states, "You can pick where you will meet me or when you will meet me, but not both"

I couldn't get that quote out of my head. It's sort of one of those unwritten laws of cruising. When someone wants to come visit, you don't want to be tied to being any certain place at any certain time or you may find yourself heading out in undesirable conditions. But when I'd talked to Sheryl several weeks ago and we made plans to meet up in Hawaii, the last thing I expected was a major weather disturbance to crop up in my path. After all, it was May and hurricane season doesn't start in the North Pacific until June, so it should have been the ideal time to make the passage. So I happily set off from Fakarava, that beautiful atoll with the funny name in the Tuamotu Archipelago of French Polynesia, with Honolulu as my destination. I was sailing blissfully along until two weeks into the journey when I got the bad news.

Listening to the high-seas weather forecast, I felt like I'd been punched in the stomach when the weather prognosticators announced that a troublesome low pressure system, which I'd been tracking, suddenly ballooned into a Tropical Depression. Unpleasant, yes, but it could be worse. That's what worried me the most: that it might get worse. And what is worse than a Tropical Depression? A HURRICANE. Jack and I had enough of hurricanes when we were treated to hurricane Iniki in Hawaii years before, and neither of us wanted to go through anything like that again. The robotic voice on the radio told us without emotion that *Casablanca*, Jack and I were going to be served up a portion of nasty weather pie.

I spent the next several hours trying to reason out what direction the massive storm would take and how I could put the greatest distance between us and the nasty weather system. Turning back south seemed out of the question because the storm's predicted track would have it overtaking me before I could get to any meaningful shelter.

"*Casablanca, Casablanca*, come in Rick," the VHF radio broke into my concentration. It was Chris, on the sailboat *The Swallow*, who was about a half a day behind me. We had been more or less traveling together since leaving the Tuamotus.

"Go ahead Chris," I said through the growing static on the radio.

"Did ya get the latest weather there Rick?" Chris asked, the tension putting a distinct edge to his voice.

"Yeah, not so good is it? What do you think?" I asked, since I'm always ready to hear someone else's weather opinion.

"I think the bloody bastard is in our way and we need to go around it," he reported as his radio started cutting out.

"The storm seems to be heading southwest, I think we can try to end run the thing by going northeast," I said trying to sound as if it was no big deal.

"My bara... se..m...to....roger" came through the heavy static.

"Chris, I only got about every other word. Repeat please," I said hoping he had better copy on me.

Static.

"*Swallow*, do you read me, over," I said, raising my voice, as if it would help.

Still no answer.

"Good luck Chris.... *Casablanca* clear," I said to the silent radio as I hung up the microphone.

As I've said before, Jack seems to have an instinct about weather and he was already tucked into his favorite spot, wedged between two sail bags in the V Berth.

"You stay put," I said. I was glad to know where he was, just in case we had to get out in a hurry.

I immediately set about preparing for what could be the worst storm I've ever had to face out at sea. First I started the engine to put a full charge on the boat's six batteries. Next I dropped the main sail, secured the boom and raised the storm trysail. This small, heavyweight sail replaces the main sail and runs up a separate track. It is also free footed, meaning it doesn't attach to the boom so it can move from side to side with no danger of the boom crashing across in an accidental jibe causing serious damage to the rig or, even worse, myself. The heavier cloth enables it to take a lot of punishment from the wind without being ripped to shreds.

When I went forward to put up the storm jib, another smaller, heavier sail, I scanned the horizon and noticed that a dark cloud line had replaced the deep blue sky. Not good. I could tell the clouds had an abundance of rain stored in them and it was easy to spot heavy precipitation at their base. The squalls were very ragged around the edges, an indicator that strong winds were blowing in the dark menaces. Even though it was midday, I could see the interior of these storm precursors light up, the result of the electro static discharging. Lightening. God, I hate lightening.

I'd set a course that I thought would keep me on the outer fringes of the storm, providing it followed the predicted path. Only time would tell.

When the outer edges of the storm were finally upon *Casablanca,* all I could do was hope. I hoped the thing stayed on its present course. I hoped the direction I'd chosen, was right. I hoped that all I'd have to deal with was the fringes of the tropical depression. But most of all I hoped it remained a tropical depression and didn't turn into something even more violent.

Then another old saying came to mind: "You can hope in one hand and crap in the other and see which one fills up quicker."

The wind was soon blowing 20 to 25 knots having increased from 15 knots in just a matter of minutes. Down below I noted in the log that the barometer had dropped and the arrow was pointing to "Change in the weather". No shit, I thought.

Luckily the swell was still quite long and deep, but I knew that would soon change, as well. I double checked the cabin to make sure everything was stowed away and that all latches were secured. I also took the opportunity to heat some water for the thermos so I'd be able to fix some hot drinks or instant soups when the going got tough.

I remember waiting for the water to boil and my mind drifting to Sheryl, wondering what she was doing while I was busy preparing to meet the storm. She would have probably been packing, getting ready to leave San Francisco and fly to Honolulu for our planned rendezvous. I couldn't wait to see her smile again after being apart for so long.

Suddenly the boat lurched to its port side as we were blasted by the first wind gusts from the squalls. Hard rain began to drum the cabin top and Jack's eyes opened wide as he looked my way.

"Well, let's get started," I said with sarcasm that was lost on the cat.

In answer, the boat again went to its beam's end as if it were pushed by an enormous unseen hand. I could hear a clap of thunder in the distance. Stepping out into the cockpit, I was shocked to see how the seascape had changed so quickly. Huge waves had built and the tops were already being blown off by the gusting wind, the flying spray pelting my skin like buckshot. The sky had lost its remaining brightness and the sea had turned an ugly metal gray.

I retreated back down stairs for one last check that everything was stowed and secure. Donning my raincoat and safety harness, with its six foot tether, I went back outside to make sure *Casablanca* was sailing as best as she could be, as the wind was blowing 35 with gusts to 40. It was past sundown and the lightening was still flashing, lighting up the seascape much like a strobe light on a 1980's disco dance floor. *Casablanca's* motion below deck was not bad, especially considering the wind had increased to 45 knots. But the waves: it's always about the waves. My guess was they were 18 to 20 feet high and they looked like the side of a barn to me. The wind would shriek at the top of the giant mountains of water, then as we raced down the backside to the trough below it would be eerily silent. Then we'd struggle up the next monster for a repeat performance. All the while the lightening flashes.

After spending an hour huddled behind the dodger, I could see that the self-steering was doing its job keeping the boat on course, so I felt it was safe to leave the deck. I went down below, and with my raingear still on, squeezed into the pilot berth to try and get some sleep. It was a fitful rest at best, as I couldn't quit listening to the growl of the wind as the boat approached the wave tops followed by the silence at the bottom of the trough. Just as I was finally getting comfortable with the sounds of the storm and beginning to drift off to sleep, I heard a distinct change in the rhythm of the waves. As I swung my legs out of the bunk a thunderous roar enveloped *Casablanca* and I was catapulted across the cabin. Along with me came a sleeping bag, pillows, some cans from a now open cupboard and a pile of books that broke loose from their bungee cord restraint on the bookshelf.

Suddenly I found myself kneeling on top of the cabinets on the port side of the boat and it took me a minute to realize that *Casablanca* had taken a direct hit by a large wave and had rolled 90 degrees or more. In the dim cabin light, I could see water squirting in through the port windows, even though they'd been tightly dogged down. Then, ever so slowly, *Casablanca* began to right herself. Thankfully the boat's heavily leaded full keel did its job bringing the boat back to an upright position. Unfortunately, that same heavy keel would make her sink like a stone if too much water was taken into the cabin on such a knockdown or a rollover.

I waded through the displaced obstacles strewn over the cabin floor and pushed open the hatch.

"Oh my God," my brain was yelling as I stared at the monstrous waves, my mouth agape. They looked like a mountain range with a blizzard raging. The tops of the waves were being blown into a white spume as a result of the strengthening wind.

The sturdy life line stanchions on the port side were all bent like frail limbs of a tree and the spray dodger over the hatch was pushed out of shape, but luckily still standing. 60 knots of wind was frozen onto the face of the no longer working wind instrument. It was fine with me that it wasn't functional, for I really didn't want to know if it got any worse than that. That's when I saw my greatest loss: the 4 person life raft that had been stored on deck between the mast and the dodger was gone. Its stainless steel cradle sat sadly empty.

CHAPTER 15
THE LAST HOPE

"The only thing standing between you and a watery grave is your wits,
and that's not my idea of adequate protection."
—Movie quote, Beat the Devil

"Well, we won't have to worry about getting into the life raft, Jack," I called down to my sailing buddy scanning below to see if he was still tucked safely away.

I didn't have time to really search for him, as I had to take some quick action. *Casablanca* was drifting sideways and the huge waves were pummeling relentlessly threatening to turn us over again. Apparently the windvane, which had steered us faithfully for thousands of miles, was somehow damaged in the knock down.

It didn't take a rocket scientist to determine that outrunning the storm was no longer an option. It had already found us.

However, I did have one more trick up my sleeve. *Casablanca's* previous owner had a sea anchor on board as part of the safety gear, and I felt this was the time to give it a try. I was vaguely familiar with its function, but had never used one before, so it would be a new experience and I'd have to try to figure it out on the fly.

When I went below to get the sea anchor, I heard Jack crying. Looking in the direction where I'd last seen him, I could tell he'd been tossed just as I had been and the sail bags he usually snuggles between were all jammed on one side of the boat.

"Jack, where are you?" I shouted. I heard a weak mew from under the pile of bags. As I dug him out, I was surprised at how wet everything, including Jack, had become. I grabbed a towel and wrapped his shaking body in it. Then another wave broke on the boat sending what looked like a waterfall cascading down the companionway stairs. In my haste to get the parachute and search for Jack, I had neglected to fully close the sliding hatch.

"Dammit," I groaned through clenched teeth. The wall of water had spooked the cat and I was rewarded with deep, bloody claw marks across my face as he scrambled for a new hiding place.

The motion of the boat told me I needed to get back on deck pronto to get *Casablanca* stabilized before something really bad happened: again.

After rifling through a closet, tossing more items onto the already cluttered cabin sole, I found the sea anchor. I grabbed the bag containing the 18 foot parachute and the directions for deploying it.

Scanning the instructions quickly, I read that after attaching one end of the line to the boat and the other end to the parachute, the next step was to toss the bag over the lee side of the vessel. As it begins to sink you're supposed to give the line a hard tug releasing the chute from the bag causing it to billow out. All of this, of course, is easier said than done, especially since I would be attempting it on a wildly thrashing boat with waves threatening to wash me over at any moment. But it was the only way I could get *Casablanca* out of the dangerous position she'd fallen into.

Reading on, the directions said to play out enough line so that the boat would be two wave sets behind the parachute, and the boat and chute should each be on top of a wave crest at the same time. This brings the bow of the boat head on into the waves and the fully blossomed chute disturbs the wave pattern keeping them from breaking on the boat with destructive force. Sounds like a good plan, I thought.

I was tethered to a pad eye in the cockpit as I went over in my mind step by step what needed to be done to safely deploy the sea anchor. *Casablanca* was riding "hove to", which, simply put means she's turned in such a way to the wind that her sail is backfilled, so she doesn't move forward, just sort of bobs like a cork with the bow about 45 degrees off of the wind. The problem was the cross swells that would hit us from the beam, and as we'd seen, some of those waves were giants. I was counting on the chute to help us ride out the storm in relative safety with no more knock downs or sheets of water below.

Before heading forward, I dug around in the cockpit locker for one last piece of equipment I thought might aid in my task: my snorkeling mask. I realized that with the wind and spray building, if I didn't have some eye protection, I wouldn't have a chance at seeing anything up on the bow.

The lightening flashes weren't as frequent as they had been, which did help my nerves a bit, but the downside was it was darker without the little bursts of light. So, in another attempt at improving my visibility, I switched on the spreader lights, which are small spot lights mounted on the mast facing down to light up the deck. Unfortunately, most of their light was lost in the blowing gloom.

"Here goes," I said, but I couldn't tell over the din if I'd actually vocalized it or just thought it. I removed my tether from the pad eye in the cockpit and hooked it to the "jack line," which is a one inch wide piece of webbing that runs the length of the deck. This would allow me to stay safely attached to the boat as I moved forward to the bow. With dive mask on and the heavy bundle containing my last hope tight in my arms, I rolled out of the cockpit and started to slither on my stomach, pushing the bag with the sea anchor ahead of me.

Torrents of water would wash down the deck as wave after wave broke on the pitching 35 foot boat that I was clinging to for dear life. When *Casablanca* would slide down the back of a wave, I would momentarily be weightless and would desperately cling to my precious cargo, knowing if it was lost over the side, the outlook would be pretty grim.

Exhausted, I reached the bow of the boat, only to find that the safety tether was about a foot short of where I needed to be to properly attach the sea anchor. Reluctantly I unclipped the tether from the jack line, knowing that this could have some very bad results if I lost my grip and went over the side. That's the downside of having a cat as your 1st mate: they aren't very good at search and rescue.

Wiping the rain and salt spray from the mask did little to help my vision, so I blindly reached for the handle of the rope locker. When I opened the hinged hatch, the 60 knot wind tore it from my grasp and slammed it open against its stops, then immediately slammed it shut. I barely avoided having my fingers smashed by the wildly flying door.

Once I pried the rope locker door back open, I leaned my body against it. After retrieving the 200 feet of heavy line that I needed to attach the sea anchor to the bow of the boat, I let the door slam shut. With the extra weight of my body the boat's nose would dig deeper into the up coming waves, resulting in even more water cascading over me and down the decks. I needed to hang on.

Making fast the anchor line to a cleat required me to use both hands: so much for hanging on. As I released my grip I began sliding around the front deck like a hockey puck on ice, which was not a good feeling.

It took me about 10 minutes to get the chute ready to deploy. I made one more check that every thing was attached properly. The strong gusts had become more frequent, which really meant that it wasn't "gusty" anymore, just hard-ass wind.

Weaving the bundle under the life lines, I said a little prayer as I tossed the sea anchor to the lee side of the boat and gave it the prerequisite pull..... and it stayed tightly packed. I got to my knees and gave it a bit stronger pull, but at the same time I lost my balance and landed on my back. With the crazy pitching up and down, I struggled to get up. Finally scrambling to my knees, I wiped the facemask with the back of my hand and could see that the sea anchor was partially deployed and the line was playing out at an astonishing speed.

Suddenly I was jerked from my kneeling position and heading head first for the edge of the deck. Somehow my unfastened harness tether had wrapped around the out-going line and was pulling me toward the billowing chute. It seemed the entire Pacific ocean had filled the fully-blossomed canopy and my head and shoulders were torn through the lifelines. I flailed my arms trying to grab anything to keep me from going over, knowing that it would be virtually impossible to ever get back on board, even if the chute did its trick and kept *Casablanca* relatively in one place.

My dive mask was torn off, but I managed to get a death grip on the 1 inch stainless steel tubing of the bow pulpit. The boat was pulling at the anchor in protest, with me being caught in the middle struggling to keep the rest of my body on board. Holding on with all my might watching the tumultuous waters running beneath me I managed gulps of air, between slaps of water, as I tried to figure out how to get myself out of this latest mess.

Desperately trying to pull myself back to the relative safety of the deck, I was beginning to fear I was fighting a losing battle as my strength was rapidly being sapped. I knew that getting the tether undone from my harness was the only way I could save myself, but that would involve letting go of the boat with one arm so I could unclip the carabineer hook of the tether from the D ring on my harness. I was terrified. I didn't know if I could hold myself on with just one arm.

As the waves passed under my little boat, the anchor line would pull tight, forcing me to use all my strength to keep from being drug through the lifelines and into the churning sea. Conversely, on the back of a wave the line would slacken, just a bit, and give me about a 10 second period of relief from the excruciating pain as the pull on my harness lessened. I would have to time my move for that slight slack period.

Another flash of lightening exposed the wildly chaotic seascape, and I knew it was now or never as my strength was nearly gone. When I felt the bone-crushing pull begin to subside as *Casablanca* slipped down the wave, I hesitantly let go with my right hand keeping my left arm wrapped tightly around the pulpit. I silently counted to myself, knowing that by the count of 10, I would either be free or drug off the boat and into the darkness of the sea in front of me.

At first I fumbled awkwardly with the carabineer clip, my hand being stiff from the death grip it had maintained. Three.....four.....five...... don't panic I thought as I remembered this harness needed some slack to be able to unclip. I eased my body forward ever so slightly in the direction I really didn't want to go, over the side of the boat, in hopes of getting that millimeter of slack. Seven....eight.... I finally managed to open the clip and slowly slip it through the D ring....TEN!

With a loud SLAP the tether bolted off the boat into the rain swept gloom. About as quickly, I pushed my body back in the opposite direction away from the raging sea and on to the wave swept deck, fully aware that without the tether, I was very vulnerable. Completely drained, I laid flat on my belly with my arms wrapped around the jack line and my salt encrusted face lying on the cool deck.

Once I regained a little strength, I checked to make sure the sea anchor was out far enough and tied off securely. After a minor adjustment to the anchor line, I began a slow crawl back to the cockpit. With the anchor fully deployed and the proper amount of line out, there was a huge change in the motion of the boat and I began to feel confident that I was getting things under control.

As advertised, the sea anchor was keeping *Casablanca's* bow into the oncoming waves. With the parachute about two wave lengths forward of us, it was doing a good job of disturbing the wave pattern and the monsters were breaking on either side of the chute, leaving a relatively smooth slick in front of the boat.

As I pulled myself up to climb into the safety of the boat's center cockpit, an errant wave hit *Casablanca* on the port side just as I was stepping into the enclosure. The jolt and blast of water knocked me off balance and I crashed head first into the steering pedestal. Pain shot through my arm as I tried to roll onto the cockpit seat. Then blackness enveloped my consciousness.

The pain that had caused me to blackout was the same pain that brought me back to reality. I slowly opened my eyes trying to come to grips with what was happening. I was relieved to hear Jack's muffled meows from the other side of the hatch, which told me he was OK and had survived the mayhem down below.

Still flat on my back, staring straight up at the mast and not knowing how long I'd been out, I was thankful that the darkness of the night was beginning to lift. In the growing light, I could tell the clouds weren't scudding by as fast as they had been. The waves were still incredibly large and when they would smash into the side of the boat, the jarring would send stabbing pain up my obviously broken arm.

My head was throbbing, so before trying to sit up, I went over what I needed to do for my arm. In my Offshore First Aid Kit there was a splint that you slide on and blow up to immobilize the damaged limb. I would have to somehow get that on to protect my arm until I could get proper attention. Unfortunately, it was still a long way to Hawaii.

CHAPTER 16
WORLD OF HURT

"The sweetest thing afloat, that's my boat."
—James "Sunny Jim" White

Making my way down below, I wasn't sure if it was the hit I had taken on my head, courtesy of the steering wheel, or the intense pain of my broken arm that was causing me to be nauseous. The boat was riding very smoothly on the dying storm swell, so sea sickness was not the problem.

I was horrified at the condition of *Casablanca's* cabin. Books, cans, and papers were sloshing back and forth in an inch of oily water that covered the cabin sole. Hitting the electric bilge pump switch brought no change in the water level. Checking the voltage meter that monitors the amount of charge in the battery banks, the needle didn't move. Obviously the water that had come on board in the knock down had shorted some of the electrical systems.

"OK, first things first," I said out loud, as kind of a personal motivational speech.

Staggering to the cabinet that held my First Aid Kit, I was relieved to see that it didn't appear to be water damaged. With my good arm, I grabbed the bag and emptied the contents on the galley table. Several prescription bottles rolled around as I searched for the air splint. Finally finding it in a side pocket of the medical bag, I tore open its plastic container, using my teeth.

My left arm was broken just below the elbow and a large lump showed around a deepening black bruise. Putting the splint on sent pain coursing through my arm and shoulder, beads of sweat blossomed across my forehead and I had to choke down the urge to vomit. Once the splint was in position, I needed to blow it up. The simple motion of bringing the tube up to my mouth shot even more pain through my already raw nerves, but I managed to get the splint inflated.

A large swatch of cotton material to make a sling was also in the First Aid Kit, so I was able to further immobilize my splinted broken arm.

I then found the Aspirin bottle and unloaded 8 tablets onto the counter top. I picked them up and downed them dry, praying they would help. I carried stronger pain killers aboard, but I was reluctant to use them until things on *Casablanca* were squared away.

Seeing Jack in an unaccustomed spot on the book shelf, I said, "Hey Buddy, how ya doing?"

He still looked wet, so I grabbed a towel and using my good arm, I rubbed his cold fur. Then it hit me why Jack was on the shelf: it was empty of the twenty or more books that usually occupy that spot.

The next step was to get the inside of the boat back in order. I felt exhausted, but seeing the water and mess floating in it compelled me to find the manual bilge pump handle and go to work.

A couple hours and several rest periods later, the floor was dry and all of the damaged books were picked up. Of course, they were ruined, but the sleeping bag, pillow and assorted cans could be saved.

I was satisfied that the cabin was once again livable, at least until we made it to Hawaii. Then with great difficulty, I opened a can of tuna for Jack. I was finding that even the simplest tasks were very difficult and time consuming only being able to use one arm. He hungrily ate as I stroked his fur, contemplating my next move.

With no power in the batteries, I wouldn't be able to start the engine, run electrical lights or use the SSB radio. I couldn't believe my brand new engine was out of commission. But, on the plus side, I was in a sailboat, I had oil lamps and flashlights for light, and when the time came I had a hand held VHF radio that I could use for short distance communication. And my trusty GPS was a hand held model as well, which ran on its own battery power.

Before I knew it the sun was beginning to set and I was surprised how quickly the day had gone. *Casablanca* continued to ride gently behind the sea anchor. I needed to rest, but a voice in my head was playing doctor, telling me not to fall asleep in case I had a concussion.

"Tomorrow!" I yelled, startling Jack, and jarring my arm sending new streaks of pain through my body. Then, finishing my sentence with the same determination, but a bit more calmly, I added, "We start sailing again to Hawaii."

I cat napped that night, trying to sleep for only 20 minutes at a time, fearing that I might not wake up since I didn't know how bad the concussion was. Finally around 3 in the morning I said to hell with it, I needed some real sleep.

It was the throbbing in my arm and not the sunlight shining in through the portholes that woke me up 4 hours later. Before climbing out of my berth, I pondered on the best way to retrieve the sea anchor. The parachute which had likely saved *Casablanca*, was now a burden keeping her from sailing on to Hawaii. In ideal conditions I would motor up to it, hauling in the one inch line hand over hand. Well, I had no motor and only one good hand, so it was definitely far from ideal conditions.

It was with a mix of reluctance and sadness that I walked to the bow of the boat. I silently thanked the inanimate object for keeping us safe through the brunt of the storm, then I cut the line, releasing the sea anchor. After I released the sea anchor, I loosened the halyard for the small front storm sail and let it fall to the deck. I knew I should try to bundle it up, but I just didn't have the strength or energy so I simply left it lying there with hope of taking care of it later. I decided to leave the storm trysail in place since I knew I wouldn't be able to manage putting up the large mainsail in my present condition.

Almost immediately, *Casablanca* acted like a horse wanting to get to the barn. She took on a livelier motion as I carefully made my way back to the cockpit.

With my right arm, I cranked out the Genoa headsail, adjusted the sheets and set a course for Hawaii. Although streaks of pain shot through my arm, I felt very pleased with myself. We were again underway and I was sure nothing would stop us now. As it was we were probably only few days behind my projected schedule, and I knew Sheryl wouldn't be concerned.

Casablanca would have to be a lot more overdue than that to cause her any worry because she knows that the length of a passage is variable, being affected by winds or lack there of. I also knew that the absence of radio contact wouldn't alarm her, since she also knows all electronics are subject to failure in the marine environment, and those failures always occur at the most inopportune moments.

A short time later the euphoria wore off and I came to my senses when I realized I wouldn't be able to hand steer the three hundred or so miles left to go. I'd overlooked the fact that the self-steering vane had been damaged in the knockdown. I hadn't had a chance to investigate what the problem had been, but a cheery voice in my head said there was no time like the present.

It was a real pain, in more ways than one, leaning over the stern rail to check out the steering unit. Surprisingly enough, I found the problem rather quickly. A quarter inch line, or more accurately, a small rope, had worn through and parted. The absence of this line prevented the windvane from turning the boat's steering wheel. This discovery made it evident what had happened to us at the height of the storm. After the rope broke, the boat wandered off course, got sideways to the wind and seas, then BAM: Knockdown – Bob's your uncle.

The repair to the windvane would normally have been a five minute fix, if I could have used two hands. But, in my limited condition, it took over an hour and the tedious work brought the pounding headache back.

I managed to hook up the self-steering and then I laid my head down in the cockpit. Again, I was totally spent. I felt drained like I had no reserves left, that all my strength was gone. I still had at least three days at best before I made landfall. The first faint twinge of fear began to creep into my thoughts. What if.......

Little did I know that right about that same time, 300 miles away in Hawaii, another drama was being played out.

Sheryl had checked into her hotel after her long flight from San Francisco and was surprised when the desk clerk said that she had a message waiting. Thinking it was from me, possibly saying I had already arrived in town, she eagerly took the note from the man. She grew concerned when she saw it was from my mom. The concern turned to dread when she read that Mom wanted her to call her immediately.

After several frustratingly futile attempts she finally got through and she could tell by the strain in my mom's voice that something was seriously wrong.

Mom explained to Sheryl that the Hawaiian-based Coast Guard had contacted her earlier that day. They'd told her that a massive search and rescue effort had been launched, south of Hawaii, for a boat that had sent out a Mayday call.

Although I hadn't put out a Mayday, and pretty sure Jack hadn't either, the Coast Guard had us on a list of possible search targets. The reason for this was simple: A C-130 rescue plane had been out looking for the boat that had sent out a distress call when they'd spotted an inflated life raft. A bulk oil tanker, *The New Horizon*, on a run from Panama to Hawaii, was diverted to the location of the bobbing raft to make the rescue. What they found, however, was an empty raft. The captain of the tanker had it hauled on board for closer inspection. It was learned from the serial numbers inside the raft that the small survival boat belonged to *Casablanca*, and my mom was the emergency contact.

The Coast Guard then contacted Mom as they were looking for any information to aid in the search for *Casablanca*: point and date of departure, intended course and destination and whether there had been any contact, before, after or during the storm. Since Mom really didn't have any of that information, she contacted Sheryl and as soon as Sheryl got off the phone with Mom, she called the Coast Guard to give them all the information she had. Then she called the airlines to arrange for Mom to join her in Hawaii.

While I was thinking that there would be no worries about us back home as we limped our way to Honolulu, the two very special women in my life were spending several very long and agonizing days awaiting word of the fate of *Casablanca* and her motley crew.

The next two days went mind-numbingly slow as we inched our way to Hawaii. The pain in my arm continued to increase and the skin was itching like crazy under the plastic splint. I'd toyed with taking off the splint, but was afraid it would end up making things worse and I knew I wouldn't be able to get it back on again if I needed to. *Casablanca's* once cozy cabin was looking quite grim, as I hadn't been able to do much in the way of cleaning up. It was all I could do to open some cans of tuna, which Jack and I would share. I didn't have any appetite, so the one can meal seemed to suffice. I couldn't even concentrate to read, so I found myself napping most of the time. I was just plain miserable.

At sunrise, three days after the storm from Hell, the faint smudge of Honolulu's skyline replaced the endless horizon I had been staring at for nearly a month since leaving the Tuamotus. Sitting in the cockpit, I looked up when I heard the thwunk-thwunk-thwunk of an approaching helicopter. As it came closer its white body with a bold red stripe, clearly marked it as a USCG aircraft. Spotting it, I felt relief, because it was another sign that I was nearing land and civilization.

I retrieved my handheld VHF, and with my one good hand, fumbled with the on-off switch. Almost immediately it boomed to life with a loud voice asking the white hulled sailboat, me, to respond. I was thankful my handheld actually worked as there had been no way for me to test it earlier. But it was also strange to hear another human voice after so long. Chris on *The Swallow* was the last contact I'd had.

I took a deep breath, getting my thoughts together and identified myself and then phonetically spelled out *Casablanca*. I answered the Coastie's questions about number of people on board, whether or not I had a life jacket and if I was in any immediate danger. I responded that I wasn't in any immediate danger, but I would like some assistance. I'd asked if I could get a tow once I was closer to the city, since my engine was out. I also advised them that I had a broken arm. What I didn't tell the Coast Guard was that I had a blinding headache and a very high fever. They responded that they would contact Vessel Assist, wished me a good day, and then flew off in a southerly direction.

Six long hours later, and about one mile offshore, a bright red and white motor vessel was cutting through the moderate swell toward Jack and me. I figured this must be the Vessel Assist boat, sent by the Coast Guard, to help me in. Vessel Assist is a great thing: like Triple A on the water.

As they neared, I could see there were two occupants on board the workboat.

"*Casablanca, Casablanca*, this is Vessel Assist," came the call on the radio.

"This is *Casablanca*, go ahead," I replied, practically yelling into the handheld VHF, as the adrenaline was kicking in.

"We will come alongside on your port and transfer a line handler to your vessel. We understand you have a broken arm. We will then hook up a tow line and proceed into the Ali Wai Yacht Harbor. Please drop your sail then center your rudder and lock it off if possible. Over."

"Roger that," was my only response. I was worried about blacking out as I was covered in a cold sweat and the pain in my arm was starting to build again, but I somehow managed to roll in the Genoa.

I was also thinking about the irony of again having to have help in making landfall in Hawaii. The first time was when I sailed into Hilo after the long crossing from San Francisco. Low on fuel with a hurricane on my tail, I was attempting to enter the port at night (a big no-no in cruiser-land). I had happily accepted the assistance of a local fisherman that swam over from another boat to *Rick's Place* with diesel, beer and local knowledge. Ahhhh: the spirit of Aloha.

This time it was more official and a bit more dire straits. As the captain of the 27 foot boat came nimbly alongside, his helper dressed in full foul weather gear and a baseball cap, waited on the rail. Just as both boats were in synch on the swell, he deftly jumped aboard my boat and quickly ran forward with a small rope line. That line was, in turn, connected to a larger diameter line that was neatly coiled on the stern of the Vessel Assist boat.

I didn't leave the wheel for fear of the two boats smashing against each other, plus with the bum arm and blinding pain I wouldn't have been much help. I was also beginning to feel nauseous again.

After the large line was hauled over and tied around *Casablanca's* forward mooring cleat, the line handler signaled the small boat to ease forward and take up the slack. As I bent over to lock the wheel in place, Jack poked his head out to see what all the commotion was about.

"There's my Jackie Boy," came the feminine coo.

My head jerked up to see the line handler standing in front of me, but backlit by the sun. Had he, or I guess she, really said what I think I heard? The bump on my head must have been worse than I thought.

"Well, what kind of reception is that?" she said and I could hear the smile in her voice. Then she removed the baseball cap and her long blonde hair blew in the wind.

"Sheryl! What, how?" I exclaimed. Then darkness once again enveloped me.

CHAPTER 17
DOWN AND OUT IN HONOLULU

"What do you give a man who has everything? Penicillin."
—Jerry Lester

"Hey sleepy head, it's about time you woke up," I heard Sheryl saying softly to me.

In my groggy state, I tried to answer her, but my throat was dry and raw, so I only managed to mumble, "Hey..." Not knowing if it was just another dream, I attempted to reach out to her, but couldn't will my arms to move.

As I regained consciousness, my senses were assaulted by the bright lights and antiseptic smell of the room where I found myself. Without moving my head, I slowly moved my eyes to assess the situation and saw that my left arm was snugged in tight to my body in a brand new cast and sling, while the other one was strapped down with an IV attached. I realized I was in a hospital room.

"Water," was the next word I managed to get out, looking for relief for my sore throat, and Sheryl quickly acquiesced, handing me a plastic cup with a bendable straw.

"They said your throat would be sore, from the ventilator tubes they used during the surgery," Sheryl said to my unasked question.

Seeing the confusion in my eyes, Sheryl, in a soft, even voice, recounted the events that had transpired since she surprised me aboard *Casablanca*. She said the doctors figured my relief at seeing her aboard the boat had been a signal to my body that all was well and I'd be taken care of, so it just shut down after having been pushed to the limits during the storm and its aftermath. I guess I passed in and out of consciousness several times, because everything was extremely fuzzy between seeing her that day and when I woke up in the hospital bed.

After the Coast Guard helicopter had spotted *Casablanca* and spoken with me, they passed the information back to their base, and they in turn contacted Sheryl. Learning that Vessel Assist would be going out to tow me in, she made arrangements to get on that boat. When they made their rendezvous with me and she saw the seriousness of my condition, she immediately called to have an ambulance waiting at the dock.

Sheryl rode to the hospital in the ambulance with me, then went down to *Casablanca* and snuck Jack back to her hotel room, thinking the boat didn't look like a good place for man nor beast at that point. After getting Jack settled in and showing him the toilet, she took a cab back to the hospital.

In addition to being broken, my arm had become badly infected. Apparently I'd scraped it and the fresh wounds had become a breeding ground for the bacteria trapped in the warm environment of the inflatable cast I'd had to use to stabilize the broken bone. Sheryl said the doctors were great and had quickly gotten the infection under control. Unfortunately, they had to re-break my arm so that it could be set correctly and some pins were surgically placed to aid in the healing, or more accurately, the re-healing process.

She also told me the doctors said the source of the mind-numbing headaches I'd experienced were due, as I'd suspected, to a slight concussion I'd received on the fall that broke my arm. Luckily, it hadn't been severe or life threatening.

While Sheryl continued to get me up to speed on where I was and why, the comfort of her soothing voice soon had me drifting off to sleep. Sometime later, when I once again opened my eyes, my previously quiet hospital room had begun to feel like Grand Central Station.

A nurse was standing at my bedside, and with quick efficient movements, she replaced the IV bag that hung on a stainless steel pole near my head. With my eyes, I followed the clear tube from the bag to what appeared to me to be an enormous spike driven into my right forearm.

Before I could ask, she volunteered, "It's a saline solution. You were very dehydrated when you arrived."

I looked around for Sheryl, but couldn't find her, and I was afraid that my seeing her before had been a dream. But then, a familiar voice from the hall filtered into my room. Bending over my face and kissing my forehead, she said, "Ricky honey, how are you feeling?"

Through a parched throat I croaked, "Good Mom," then, feeling quite confused I asked, "What are you doing here?"

"Oh, Sheryl got me a flight right after I told her about the Coast Guard calling me," she replied.

"Coast Guard?" I repeated, very puzzled. I didn't know why my brief encounter with the helicopter would have elicited a call to my mom. My headache was starting to come back full force.

Just then, a thin tan man, about 5'10" with almond-shaped eyes behind round wire-rimmed glasses came in and stood at the foot of my bed, holding a folder. His white lab coat had the name Dr. Kim embroidered in red stitching, opposite a breast pocket that contained a pen and pencil. Hanging around his neck was a stethoscope.

"Hello Doctor," my mom spoke first.

"Good afternoon. How's our sailor today?" he asked with a smile.

Guessing that I was the only sailor in the room, I responded, "Well, my throat hurts, I've got a headache and a dull pain in my arm." I sounded pretty whiney, even to my drugged up self.

"The arm needed some fixing up. Once the infection was under control, we did some surgery to reset the break and put a pin in the arm. When the cast comes off in about 6 weeks, you'll be as good as new." Then he added, "Well, you might need a little physical therapy."

He checked my eyes with a small penlight and said, "The ventilator tube caused your raw throat. I prescribe some ice cream," as he chuckled at his own joke.

"We'll get you some Tylenol for the pain and the headache should go away once we get a little more fluid into you," he advised. "By the way, did you have any water on that boat? You were horribly dehydrated," he added.

Before I could answer with something witty about not being thirsty because I was surrounded by water, my mom chimed in with, "Oh, I always had to be after him to drink more water. You know how boys are. When will he be able to go home, Doctor?"

"Rick can leave just as soon as his systems are functioning normally," then adding more specifically, with that same clever smile, "as soon as he can go to the bathroom on his own."

"Hey, thanks Doc, for everything," I said, hoping to sound more grateful than I had with my first complaining statements.

"No problem, Rick. You're doing great. I'll see you in the morning, and I imagine you'll be ready to leave us tomorrow afternoon. Looks like you'll be well taken care of," he added, nodding towards Mom.

With that he disappeared out into the hallway.

"Where's Sheryl?" I asked with a raspy voice, still wondering if her vivid image had just been a figment of my imagination.

"She's at the hotel, Ricky. After you were admitted to the hospital, she spent the night here. I stayed with Jack back in our room and we've been trading off looking after you and the cat ever since," she informed me. "Sheryl was here this morning when you woke up, and came back to our room to get me when you took another nap."

"How's Jack?" I asked, my throat starting to feel better even without the ice cream.

"Good. Except when I got him to the hotel room he chose to poop in the sink instead of the toilet," she said with a trace of disgust on her face.

That made me smile.

"Oh Ricky, we were so.....," she started to say, as a tear formed in her tired eyes. I'm glad she didn't finish the sentence.

A light knock at the opened door, announced another visitor. We both looked up to see a young man, in his late 20's, lean and tall with close cropped hair, standing there in a Coast Guard uniform.

"May I come in," he politely asked.

"Sure," I responded a bit hesitantly, wondering if I was in some sort of trouble, but not knowing why I would be.

Mom squeezed my shoulder and said, "I'll be right back." Then she disappeared into the busy hallway.

"I hope this isn't a bad time, Sir. My name is Jackson, Lieutenant Jackson," he said very officially.

I still couldn't imagine why he was there, and I answered his question with, "No, the timing's just fine. You're here to give me my sponge bath?" My small attempt at humor brought no change to his serious demeanor.

"Sir, I'd like to ask you a few questions," he stated.

"Fire away," I replied, wanting to find out what this was all about.

"During the storm you were in, did you send out a Mayday call?" he asked, looking down at a notepad he'd pulled from his pocket.

"No, I didn't." I answered matter-of-factly, wanting to add that I wasn't sure about my cat, but I could tell this guy wasn't up for any more of my lame jokes.

His next question was, "Are you familiar with the boat *The Swallow*?"

"Yeah, we'd met up a few times in the last several months and we started out from Fakarava near the same time," I informed him, wondering where Chris was now.

"Did you talk with him on the radio any time after leaving Fakarava? Particularly during the storm?" he quizzed me further.

"We tried to keep in touch, but I lost him pretty early on in the static." Getting a sense of where this was going, and feeling an uncomfortable knot forming in my stomach, I asked, "Is he missing?"

"Yes Sir, his family has reported him as overdue. And we suspect he was the source of the Mayday call, since you didn't send one." He added in his practiced emotionless tone.

I told the lieutenant the approximate position of *Casablanca* when I'd had my last contact with *The Swallow* and I also relayed to him how our conversation had been cut short due to the intense static interference.

He finally offered, "We found a life ring with the name *The Swallow* on it the same day we found your inflated life raft."

"My life raft?" This was news to me.

"Yes Sir. An oil tanker picked it up. That's where we got the contact information for your mother," he informed me.

Then I remembered and told him, "After a big wave hit *Casablanca*, the life raft got washed over," adding as an afterthought, "I didn't see it inflate."

My mind started to drift off, picturing the huge waves and the chaos of nearly being pulled over in to the dark sea. When a hand touched my good arm I nearly jumped out of the bed as it jolted me back to the present. It was Sheryl.

"Hello Lieutenant Jackson," she said warmly to the Coastie.

"Nice to see things have worked out here," was his reply.

"You know the Lieutenant?" I inquired, still trying to piece it all together.

Sending a smile of appreciation his way, Sheryl answered me with, "Yes, he's been kind enough to keep your mom and me in the loop while they were searching for you. Lieutenant Jackson called me as soon as the helicopter made contact with you that day, so we'd know you were alright."

Then turning to the Lieutenant Sheryl said, "I can't thank you enough for your consideration in contacting us so promptly and putting an end to all our worries."

Looking slightly embarrassed, Lieutenant Jackson turned and headed for the door. He stopped at the threshold and said, "If you happen to hear from *The Swallow*, or remember anything that could possibly aid in our search, please give us a call." Then he, too, disappeared into the busy hallway. I was beginning to think of that doorway as a portal to another world, as people seemed to randomly appear and disappear at it's threshold, while I lay confined in my bed not knowing what was on the other side.

"Hi Honey," Sheryl said, kissing my cheek. She looked wonderful in a simple flower print cotton sundress, her hair clean and flowing and the worry lines that were on her face earlier were now no where to be found. Then she said, "So whatcha been up to?"

"Very funny," I managed.

She went on to tell me that she'd just come back from *Casablanca*.

"I hired a couple locals to help clean up your version of *Animal House*. They'd been at it for a whole day. They just have to get the cushions back from the cleaners and we can move back on board," she said with growing excitement.

Turning more serious, she said, "Rick, I can't imagine what that was like out there by yourself... sick and hurt..."

"I had Jack," I joked, wanting to bring her back to the happier mood she'd just been in.

Just then, Mom returned and she was carrying a small bag that had ABC Store printed on the side.

Squeezing in next to my girlfriend, Mom cautiously looked around and asked, "Is the coast clear?" as she reached into the mysterious bag and pulled out a large cup of golden French fries and a chocolate milkshake.

Knowing these were two of my favorite food groups, Mom said, "You're probably not getting a lot of fried foods through that tube," as she pointed to my IV, then continuing, "So I went to McDonald's for the shake and fries then hid them in this bag from the corner ABC store." She was beaming with pride at the success of her clandestine operation, and I was happy to see her worry lines were diminishing, too.

After our impromptu snack, Mom bid us aloha, saying she should get back to her "house guest". As she exited the room she said, just loud enough for all to hear, "I can't wait to have Jack in bed with me tonight."

"You're mom is so funny," Sheryl said smiling.

I just rolled my eyes.

Sheryl again sat with me and patiently filled in the blanks of not only the past week, but on the past several months since we'd last seen each other.

Then, almost as if to steer the conversation in a new direction she said with a big goofy grin, "Dr. Kim says that if you're a good boy and use the potty by yourself, you can go home tomorrow."

I guessed that she thought we were headed to the marriage proposal area of conversation, something I really didn't want to get into right then either, so I went with her change in direction and stated, "Yeah, it just takes one little poop to get me out of this hospital room."

I was starting to feel tired again and I could tell by the amount of sunlight filtering in through the curtains that sunset was closing in.

"How long are you able to stay in Hawaii?" I asked hoping that it would be a bit longer than my release date.

As Sheryl started to answer, I could tell she was uncomfortable, but she gave me a vague run down of things she needed to do and before she got to answering my question, sleep pulled its veil over my eyes.

That night, the scene that had terrified me the most during the storm, replayed itself in my dreams.

I was being pulled into the dark angry waters, the wind howling and water splashing hard against my face. Struggling to hold on, then eventually losing my grip. Finally sucked into the water, I watch helplessly as Casablanca sails away, leaving me fighting to catch up, until her lights were swallowed in the gloom.

Waking up with a start, I was so drenched with sweat, I felt as if I really had been in the water. I laid awake listening to the light traffic sounds drifting up from the street below, punctuated with the occasional high pitched whine of a siren.

"I'm really looking forward to getting back to the boat," I said out loud.

A nurse, who must have heard my rhetorical statement, stuck her head in the door and asked if everything was OK.

"Could I have some prune juice?" was my simple request.

The next morning, with an audience made up of my mom and girlfriend, I waited for the most important bowel movement in recent memory. Around 11 in the morning I got out of the hospital bed and gingerly made my way to the toilet. With my business complete, I came out and took an awkward bow. The nurse was called in for confirmation of my achievement and plans were made for my afternoon departure. The Doc breezed in for one final exam and pronounced me good to go.

"Continue to drink plenty of fluids, get plenty of rest and no sailing for awhile," he said smiling, then added, "We'll need to change that cast in about 3 weeks, so call my office and schedule an appointment."

"Thanks for everything, Doctor," I said, excited to be going back to *Casablanca*.

Once the three of us, Mom, Sheryl and I, were squeezed into the small rental car, Sheryl informed me that we'd be spending the night at the hotel, because all the work being done on *Casablanca* to make it livable again, hadn't yet been completed.

As we made our way through the heavy Honolulu traffic to the hotel where Jack was waiting for us, I reflected on my fate of the past few weeks. As horrible as my ordeal had been, I was very lucky. While I was in the hospital recuperating, the Coast Guard had continued their futile search for my friend's boat, *The Swallow*. It gave me chills every time I realized that my last short static ridden conversation with Chris was the last anyone had heard from his boat.

CHAPTER 18
THE GATHERING

"Love is the exploding cigar we all willingly smoke."
—Lydia Barry

I was standing on a beach near Honolulu holding Sheryl's hand and staring out at a magnificent sunset. The sand was still warm beneath our bare feet and I was thinking I'd never felt happier in all my life. Then the heavyset Hawaiian man standing in front of us wearing a long flowing ceremonial robe said, "You may kiss the bride."

For once it wasn't a dream, and after I gave her the kiss, I held Sheryl with my good arm and turned to face the gathering of family and friends that were scattered on the beach behind us. Clutched in her hand and held close to her heart were the black pearls I'd gotten on Makemo. I'd surprised her with them in the ceremony and I intended to have them made into a ring, if I could ever pry them out of her hand.

Tiki torches had been lit to provide light as the sun sank into the sea. To one side of the hotel's everlasting pool, that was just steps away from the beach, sat a long table covered with an elegant white cloth. That table was overflowing with food and drink. Arranged around a centerpiece of Bird O'Paradise and other tropical flowers were two large punchbowls and many trays of artfully prepared appetizers, or poupou's as they are called in the islands. A second, smaller table held a beautiful three tiered wedding cake adorned with delicate Plumeria flowers. On the top, in lieu of the traditional little bride and groom statues, sat a sailboat that looked much like *Casablanca*.

On the other side of the pool, our good friend Dave Calhoun was setting up his equipment. His great musical entertainment would be his wedding gift to us and I walked over to thank him.

"Dave, I can't believe you could make it here for this. I can't thank you enough. It's great to see you," then turning to look around I asked, "Where's Marcia?"

"Don't you worry, she's here. I wouldn't have missed this for anything! She just ran back to our rental car to get something for me. That was a great ceremony, short and sweet. Now let's party!" he said as he started tuning up.

"Hey, congratulations man," Sparky said in his slow drawl as he sauntered up behind me, his wrap-around Maui Jims still covering his light blue eyes in the fading light. "I knew she'd finally say yes to your proposal," he added with a smile.

"Well, the funny thing is, she never did really answer my proposal," I told him, going on to explain, "She just arranged this whole thing while I was recuperating in the hospital. She didn't want any additional stress weighing on me so she kept it a secret until yesterday."

"So you didn't have a clue?" he asked.

"Well, I had a feeling something was up. Sheryl was acting kind of strange, sort of preoccupied. To tell you the truth, when she wanted to take a walk and talk the other day, I was afraid she was going to dump me, I was feeling pretty devastated and then she told me about all this," I confessed.

"Here you are all married and we didn't even know you were engaged!" this from Liz Bates as she gave me a warm hug. Her husband Tom was right behind her and reached out to shake my hand saying, "Way to go Rick."

"So how did Sheryl happen to get hold of you guys? She'd never met you, had she?" I asked trying to piece this one together.

Tom replied, "She called us up and explained who she was and wondered if we'd like to come to the wedding since it was kind of in our neighborhood. She said she found our names and phone numbers on a piece of paper on the boat. Must have been from when we exchanged our contact info back in Zihuatanejo."

"Sure, that makes sense. She knows all about you guys even though you hadn't met. I'm sure glad she was able to get hold of you and I'm really happy you could make it to the wedding," I said sincerely.

I went on to tell them that besides the wedding, the other surprise Sheryl had for me was that she'd just signed the papers to sell her flower shop in San Francisco.

"So your solo sailing days are over now?" asked Liz with a heartfelt smile.

"Yes they are I'm very happy to say," I replied, adding, "I'd gotten pretty used to having her around when we sailed down the coast together, so when she had to leave me in Zihuatanejo to go back to her shop, seemed all I could think about was when she'd be able to return to *Casablanca*. I could tell Jack missed her, too."

"So where is Jack? He couldn't make it to the wedding? I was hoping to see the big fur ball," Liz jokingly asked.

"Come on down to the boat tomorrow. It's moored at the Waikiki Yacht Club. I know he'd be happy to have some more attention lavished on him. Sheryl's been pretty busy lately, as you can imagine."

"Oh can we? That would be great!" Liz said enthusiastically, adding, "We'd better let you get on with your other guests. See ya tomorrow Rick."

Finding myself momentarily alone, my mind drifted back to that tense moment the day before when Sheryl started out the conversation by saying she was sorry she'd been in kind of a weird mood since my release from the hospital, but she'd had a lot on her mind. I was expecting the worst when she surprised me first with the news about selling the shop and then she really blew my mind with the wedding plans. What an emotional roller coaster that had been.

Then, Tami, Sparky's wife, ran up and gave me a big kiss on the cheek breaking into my thoughts and bringing me back to the party, saying, between sobs, "It was a perfect wedding, Rick!"

I had to agree with her, because it certainly felt perfect to me. And it was all thanks to Sheryl. She'd made the arrangements for our simple ceremony on the beach and put out a call to all of our friends. I was really surprised and humbled at the number of people that could make it the long distance on such short notice.

As I was finishing up my conversation with Tami, I started to get a familiar, but weird sensation, as if the hairs on the back of my neck were prickling up. I turned to look behind me and there, about 10 feet away, stood the always mysterious, Alien Allen. I couldn't believe my eyes.

"Allen, how on earth did you get here?" I asked, secretly wondering if he'd had to stash a spaceship somewhere or just beamed in. I hadn't seen Allen in quite a while and his appearance always gave me a bit of a start, with his hairless porcelain skin and those royal blue eyes that seem to have their own light source behind them.

He never did say how he got there, but in his short clipped manner of speaking went on to explain that when word of my impending marriage got down to the marina, he was chosen to come as a representative of all my friends there, since he was the only one who could make the trip on such short notice. I'm guessing he beamed in.

After catching up with Allen about the goings on down at the docks in Gig Harbor, I told him to give everyone my best, then excused myself.

I was starting to feel a little fatigued and overwhelmed and I still wasn't entirely with the program. After all, I'd just gotten out of the hospital two days before and found out about the wedding the day after that.

Looking back, it certainly explains a few things that had me pretty puzzled: like why my mom was sticking around after I was out of the hospital. She said she wanted to stay and explore the beaches of Hawaii, but it was so out of character for her since she likes nothing better than to be in her own house knitting, and the only exploring I've ever known her to do was looking under the bed for dust bunnies.

Glancing around I spotted my new wife surrounded by my mom and her mom and I could tell she was being grilled about when we were going to settle down. That seemed to be a common agenda with the two of them. It was too bad Sheryl's sister Joni hadn't been able to make it to the wedding, so she would have had a little support dealing with the two moms, but since she was expecting twins, the Dr. advised her not to fly.

Then Dave announced that the next song was for Sheryl and me, so I took my wife's hand and led her back to the beach, where we'd just said our I do's, for our first dance. Dave played the perfect song for the two of us, one he'd written called: *We're Goin' Sailing*.

When the song ended, Mom walked up to me and said, "That was wonderful, honey," smiling up at me with tears making tracks down her cheeks. She wrapped herself around my good arm and leaned her head against me and sighed. She'd been through quite an ordeal, too.

A tap on my shoulder had me turning to face my new bride. A flower lei adorned her head and her shoulder length blonde hair floated lightly in the breeze. Her white cotton dress was in breathtaking contrast to her golden brown tanned skin.

"So what did you think of the wedding?" she said beaming with pride.

"I think you were taking a pretty big chance, assuming the proposal was still on the table after all this time," I teased.

Putting her arm around my neck, she whispered in my ear, "I love you Rick. I am so happy. Whaddya say we sail off into the sunset for our honeymoon because I can't wait to see what I've been missing not being on the boat with you and Jack?"

"You really haven't missed much," was my understated reply.

EPILOG

It's been 4 months since Sheryl stepped off that Vessel Assist boat onto *Casablanca* to help me into Honolulu after being battered by the storm, and it's been 1 week since we pulled into our slip at Old Town Marina in Gig Harbor.

Sheryl's honeymoon plans to sail off into the sunset had to be put on hold, but we did enjoy a glorious 3 week honeymoon on Maui. Our good friends Liz and Tom let us housesit for them when they went off on a long vacation to the Greek Isles. I was able to point out to Sheryl where *Rick's Place* had been anchored during the hurricane and where Liz had found Jack and me after we'd been taken off the boat.

We took daily walks and when the cast finally came off I built up the atrophied arm by swimming in the warm aqua water in front of the condo. It was a great way to relax and recuperate.

While on our honeymoon, Sheryl and I were contacted by Lt. Jackson of the Coast Guard. He had received word that a Panamanian registered freighter had spotted a flare several miles off their intended course. Further investigation revealed a dismasted and badly battered sailboat. Its lone occupant was dehydrated but otherwise unhurt. *The Swallow* had been found! Chris had been taken aboard the ship and was headed for Guam, their next port of call.

With the approach of fall, it was time to get on our way before the North Pacific got nasty. I had a job offer in Gig Harbor and Sheryl and I had decided we should work a while to build the cruising funds back up for they'd taken quite a hit with my hospital stay and the boat repairs. Once the honeymoon was over, we got to work on *Casablanca* to ready her for the crossing to Washington.

We got all the systems back in working order, replaced the damaged electronics, torn canvas and bent stanchions. When we were done it was nearly impossible to tell that *Casablanca* had been in such a major blow. I also purchased a new life raft and a new Sea Anchor – just in case.....

Once the repairs were complete and the boat provisioned, we untied the dock lines and with little fan fare, slipped out of Honolulu's Ali Wai Harbor. For the most part, the return trip was uneventful. The big North Pacific high was occupying its usual late summer position, blocking the rhumb line course to the West Coast. *Casablanca* doesn't carry enough fuel to motor through the completely windless center of the high. To find the best wind, we had to head north toward the Aleution Islands to skirt outside of the dead zone. It was the first time in a very long time that I needed to dig out warm clothes for the cooler days and nights.

We arrived at the Washington coast 28 days after leaving Hawaii where we made a very brief stop at Neah Bay for fuel and some fresh food supplies, then we harbor hopped down to the South Puget Sound, enjoying wonderful stops at Port Townsend, Kingston and Blake Island along the way. It was great to see the excitement on Sheryl's face as she discovered, for the first time, these great cruising grounds that were so familiar to me.

By the time we reached Gig Harbor, Mom had about a dozen people, some I hadn't seen in nearly 4 years, ready to greet us when we pulled into the marina. It was a good feeling to see the smiling faces as they grabbed our dock lines and welcomed me back.

Sheryl, Jack and I have settled into a very comfortable routine aboard *Casablanca* at the dock and the late Indian Summer is giving way to the coolness of fall. We are looking forward to spending a year here before once again heading to points south and warmer climes.

I'm sitting in the waiting room at the doctor's office, reading a three year old *Time* magazine, waiting for Sheryl. The sea sickness which started about two weeks into the cruise to Washington never got much better once the passage ended so she's having it checked out.

"Rick," Sheryl says approaching me with a wide smile on her face, which is reassuring that it's nothing serious.

"Hey Hon, what did the doc have to say?" I ask, searching her face for a clue.

Sheryl reached over and gave me a big hug and whispered in my ear, "Have I ever got some interesting news for you...."

AUTHOR'S NOTE

S/V Casablanca was inspired by my family's nearly four year cruise from Gig Harbor, Washington to Mexico, French Polynesia and then on to Hawaii. Most of the major events are true, but of course names have been changed—well, you know why. In fact, most characters are really a composite of people I know or have met along the way. I'll take a name from one and a characteristic or description from someone else and it's all in good fun.

One name that showed up in the first book, *Rick's Place*, is Sparky and he shows up again in this sequel. Sparky is the name of a good friend of mine, and I can assure you he is not the flaky character that I have created in the book. It's just a great name for that character. I've also borrowed the names of his wife, Tami, and their three kids for various characters in the book – so a big thanks to the whole family for letting me intrude into their lives. Also, keeping it in the family, a big thank you to the Johnston's son, Travis, who is the talented artist whose amazing drawings grace the pages of this book as they did *Rick's Place*.

Another couple, whose names I "borrowed" for this book (I guess maybe I didn't really change that many names, did I?) are those of Liz and Tom Bates. Our family has had the good fortune to be spoiled by these two for many years. At various times Liz has handled our mail, fed our cat, picked us up at the airport, flown to Mexico to visit, made us countless dinners (and a better cook you could not ask for) and they've opened up their home to us (the Kotas Wing) – a regular Bed & Breakfast when we'd come back for a visit. As for her husband, Tom, I'm not exactly sure what he contributes, but there must be something.... Oh, I know, it's his great Margaritas! Thanks for everything Liz and Tom.

A tip of the hat to the talented Dave Calhoun – another real life character (the lawyers must be licking their chops by now) who plays the best Trop Rock music around.

Thank you, Mike Fak, for being there to edit both books and for offering good advice as well as encouragement.

Our daughter Carly did fact checking and has read the manuscript numerous times and helped me right some wrongs and reminded me of details I had forgotten. She was a great cruising kid and lived aboard boats with us from age 2 to 16. She is now a young adult and I'm very proud of her.

Heidi, my wife, deserves more credit for the completion of *S/V Casablanca* than I could ever express. She has read and re-read, typed and re-typed the pages so many times she must know them by heart. She gently nudged me when I needed nudging, pushed me when I needed pushing and when all else failed she kicked my butt to get me going. Her patience during the writing of *S/V Casablanca* reached new heights. Thank you for always being there.

Again, thanks to Reagan Rothe and Black Rose Writing for putting my words in print and helping me tell my story.

To all my friends and supporters, too numerous to mention, (you know who you are) you have my heartfelt thanks.

ABOUT THE AUTHOR

Terry and his wife, Heidi, live aboard their Fantasia 35 sailboat, *Cetus*, with their cat, Rosie. They have sailed across the South Pacific twice, once in *Cetus* and the first time in *Cassiopeia*, a Golden Gate 30 that they built in their back yard. They continue to cruise and are currently in the Sea of Cortez with plans to sail to the Galapagos and beyond.

NOTE FROM THE AUTHOR

Word-of-mouth is crucial for any author to succeed. If you enjoyed *Adventures Aboard S/V Casablanca*, please leave a review online—anywhere you are able. Even if it's just a sentence or two. It would make all the difference and would be very much appreciated.

Watch for my latest novel *Adventures Off The Beaten Path* coming September 2021 and thus completing this cruising adventure trilogy.

Thanks!
Terry J. Kotas

Thank you so much for checking out
one of **Terry J. Kotas's** novels
If you enjoyed our book, please check out our recommended
title for your next great read!

Adventures Aboard Rick's Place

Adventures Aboard Rick's Place is a story of a solo sailor, based on the author's true-life adventures.

Follow Rick through his carefree youth and then later in life as a series of events leave him jobless and wondering just what comes next.

Live vicariously through this charming landlubber turned sailor as he fulfills his dream of escaping the rat race and sailing off into the sunset.

Culminating with a life-changing event, this humorous tale gives a realistic look at the adventurous cruising lifestyle and will leave you longing to visit the beautiful isles Rick explores as he sails the Coconut Milk Run.

CPSIA information can be obtained
at www.ICGtesting.com
Printed in the USA
FSHW011741050421
80150FS